The Color of Equality

THE COLOR OF EQUALITY

The Story of a Failed American Colony

A Historical Novel by Annette James-Rogers

Appreciation

Appreciation is given to those who listened, read drafts, questioned
and supported the writing of *The Color of Equality.*

To my brother, Dr. Keith A. James, who let me roam the university
stacks for source material; to my critique group members, Sharon and
Rene, there from the beginning with valuable input and suggestions;
to my friend and jogging partner Judy, for her role as "aunt" to
the developing story; and a special thank you to my manuscript editor,
Lois Winsen, who tweaked and polished things to perfection.
My apologies to anyone I may have overlooked.

Dedication

The Color of Equality is dedicated to my great-grandfather,
Sergeant Henry Joseph James, 26th Regiment, N.Y. USCT, and other
free men of color who "stood for the cause" and fought for equality.

Entries

REFERENCES ON PAGE 183

Preface

When I was a young adult, I spent an afternoon with my elderly paternal grandfather. It was an opportunity to get to know a relative I had seldom seen. While we sat together he told me that when he was twelve he and his mother made a journey to Springfield, Massachusetts, where his older sister lived, bringing with them the body of his father, a Civil War veteran, for burial. Grandfather said both of his parents were of mixed race, free born mulattos, a surprise to me. He also said his father harbored a dislike for President Lincoln although he didn't know why. But my biggest surprise was hearing that my great-grandparents had lived in Haiti before grandfather was born.

After this visit I tried to learn more about my family history, but my father, aunts and uncles were unable to add much to the scraps they had heard. That is when I began a journey to piece together the lives of my Civil War family. I found information about where they were born and traced their moves to different states prior to the war.

Reading about this period in the history of America uncovered buried facts regarding the position and treatment of free people of color by President Lincoln and his administration. I was unaware that when recruitment for the Union Army began, free men of color asked permission to enlist from President Lincoln. He denied their request and instead recommended they emigrate to the Caribbean and establish a separate country.

My great-grandparents and their children participated in an attempt to form a colony in Haiti. *The Color of Equality* is a novel based on their experience, written as imagined from their daughter's point of view.

Major events, including newspaper articles actually happened, but other details and some names have been modified or created to suit the narrative. Lincoln met several times with representatives from different groups within the community of color, and the content of the fictional letter from President Lincoln in Chapter 4 was assembled by the author from records of face to face meetings between Lincoln and the African American delegation, as recorded in *Abraham Lincoln, Complete Works.*

President Geffrand of Haiti, William Lloyd Garrison, Mary Ann Shadd and Joseph Redpath were real people. Mr. Garrison published *The Liberator*, Mrs. Shadd, *The Freedman's Journal.* Mr. Redpath was the U.S. Ambassador to Haiti, as well as the author of *A Guide to Hayti*, and editor of *The Pine and Palm*, the colony newspaper published by *The New York Times.*

I read many books and hundreds of documents in the search for information. Along the way I located the grave of my great-grandfather and obtained his military record. As you read the following pages, I hope you will find what happened as interesting as I did, and enjoy a greater understanding of a little known, but important, aspect of the events and people affected by the Civil War.

The author is a member of The Daughters of Union Veterans of the Civil War, 1861–1865, and The Los Angeles Civil War Round Table. She has made presentations about her great-grandfather to chapters of both organizations. She is also a Docent at the Drum Barracks Civil War Museum in Wilmington, California.

Annette James-Rogers earned a Bachelor of Psychology degree from the University of Massachusetts at Amherst and a Master of Science in Social Sciences degree from Boston University, Boston, Massachusetts, and was employed as a Clinical Therapist/Patient Education Specialist. This is her first novel. She currently lives in Los Angeles, California.

Chapter 1

Spencer, New York, December 1861

Miri watched her mother add milk to the bowl of mashed potatoes. It seemed there was always a spoon or pestle in her hand. Either she was making something to eat, or blending an herbal remedy for someone who sought her skill as a healer.

"Do you think there will be rioting here, Mother?" Miri asked.

Her mother stopped stirring. The lamplight danced on her ebony hair. "I don't think so. And you need to see about getting the sideboard set up."

"Then why is Mr. Garrison coming to the meeting tonight?" It was the first time a newspaper publisher had been invited, and Miri was certain it was because he'd written an article about the race riots in Detroit. The article called the attacks by white mobs on free people of color like her family, "vile and despicable."

Her mother said, "Your father asked Mr. Garrison to come because he's an advocate for the rights of freedom and equality for all people, not just those who are white. As for riots happening here, I wouldn't worry. Spencer's far from Detroit and there aren't many of us here. Now please go finish the parlor."

As Miri turned, Georgie dashed through the door and bumped her. The spoons, forks and napkins nearly flew out of her hands.

"For heaven's sake, Splinter," she said, following tight on his heels, "watch where you're going."

Her brother ignored her and plopped down into the overstuffed wing-back chair.

She frowned. No one but Father was supposed to sit in that chair, but Georgie often got away with such boldness. The fever deaths of six-year old twins Freddie and Teddy last year left Georgie the only remaining son, and their parents doted on him and treated him like a prince.

He was the image of their father, and the nickname "Splinter" fit Georgie like a glove. Father and son had the same skin color, apple cider brown with a hint of yellow, and both were slightly bow-legged. Only their eye colors differed. Father's eyes were coal black while Georgie's were gray as an overcast day.

For Miri, however, the biggest contrast between the two was that Father was a caring, if strict, parent and Georgie simply an eleven-year-old torment.

Miri arranged the utensils and napkins atop the sideboard, then turned to go back to the kitchen. A newspaper lay on the parlor table and she was stopped by the headline.

RACE RIOTS NOW IN NEW YORK

Pins and needles prickled her scalp. New York City was just a hundred miles from Spencer. She picked up the paper.

> Race riots have spread from Detroit to New York as Irish mobs chase and beat Negroes and torch their homes. Angry white dockworkers complain they can't find work. They went on strike for higher wages and employers hired free colored people. Employers say they prefer them to whites because free coloreds are skilled and reliable. White workers have also been drafted into the Army and colored men are not eligible, so there is no loss of manpower.

Miri's stomach constricted at the thought of violence and she recalled unpleasant images of a visit to New York City where the family had gone for the funeral of a relative. She was shocked by the sight of black and white children, shoeless and in tattered clothes, lining the streets and begging for handouts. There were also gangs of urchins along with stray dogs, pigs, cats and birds, picking through piles of garbage, all searching for something to eat. Spencer was nothing like New York and Miri felt fortunate to have loving parents and a comfortable home.

Mother's probably right, she thought. *Trouble isn't apt to come here. Father's not taking work away from anyone. As the town's "Boss barber" he has two shops, one for white customers and one for colored. He's respected, we're churched and attend regularly, Mother is a successful midwife and healer, and Georgie and I are in school.*

"Miri? Are you finished?"

"Almost." She fiddled with the newspaper and tried to shake her uneasy feelings. Her mind went back to the riots. Why did skin color create such anger that otherwise ordinary people burned houses and harmed women and children?

Her mother looked into the parlor as the knocker on the front door clacked. "Miriam," she said. "Get your nose out of that paper and answer the door."

It was her uncle and his daughter, Portia. "Hello, Miri," her uncle said. They stepped inside and he gave Miri a quick hug. The mingled odor of horse, wool and tobacco filled her nose.

"Good evening, Uncle Will," she answered, grateful the embrace was brief.

She looked at Portia and wondered why on earth her entire outfit was brown. The dull color didn't suit either her complexion or sunny personality. She thought of her own winter coat, and smiled. The cranberry-red woolen coat with its black velvet collar reminded her of the cardinals that appeared each winter. Both bird and coat never failed to brighten even the dreariest day.

Teased by a spicy aroma rising from the wicker basket swaying on Portia's arm, Miri lifted a corner of the checkered cloth covering and inhaled. "Mmmm, smells wonderful."

"Two pies made with apples from the last picking," Portia said as she followed Miri into the kitchen.

"Aunt Rachel sent fresh pies, Mother," Miri said. She placed one pie on the shelf above the rear burner of the stove to keep it warm and the second on a trivet next to the honey cake cooling on the table.

"Your mother didn't come, Portia?"

"No, Aunt Sarah. She's busy putting up eggs for tomorrow's deliveries."

"That means you girls will have to serve refreshments," she said and handed each an apron. "Put these on while I go check the parlor."

"I wish we could attend the meetings," Miri said, as she tied the apron on.

"Why?" Portia asked. "They're meant for adults."

"Hmmph!" Miri said. "I'm sixteen, almost an adult, but because I'm a girl I'm expected to serve and clean up. It's not fair."

Her mother came into the room, eyes flashing. "I heard that comment, Miri," she said, "and let me tell you, girls have no business in these meetings."

"I'm not a girl anymore, Mother. You told me so several years ago. You said it was time for me to wear a corset and hoop because I was a young woman."

"It doesn't matter if you are young or old, Miri. Women are not meant to participate in political discussions. Anyway, why bother? We can't vote."

"But, Mother, women are speaking out to get equality and the same rights as men. They want to be more involved in politics. Women should be involved and able to participate in decisions that affect us."

"Stop arguing, Miriam," her mother said. "I don't have time to listen to such foolishness."

At the sharp tone in her aunt's voice, Portia scurried from the kitchen with a handful of plates.

Meek as a mouse, Miri thought watching the hasty exit. *Portia ought to show some gumption once in a while.*

Unable to drop the subject of women's equality, she said, "I've been reading articles about white and colored ladies speaking out for the same privileges as men, Mother, and I agree with them. We ought to have equal rights."

"Oh, for heaven's sake, Miriam, is that where you're getting these ideas? From the newspaper? That so called 'Suffragette' movement is foolishness." She shook the box in her hand and the wooden matches rattled. "Women have enough work to do without meddling in politics."

"It wouldn't be meddling, Mother. If we were involved..."

"Miriam Hazel Rose, enough! Come help me arrange the chairs."

With a sigh of resignation Miri set the chairs they'd borrowed from the church, in rows in the parlor.

How can Mother and I look so alike yet be so different, she wondered. *Why shouldn't women be concerned with what goes on in the world? We live in it and everything we do helps keep it functioning.*

Her mother moved about igniting wicks. Lamplight filled the room, and its honey-gold color took Miri's mind in another direction. Afraid all the refreshments would be eaten during the meeting she asked, "Would it be alright if Portia and I have our sweet now, Mother?" Out of the corner of her eye she saw Portia nod.

"No. There'll be time later," her mother said, tucking several stray hairs back into the bun on her neck. "I'll save some honey cake for you, Miri. And what would you like, Portia? A slice of your mother's pie perhaps?"

A smile broke across Portia's plain as pudding face.

The promise of her favorite cake softened Miri's peevish mood and she volunteered to put on the teakettle.

Moments later she accepted the coats of several men and one from a short, toffee-colored woman with a round face and piercing black eyes.

The men, unaccustomed to a woman being present at the meetings, looked at the newcomer with curiosity. "I'm Miss Amelia Shadd from Canada," she said. "Perhaps you've heard of my newspaper, a weekly called *The Provincial Freeman*."

A man said, "I know of it and I've read it. You're located in Dresden, Ontario, correct? Dresden was the destination of most of the runaway slaves we've helped pass through Spencer."

"Dresden is one of several Canadian settlements of free-born people of color," she told him. "We welcome our escaped brethren and help them build new lives among us. I also belong to the African-American Female Anti-Slavery Society which recently held its second Free Colored Women's Convention for Women's Rights."

Miri listened, transfixed, as Miss Shadd spoke her mind and held the attention of the men. The ease and confidence Miss Shadd exhibited impressed her and she thought about asking her to describe her work on women's equality.

Portia whispered, "Your mother's coming," and startled her into taking coats again.

People continued to stream into the house. People she was acquainted with like Reverend Grady, Mr. Saxton, owner of the General Store, Mr. Chapel, the town cooper, and a cobbler named Reeves. She didn't know the farmers in the crowd by name but recognized them by the pungent animal smells that clung to their rough clothes. When it seemed there would be no more arrivals, Miri brought a tray of refreshments from the kitchen. Bits of conversations filled with opinions about the war and the riots floated around her as she moved about offering slices of cake.

Seven bells sounded from the mantle clock. A moment later the front door opened. The attention of the crowd shifted and quiet fell over the room. A man had come in with her father and Miri eased forward to get a better look at him. He was tall and pale. A pair of wire-rimmed glasses perched on a sharp nose. The hat he removed exposed a head that, except for a fringe of dark hair above the ears was bald.

Is this Mr. Garrison? Miri wondered. He didn't look in the least robust or hearty. More than once he and his newspaper had suffered injury at the hands of anti-abolitionist hooligans and yet he continued to publish editorials against slavery. *Where does the strength of his convictions come from?*

The chattering resumed and rose in volume.

She peered between the shoulders of a two men and saw her father wave his arms over his head.

"Quiet please," he called. "The meeting of The Society of Free People of Color is now in session. I'd like you to welcome our guest, Mr. William Lloyd Garrison of Boston. As you know, Mr. Garrison is the publisher of *The Liberator*, and a staunch advocate to end slavery. He is also a true friend to free people of color."

Mr. Garrison stood in front of the fireplace to address the group. He shared his belief that all men should be free and described the work he was doing to end slavery. His high-pitched voice shook with passion as he said, "Most of you here are mulattoes, born into families that have been free for generations. Yet despite your free status, you carry a special burden because you are classified as non-white. Now the conflict between North and South, and impending war, has placed your lives in peril. Violence against you is increasing...."

Miri recalled the beatings and burnings she'd read about. With an unsettled stomach she lingered at the back of the room to listen.

Her father interrupted Mr. Garrison. "It troubles me that we're not taking any measures to protect ourselves," he said.

"There's no reason for us to do anything rash and create a riskier situation, Henry."

Miri recognized the voice as Uncle Will's. *What did he mean? There was every reason in the world to want to stay free. I can't imagine any person in the room wanting to become a defenseless victim of an attack.*

Her uncle said, "I think Lincoln's idea for colored and white people to live apart, and his recommendation we establish a colony in Haiti are both good. I, for one, will be glad to be quit of this infernal place."

A few men cheered and some clapped approval.

A colony? In Haiti? Miri's stomach lurched. She couldn't believe the idea was being seriously considered.

"What in blazes are you thinking, Will?" her father said bitterly. "The United States is our country, and we have the right to live here. Ever since Haiti became a republic it has been struggling to bring itself out of poverty, and only a few countries recognize its existence. I plan to stay right here and continue efforts to gain full equality. The feud of slavery versus freedom for black people is our battle, too. If we leave, it'll be like running away, and that's exactly what Lincoln would like to see happen."

Miri was proud to hear her father speak up and advocate against leaving. Spencer was home.

Uncle Will replied, "Lincoln said he won't fight a war to free the slaves, and I'll wager he won't protect us either. It's bad enough we have to carry our registration papers to prove we're free if anyone questions us. Soon, I suspect, even registration papers won't be enough to ensure our safety."

Miri reached under her apron and touched the velvet purse tied to her waistband. In it was her registration paper and every word was etched in her memory. *Miriam Hazel Rose Whitfield, a mulatto female of a milk tea color, infant, two months old, with hazel eyes, high cheekbones and an ink mark near the eye. Born free, registered in my office this 11th day of November 1848 by her parents Henry and Sarah Whitfield. County Court, October 11th, 1844.*

An embossed impression of the County Seal was on the right side of the paper above the official endorsement. *The Court doth certify the register of Miriam Whitfield as taken by the clerk thereof to be correct and true. Testimony whereof I hereby set my hand to and affix the seal of my office at the courthouse this 11th day of November 1844. John Monway, Justice of the Peace, County of Reneschlauer, in the state of New York.*

She hadn't been aware she had a registration paper until her father handed it to her and explained that although their family had been free for several generations, because they were mixed race, they were required to be registered with the county.

"The government," he said," considers any person who has one drop or more of black or Indian blood not white. The law specifies all free black and mixed race births to be officially documented. With the number of runaways increasing, bounty hunters are looking everywhere for escaped slaves. Any person of color found without a registration paper risks being sent south. So don't ever be without yours."

"But isn't Spencer safe, Father? We've never had any trouble."

"While I'd like to think we're in no danger," he said, "this is not a time to be foolish. Carry your paper and be cautious when you are out and about."

Although it seemed odd to need registration papers in the city where she'd been born, Miri followed her father's advice. She could be stopped any time she was on her way somewhere.

Her mother's father, Grandfather Minifee, didn't need papers because he was German. Townspeople sometimes referred to him as

"Mulatto Minifee" because he was married to a mixed race woman.

Her father's racial mixture was inherited from the white indentured servant who was his grandmother. Her husband was a black man who bought his freedom. They married in North Carolina before the state passed laws prohibiting such unions. The couple's daughter, Mary, married Ethan Whitfield, a freeborn mulatto and after the wedding, they moved to New York where her father was born.

"I'll say it again," Uncle Will shouted over the noise, and Miri's attention snapped back to the discussion.

"Our papers will be no protection." He pointed around the room. "Each and every one of us is still in danger of being kidnapped by some slave tracker interested in earning a bounty."

"That's right," a man said. "And even though we're free we have no legal rights. There is no justice for us in any court."

"Nevertheless, this is still our country," her father said. "And we need to pursue full equality and citizenship. I don't relish the idea of becoming a stranger in a strange land."

The ferocity in his voice fired up Miri's heart. She also opposed moving to some foreign place.

"How can you want to stay?" Uncle Will thundered. "Honestly, Henry, I see no peace for us here. Let us try and find it elsewhere."

Random applause, like firecrackers, came from the crowd and scattered exchanges broke out.

Her father swiped a hand across his mouth and tugged at his beard. *He's trying not to lose to his temper,* Miri thought.

"You know perfectly well…" he began. His brother-in-law turned, shoulders squared. They were almost nose to nose. Miri had never seen her father and uncle so at odds.

Mr. Garrison stepped between them. "Some abolitionist groups," he said, "although against slavery, agree with President Lincoln on the subject of colonization for free people of color. However, the advice of my group, The New England Abolitionist Society, is for you *not* to accept the proposal of relocation or assistance from The Emigration Association."

Discussions that sometimes bordered on arguments resumed and went on until the evening grew late. The few men still present agreed to adjourn and vote on the question of colonization at the next meeting.

"Honestly, Portia," Miri said as they cleaned the parlor after the meeting. "It's sad to realize how little Mr. Lincoln cares about us. You should have heard my father. He said Old Abe wishes we didn't exist." Anger constricted her chest and made it hard to breathe.

Portia said, "My ma believes Lincoln will put an end to the war soon. She says he'll make peace with the southern states and the problems will be over."

Miri lowered a pile of plates into the pan of soapy water. "I hope your mother's right," she said, "But I have my doubts."

Later, she tossed about, unable to sleep. The thought of creating a new home in Haiti swooped around in her head like a bird with no place to perch. *Spencer is a wonderful town and I love it. My grandparents are here and so is Clarice. We've been best friends since first grade and she's like a sister. What would I do without her? Who would I confide in and share secrets with?*

She traced the outline of moonlit roses on the wallpaper and listened to the familiar sighs and creaks of the house. At last, exhaustion overtook her. The moon started its decent, her eyelids drooped and she fell into a restless sleep.

Chapter 2

February 1862

As she stood outside the parlor, Miri heard her father introduce the guest speaker, Mr. James Redpath, Ambassador to Haiti and representative of the New York office of the Emigration Aid Society. With attention on the speaker, no one noticed Miri slip into the room.

The two men with Mr. Redpath stood to his right. One was short, gray haired and walnut colored, the other was closer to Miri's age, tall, with wavy hair. When she had taken his coat she noticed he smelled of coffee. They had nodded to one another out of politeness but since no introductions had been made, didn't speak.

Mr. Redpath began, "I come with a message from President Geffrand of Haiti. Like many of you, he is mulatto and feels he understands your predicament here. He wants me to assure you Haiti will cordially welcome colonists. Each family will be allotted a portion of land and given supplies during their first year. President Geffrand also guarantees colony residents will be permitted to worship as Protestants without fear of harassment."

The young stranger bent to speak to the older man. Miri realized he was translating. *Who were these men and why were they here?*

Mr. Redpath continued. "That concludes the kinds of assistance that will be available from the Haitian Government. President Lincoln has authorized the provision of materials to build houses, a church, and a school for the education of the children. You will receive funds from private donors of the Emigration Society to purchase supplies for the school. An infirmary will also be built to assure a place where colonists can receive medical care." He motioned to the strangers and they stepped forward.

"Dr. Lazarre is from Port-au-Prince," Mr. Redpath said, gesturing toward the older man. "He was educated in France and can provide medical care if none of your own doctors decides to participate in the emigration. And if there is a physician in the colony, he will be able to avail himself of assistance and consultation from Dr. Lazarre. The young gentleman is Philippe Lazarre, the doctor's nephew and apprentice. Philippe is fluent in both French and English."

Miri wondered how and where he learned English.

"Until the colony is established Philippe will remain in Spencer and study with Dr. Stillman." With that, Mr. Redpath smiled and said, "That ends my presentation. Are there any questions?"

Miri's father asked if either President Lincoln or President Geffrand could guarantee jobs for the men. "Several earlier attempts by free people of color to settle in Haiti ended in failure," he said, "because jobs weren't available. We need paid employment in order to provide for our families."

"You will have every opportunity to prosper," Mr. Redpath said. "Haiti has an abundance of land, the climate is mild and crops grow well."

Father's a barber, Miri thought. *He doesn't know a thing about raising crops.*

"There are few among us who are farmers, Mr. Redpath," her father said. "Most of us are craftsmen...teamsters, coopers, cordwainers, tailors, barbers and carpenters. We're city people with little knowledge or experience with farming, and our lives have been for the most part comfortable and civil."

"Mr. Whitfield, those men who wish to, may seek employment in Port-au-Prince or the other large cities of the island. In Haiti, there will be ample and unrestricted opportunities to improve your current situation which is a precarious existence betwixt equality and slavery."

How could Haiti be better than Spencer, Miri wondered. The family had never had any problems, and the idea of leaving the only home she ever knew sent a shudder through her. She wanted to hear someone say the notion of forming a colony was absurd. Instead, a noisy debate broke out between a faction favoring relocation to Haiti and those in opposition.

Her father raised a hand and as quiet came over the room, he said, "We will do this properly and vote on the proposal to emigrate. I shall abide by what is decided by the majority."

People immediately began talking again and once more his hand went up.

"I also propose," he said, "we take action and send a letter to Mr. Lincoln to state our position. As free people we need to demand equality unrestricted by the color of our skin, and access to every right we're entitled to. And I pray Mr. Lincoln responds in our favor and ends any thought of emigration."

Surely if Father brings our concerns straight to Mr. Lincoln, he will do right by us. Miri was confident they would not be going to Haiti.

Her father called for a show of hands from those in favor of emigration and began counting.

Portia came to her side and asked, "What's going on?"

Several heads swiveled in their direction and Miri winced. Now was not the time to be noticed. "Shush," she whispered. "They're voting and I want to hear the results."

"Thirty-two in favor and twenty-one against," her father announced.

"That settles it," Uncle Will boomed in triumph.

Miri was dismayed. Unless her father's plan worked, emigration was now her future. *My hope to go to college will be in jeopardy. It was going to be challenge to convince Mother to let me continue beyond high school anyway. If we move to Haiti it will be impossible.*

"Miri, did you hear me?" Portia asked. "What were they voting about?"

"Emigration. They've decided in favor of going to Haiti," Miri said sadly.

Her father went to his desk, sat and reached for paper and pen.

"What's he writing?"

"A letter to Mr. Lincoln. I'll tell you about it if you stop asking questions. But if you really want to know, stay here and listen. The letter is to remind Mr. Lincoln that freeborn people of color like us are entitled to and deserve the same rights and protection as white people."

After a last flourish of the pen, her father held up the finished letter. "While this is passed around for signatures," he said, "I'll write a duplicate to post on the shop bulletin board for those who aren't here tonight."

Miri sensed eyes boring into her back and turned.

Her mother was standing in the hallway, her posture stiff and unbending. "Miri," she said, "why on earth are you and Portia dallying about? Collect the dishes and bring them straight to the kitchen."

She scolded both girls while they cleaned the kitchen and as soon as they finished Miri fled to her bedroom away from her mother's lashing tongue. But the next morning the pecking resumed.

"Stop gulping your oatmeal, Miri," her mother said. "And chew your bread well."

Miri's mind was on the letter. She was desperate to read it but it was Friday, the day her father stayed at the shop until time to go to choir practice. There would be no opportunity to see the letter until after school on Monday.

She couldn't wait an entire weekend, so when her father left the house, unbeknown to him, she followed him to his shop. From a shadowy doorway nearby, she watched him go inside, raise the window shade and putter about, arranging towels on the warmer and stropping razors. He laid the razors in a row, brought the red and white striped barber pole out, placed it on the sidewalk and went back into the shop.

He emerged with a broom and Miri thanked her lucky stars he was sweeping the walkway in the opposite direction. Three doors down from the shop he stopped to chat with the tailor and Miri darted into the barbershop. She made a beeline for the bulletin board searching for the letter, and found it. Her eyes flew across the paper.

February 20, 1862
Spencer, New York
The Society of Free Persons of Color

To Abraham Lincoln, President of the United States
Dear Sir,

This letter is addressed to you by the Colored Citizens of Spencer, New York. We are aware traitors in the south are attacking the United States government to overthrow it and insure the continuation of slavery.

This will be a contest between liberty and madness.

Our feelings urge us to declare to our countrymen that we are ready to stand and defend the government as equals of its white defenders. With patriotic sentiment burning in our hearts we will do so with our lives, our fortunes and our sacred honor.

A familiar knot of fear coiled in her stomach as she continued reading.

There are many among us who do not wish to emigrate from this, the only home we have ever had. For the sake of freedom and as good citizens, we ask that you modify the laws to protect our rights and to permit us to participate in the defending of our country.

Footsteps squeaked on the walkway, and she hurried to slip out the back door and up the alley. When she got to the school she saw Portia and pulled her aside to give her the details of the letter.

"That's a wonderful letter," Portia gushed. Excitement raised a blush on her butterscotch cheeks and lit her caramel eyes. "Both of our fathers want to help win the war, and I believe President Lincoln will find a solution to our problems."

"I'm not as certain as you that Mr. Lincoln will act to help us stay here just because of a letter," Miri said. "He wants us to leave. I hate the idea of going to Haiti, but I don't want my father to go off to fight either. I'd be scared witless if he did. How would my mother, Georgie, and I survive?"

The bell rang and as they walked into the school, Miri made a last comment. "For all our sakes, I hope Mr. Lincoln makes a good decision."

Miri focused intently on her lessons and the hours passed uneventfully. At the end of the day Clarice was waiting by the entrance, and the girls fell into their regular Friday routine. It was the only day of the week Miri had no chores and was free to visit with Clarice, who matched her stride to Miri's. Arm and arm the young women enjoyed the rare warmth of an early spring afternoon on the walk to Clarice's house.

"Tell me everything about the plans to move to Haiti," Clarice said. "It's going to be a grand adventure to create a new country, like the pioneers who came here from England."

"My home is here, Clarice Pynchon, and I dread the idea of moving to Haiti," Miri said. "I don't think of it as making a new country. Haiti is already a country. I'll just be a foreigner living there. If it wasn't for the growing disagreement between the North and South over slavery, this whole colony idea would never have arisen."

They reached Clarice's front porch and sat in the slatted, forest-green rocking chairs. Clarice sipped tea and nibbled the ginger cookies her mother brought to them, but Miri had no appetite.

"And another thing," she said. "Our friendship will change and probably end if I leave."

Morning glory blue eyes bright with concern, Clarice reached over to lay a hand on Miri's arm. "That's nonsense," she said. "We've known each other since we started Sunday school, Miri. I'll always be your friend. We'll write to each other."

Miri shook her head. "It won't be the same. Friends see one another and talk. How will we do that if I'm thousands of miles away?"

"We'll talk on paper," Clarice insisted. "We'll write each other every day. You'll describe the wonderful places you'll see and people you meet and I'll write about what's going on here. It'll be almost like talking face to face."

Miri was silent.

"Do you know what my father said?" Clarice asked.

Miri shrugged. *Clarice is trying to make me feel better. How can I tell her I don't care what her father thinks.*

"He said this is a glorious opportunity for your family. And I agree."

Miri felt her neck, cheeks and scalp burn. Her eyes flamed as she glared at Clarice. "You believe moving to Haiti will be wonderful for me because you're white." She bit her lips to stop their quivering. "If you were colored and this was happening to you, you'd know how I feel. Moving to Haiti is going to ruin everything. Everything!"

"Don't be upset, Miri," Clarice said. "Things will turn out alright, you'll see."

"No. It can only be terrible. My grandma and granddad M-Minifee won't be going...." Fury tangled her tongue. My family will b-break apart and I'll be far from Spencer. This is my home and nothing can ever take its place."

The conversation ended and she left Clarice's house in a foul temper. As she walked home, her anger turned to foggy gloom.

Lights in the window of Saxon's General Store penetrated her dark mood and her love of sweets drew her in. When she opened the door, the bell on the door jingled and Mr. Saxon looked up from the far end of the counter. He dropped a handful of potatoes into a burlap sack, tied it with twine and wiped off his hands on the front of his apron.

"Hello there, Miss Miriam," he said. "What can I do for you? Is your mother out of honey?"

"No, she has plenty," Miri said. She pointed to a row of large glass jars on the counter. "I'd like some salt-water taffy and molasses drops. I doubt anyone who is going to Haiti can make candy as good as you do, so I plan to enjoy it as long as I can."

"Don't be so sure," Mr. Saxon told her, with a smile that lifted the ends of his moustache. "It's true I won't be leaving Spencer. I've too much invested in the store to leave, but I do believe you'll find plenty of candy in Haiti." He wiped his hands on his apron again and opened a candy jar. "Now then, how much taffy do you want?"

She bought a big bagful of sweets for a dime, and popped a piece of peppermint taffy into her mouth. The cool flavor danced on her tongue, conquered the doldrums, and best of all lasted until she reached home, where she hid the bag in the bottom drawer of her dresser, safe from Georgie's grubby fingers.

"You seem quiet, Miri," her father commented at supper.

Not wanting to answer questions, she didn't mention her tiff with Clarice. "I'm a little tired is all," she said. "Um, why did Mr. Redpath say President Geffrand would assure colonists they could worship as Protestants," she asked him to change the subject.

"Haiti's a Catholic country, and the majority of those who'll be colonists are Protestant."

"But are Haitians restricted to the Church of Rome? Are they not allowed religious choice? Were other people who tried to form colonies there persecuted because they weren't Catholic?"

"From what I've been told they didn't suffer physical attacks," he said, "but the Haitian people made it clear they only respect the Papist church. It's also been rumored they practice some sort of paganism."

"Henry," her mother said. "I'm not sure we should bring up unproven nonsense for discussion."

"It's well known, Sarah," he said, "but you're right. We shouldn't occupy ourselves with things we need not be concerned with."

For the remainder of the evening Miri kept her face buried in a book. The next day, Saturday, she was busy helping her mother clean the house from top to bottom and baking a week's worth of bread, cakes and pies. Her mother took pride in her reputation as a fine cook and a skilled healer. She held to a standard of never being found with an unkempt house or without refreshments to offer visitors.

I'll never reach mother's degree of attention in finding each speck of dust in every nook and cranny, Miri decided as she wiped the back of a pantry shelf.

Sunday arrived and she didn't sit with her parents in church. Instead she joined her grandparents in their pew and during the service read random sections in the prayer missal, resisting the urge to look for Clarice.

When dusk arrived it brought Miri a realization. *It wasn't that hard to pass the weekend without Clarice, my former best friend.*

Chapter 3

March 1862

The smell of coffee and rattling pots woke her. Beneath the sounds of breakfast activity came the rumble of conversation between her parents. The words were muffled, but the rhythm of their voices was low and clipped. *They might be discussing the meeting,* Miri thought as she slipped on robe and slippers and hurried down to the kitchen.

Her mother was pouring milk onto Georgie's cereal and her father was reading a letter. Everything seemed fine until her father frowned and rapped the table with his knuckles. "I don't like these terms, Sarah," he said.

"What terms?" Miri asked.

Her mother handed her a mug of coffee and a reproach. "Your father wasn't speaking to you, Miri. This isn't your concern."

"But what terms is he talking about, Mother? Do they have to do with Haiti?"

"Yes," her father said. "This is a contract for colonists sent by the Haitian president." He crumpled the paper into a ball, tossed it onto the table and left the room.

Miri smoothed the paper out. The title was "Requirements for the Establishment of an American Colony in The Republic of Haiti."

Her mother said, "Now that you have it in your hands, you might as well read it to us, Miri."

"Requirement Number One. All healthy males will join the Haitian Militia immediately after landing," she said. She stopped in horror. The next requirement was worse and nearly stuck in her throat. "Boys must enlist on reaching the age of fifteen."

"I'll make an excellent soldier," Georgie said, aiming his spoon at an imaginary enemy.

"Hush, Georgie," Miri said. "You have no idea what you're talking about."

She returned to the letter. "Citizenship will be automatically granted to each immigrant after they have lived in The Republic of Haiti for two years." Miri looked at her mother. "I don't want to become a Haitian citizen. Isn't there something we can do to prevent us from leaving Spencer?"

Without answering the question her mother took the letter and said, "Eat your breakfast."

"I'm not hungry, Mother, and I don't want to go to Haiti."

"Stop tying yourself in knots," her mother said. "The decision is not ours to make. Now eat and get dressed or you'll be late."

The door to the cellar creaked. Runaway slaves, Viola Sparks and her mother, stood in the opening, silent as shadows. Most runaways never emerged from secret basement rooms until plans for the next step of their voyage to Canada were complete. "Night travelers" as runaways were called, left as soon as it was safe to continue their journey north.

Mrs. Sparks, however, was sure her husband would find his way to Spencer, and had decided to remain in town and wait for him. She and Vi were given forged registration papers. A place for them to live had been found yesterday. Today Vi would enter a school for the first time and Miri would tutor her.

"Good morning," Mrs. Whitfield greeted her guests. She filled two bowls with oatmeal. "Come and have some breakfast."

"Abby," she said to Mrs. Sparks, "as soon as the girls are off to school, we'll look through the things I've collected to see what you can use for the apartment."

Her cereal had cooled and Miri could only swallow a couple of mouths full before pushing the bowl away. She excused herself and got dressed with terms of the contract irritating her mind like a burr.

"Don't draw unwanted attention to yourselves," her mother warned before she and Vi left for school. "Come straight home and don't dawdle."

Miri muttered as she walked along the wooden walkway. "All this disruption and commotion is because there might be a war. That's why the Society accepted a plan for emigration to Haiti, of all places."

Still unused to wearing shoes, Vi clomped awkwardly alongside her. "Me and Mam heard voices down in our hidey hole," she said, "but we couldn't make out what they was saying."

"Well, I want to stay in Spencer," Miri said. "So does my father. But I'm afraid if we do stay and there's a war, he'll go to New York City and try to enlist. He might even go to Massachusetts. They're already recruiting colored soldiers, and so are Connecticut and Rhode Island.

Lord, I hate the idea of my father becoming a soldier. He could be injured or worse. We need him to run the shop. Neither Mother nor I know how to cut hair, much less run a barbershop. Ezra is still an apprentice and Georgie's a silly boy."

Vi listened quietly to Miri's complaints.

Once her objections to emigration were fully aired Miri fell silent and became aware of Vi's pensive expression. It crossed her mind that Vi might be thinking about her father.

The night one of the underground conductor's brought Vi and her mother to the Whitfield house, Miri's task was to find clothes to replace the rags Vi wore. She picked through an assortment of her outgrown clothes and donations, and asked the girl, "Where is your father, Viola?"

"No need to say Viola, Miss. Everybody calls me Vi. I ain't got no idea where Pap be. He was sold near 'bout three weeks before me and Mam 'scaped from Mississippi."

Though the answer pained her, Miri cringed at Vi's speech and grammar.

She and Vi were the same age, but their lives could not have been more different. Vi had been born and raised a slave, property to be bought and sold as her owner desired. Miri had talked to other runaway slaves and knew most were worked the same as animals. The concept appalled her.

She regretted her insensitivity to Vi then, and felt the same now. "Sorry for going on so," she said. "On the bright side, are you happy to be moving? Your apartment is right above the butcher's, not far from my father's shop."

"I'm excited 'bout Mam and me gettin' our own place," Vi answered, "but I'm more happy 'bout havin' these here papers." She patted the bag tied to her belt. "Now I got 'em, nobody can take me back down to Mississippi."

Miri held her tongue and said nothing about the uncertain protection of the registration papers. *No sense in telling Vi. It would only frighten her.*

Throughout the morning she pushed thoughts of emigration and the possibility of war aside by concentrating on classwork. At lunchtime Vi and Portia sat together while Miri took her basket of food and book to a table under a leafless oak tree. Clarice joined her and they ate in silence until Clarice said, "You're too quiet, Miri. What has you out of sorts?"

Miri's answer was curt. "Nothing." *Clarice won't ever understand how many problems emigration is creating for me. How could she? She's white.*

"You're fibbing," Clarice said. "It's about Haiti, isn't it?"

The question drew an irritated, "Leave me be. I don't want to talk about it," from Miri before she retreated into morose silence.

After school she spent an hour or so tutoring Vi in spelling and helped her work on penmanship. Turning to her own homework, Miri began reciting a poem she had to memorize for elocution class. She got lost in the middle of the rhyme and started the poem again from the beginning.

"That's coming along nicely," her mother said at the end of the second attempt. "But you'd better stop now. Your father's expecting you. Here are the clean towels, and don't forget to pick up the dirty ones."

Miri recited the poem to herself as she carried the basket of towels to the barbershop. She stepped on the stoop and rapped on the door. Her father's deep, hearty laugh rang out and she was unsure if he heard her knock.

It was customary for a woman to knock on the door of a barbershop to alert the men that a woman was about to enter their all male kingdom. The knock served to halt all discussion of male topics, crude language and bawdy jokes.

Her patience gone, Miri rapped again and opened the door. Two men were listening to Dr. Stillman read the newspaper pinned to the bulletin board. Ezra froze, his razor in midair. Her father's cough prompted Ezra to stop gaping and blurt out, "Good evening, Miriam."

She said hello, passed his chair to place the basket of towels in a corner away from falling hair, and noted his customer was the older Haitian who had been at the meeting.

She and Ezra Wright, the butcher's second son, had been in the same grade. But Ezra had shown no aptitude for schooling or at handling butchering saws and cleavers. He nearly severed a finger during his only attempt at carving a carcass, so with his father's blessing he had left school six years ago at the age of twelve to apprentice at the barber shop.

Although Miri had no interest in Ezra, and showed it, he developed a growing attraction to her. He recently hinted that when his training was completed he planned to open a shop in nearby Lansingburg and would shortly thereafter be financially able to marry.

After that, Miri did her best to avoid him. She rarely thought about him, and when she did it was to liken him to her uncle's oxen, steady and reliable, but plodding and rather dull. *But what if Ezra asked Father's permission to court me? Ezra knows I want to pursue more education at a college or finishing school.*

Becoming the wife of any man, especially him, isn't among my goals.

"Hello, Miri," her father said. "A bit late aren't you?"

Aware she was watched by the younger Haitian in her father's chair, Miri's face flushed and an unaccustomed shyness came over her. "Yes, Father. I was busy with homework."

"Well, good you're here to tidy the place up," he said over the snip of his scissors. "Best get to it."

The four men listening to Dr. Stillman placed hats on their newly shorn heads and left the shop. Miri began refilling the shakers with powder. The light, fresh scent of talcum was a pleasant contrast to the more earthy odors of hair oils and the tang of Bay Rum aftershave lotion.

Georgie should be doing this, not me, she mused as she wiped the oak countertop with a damp cloth. *I'm sixteen and I've outgrown this chore. He isn't a child and it's time he took on a fair share of work.*

She arranged four straight razors in a row alongside the combs and three sets of clippers and went over to the small coal stove. The accumulation of ash in its belly was low, so she left it.

The eyes of the young Haitian followed her.

She lifted the ball-shaped towel warmer off the stove took it to the counter and set it on a trivet to cool. Next she dusted mugs hung on a rack over the counter.

Her father ran a clean business and customers who kept personal shaving mugs in the shop could be sure they were stored clean and unused by anyone else. She glanced at her reflection in the long horizontal mirror in front of the chairs and met the eyes of the young Haitian.

He smiled.

Intent on his work, her father didn't notice the exchange. But Ezra had, and a spear of jealousy pierced his heart.

Once again Miri's face glowed with warmth. She smiled in return, stepped onto a footstool and stretched to dust the top of the mug rack. Her skirt snagged on the bottom corner of the counter and she was thrown off balance.

Ezra was immediately at her elbow. Nothing he'd ever done had caused Miri to blush or fall off her feet. When he began his apprenticeship, she was simply the daughter of his mentor, the girl who often skipped alongside her father as he walked to the shop.

Everything changed when they were fourteen. Miri began to spend time in the shop. She was a budding beauty. Her skin was a combination of milky fairness from white ancestors with a hint of those from Africa. Her face was a perfect oval, and above high cheekbones holding the rosy tint of a ripe peach, were hazel eyes. Fascinated by her unusual and somewhat exotic features Ezra would stop clipping or brushing hair from a customer's shoulders and stare at her.

When she was near he had an urge to pull the hairpins from the bun on her neck and release the heavy mane of shining black hair. He tried to imagine it unconfined. Was it wavy? If she loosened her hair would she be even more beautiful? He restrained himself from acting foolish as he did several years ago when he'd pulled a ribbon from one of her braids. Miri rewarded him with a stony look and her father rebuked him for larking about.

Conversations between them were brief and awkward. He could barely utter a greeting, but listened as she discussed her studies, the war, politics and world topics with her father. Though he admired her intelligence, Ezra didn't approve of Miri's outspokenness. He wondered why her father encouraged her to continue interests in activities that would serve her no good when she was a wife and mother.

Miri had become a young lady, mandated by custom and her social class to begin wearing a corset at age thirteen. The unwelcome garment emphasized her waist and hips, and its restrictions also forced her to move with a graceful sway that mesmerized Ezra. He was determined to court her and make her his wife.

Miri's father whisked a brush across the young Haitian's collar and waved off payment. He said, "This one's on the house, Philippe. A courtesy. You can pay for service in the future."

"Thank you, Mr. Whitfield," the young man answered in slightly accented English.

"Closing time, gentlemen," her father said as he ushered customers out.

Miri received another smile from Philippe as he left. She never heard Ezra's goodbye. *Philippe.* She liked the name. *It's the French version of Philip, different but not too much.*

Her father removed his apron, settled into the leather barber chair and propped his feet on the footrest. With a sigh he unfolded the paper and scoured it as he did every day for the latest information on the escalating war. A sausage-sized finger turned the page.

Miri marveled at how skillfully he was able to employ scissors and razor with hands that appeared thick and clumsy. It was rare to have any of his customers complain of being nicked.

She snacked on a handful of peanuts from the barrel and dropped the shells on the floor. They'd get swept up shortly along with bits of hair from today's barbering. She wiped off her hands, picked up a cloth and polished the towel warmer.

There was the sound of rustling and a snap, followed by her father exploding out of the chair. An angry scowl twisted his face. "Here!" he said. He thrust the newspaper at her and went outside.

While she wondered what he had read that upset him, he brought the barber pole inside, thumped it down and marched away.

The answer to her question covered the entire front page:

> *INCREASING ATTACKS ON FREE PEOPLE OF COLOR.*
> *COLORED DOCKWORKERS BEATEN BY WHITE MOB.*
> *VIOLENCE ESCALATING.*
> *HOMES OF COLORED FAMILIES LOOTED AND BURNED.*

There was also an editorial with quotes from a politician named Samuel S. Cox and from Archbishop John Hughes of the Roman Catholic Church. Both men believed white soldiers would not fight a war to satisfy a bunch of abolitionists.

All of the news was grim.

Chapter 4

April 1862

"Miri, time to get ready for school."

School meant facing Clarice and Portia and their cheery outlooks toward emigration. Miri considered it, then burrowed deeper under the blanket.

Moments later her mother came into the room. "Why aren't you up yet?" she asked.

"I think I'm sick," Miri answered weakly.

Her mother pulled back the covers. "Open your mouth. Say 'ahhh'." She laid a palm on Miri's forehead. "Hmmm. No fever and your eyes and mouth are clear. Come on, young lady. Out of bed this minute! Get dressed and go eat breakfast. Hurry or you'll be tardy."

The bell had already rung by the time Miri got to school. She slipped into the line filing into the building, pretending not to notice Clarice waving. *If I don't talk to Clarice again I won't have to hear why sailing off to Haiti should be such a joyous adventure.*

"Charles Addison?" the teacher said.

"Here, Miss Thackerly."

The seat in front of Miri was empty.

"Micah Boynton?"

"Present."

Miss Thackerly's eyes took a bead on Micah "Present, what Micah?" she asked.

Miri knew Micah was on thin ice. Miss Thackerly was a stickler for the use of proper titles when addressing someone.

"Present, Miss Thackerly," he answered. Miri saw the hint of a sneer in the curl of his lip but if the teacher noticed, she chose to ignore it.

"Thank you, Micah."

"Gabriel Fipps?" As the teacher continued taking attendance, Miri wondered if Vi was delivering laundry to her mother's customers.

"Viola?"

Vi slid into her seat, panting. "Here, Miz Thack-e-ly," she said.

The teacher's eyes narrowed. "It's Miss Thack-ER-ly, Viola."

"Yes, Maam. Thack-re-ly."

Vi's answer initiated snickers from some of the boys.

Miss Thackerly's sour frown quickly squelched the hilarity and she continued to take attendance.

Miri regarded Vi. *I wonder if we can become friends. She can't replace Clarice, and I'm not sure we have much in common, but she will be going to Haiti.*

When she arrived weeks ago, Vi was rough, uneducated and in ragged clothes. Now she had a selection of dresses and though she found corset and slips annoying, accepted both as appropriate to her new identity. Vi's hair had been a challenge for Miri, but after undergoing multiple washings and treatment with pomade it was tamed. Two neat plaits now replaced the many crooked little braids that made Vi's head resemble a fuzzy spider.

Vi's inability to walk properly annoyed Miri, but she held her tongue. It wasn't Vi's fault she stomped about clumsily, her feet were still adjusting to the confinement of shoes. Still, if she was going to be accepted as a free person she had to learn to move and act like one. It occurred to Miri the adjustment might come quicker if Vi was exposed to polite society more often.

"Miriam Whitfield?"

"Present, Miss Thackerly." Miri opened her reader, tapped Vi's shoulder and whispered. "Would you like to come over to my house after school?"

Vi turned, her agate-black eyes narrow as the coin slot on the drug store scale. "What about Clarice?" she asked. "Ain't y'all friends no more?"

"Hush," Miri warned. *If we became friends, improving Vi's grammar will be another thing to work on.* "Of course Clarice and I are still friends," she fibbed. "I just think it'd be nice if you and I got to know each other a little better."

"I'd like to visit with you," Vi said, "But Mam got more laundry to deliver tomorrow and I'ze supposed to help her fold it."

"Well, let's ask her anyway. She might say yes."

Later that afternoon, in the Starks' small kitchen, Mrs. Starks was ironing. Heat radiated from the stove, making the room almost unbearable. Vi and her mother didn't seem affected, but to Miri it felt more like

August than April. The heat, along with the stench of blood, offal and rancid meat rising from the butcher shop below made the atmosphere intolerable. She feared that in another moment she might vomit, and wanted desperately to get outside.

Mrs. Starks listened as Vi asked if she could spend time at Miri's house.

"There's a load of work, Viola," she said, "and I needs you doing your share."

Miri said, "I'll help Vi with her work, Mrs. Starks."

Vi's mother chuckled. She placed the cool flatiron on the stove, moved a hot one to a trivet and positioned a shirt on the ironing board. "These is Vi's chores, Miss Miri," she said. "You cain't be doing work like this."

Disappointment erased the eager light from Miri's face. Vi said nothing. Mrs. Starks looked at them, sighed and ran the iron along a sleeve. "Go along then, Vi, and visit Miss Miri. She seems to need of a bit of comforting."

Vi grinned and her cheeks puffed out like shiny, brown gourds.

Her mood bright again, Miri swung her hat by its ties as they walked up Hill Street. "I'm glad we'll get a chance to know each other better before we go to Haiti," she said. "Being friends will be nice."

Vi said, "I ain't going to Haiti."

Miri stopped walking. "What do you mean you're not going?"

"Mam was told she won't get no land if she don't got no husband with her, and she thinks it be hard to find enough work in Haiti to support us. 'Sides, we want to wait here for Pap."

Miri's spirits plummeted again. "This is unbelievable," she said. "Half of my family will be staying here and none of my friends are moving to Haiti. How much more am I going to lose?" Tears fed by deep sorrow wet her cheeks and the walk home was punctuated by her sobs.

At Miri's house, the two girls sat on opposite sides of the kitchen table. Vi extended a hand across to Miri, hesitated, and let it drop. "Sorry I ain't going to Haiti," Vi said, her voice filled with concern, "but Mam say we be better off in Spencer. We got a place to live, she have regular customers for laundry an' ironing, and like I sayed, my Pap is going to come lookin' for us."

Miri sat unmoving as a block of ice, cold as the pond in January.

"Cheer up Miri," Vi said. "Portia and lots of other girls are going to Haiti and you'll make new friends aplenty."

I don't agree, Miri thought, *but I don't have the energy to talk about it.*

Vi gave up on the one sided conversation. "See you tomorrow, Miri," she said.

The door latch dropped into its slot and tears poured down Miri's face. Georgie entered with an armful of kindling, and heard her sniffling. In a hurry to flee the mysterious, frightening presence of a crying female, he dropped the wood as if it was on fire. It clattered into the bin near the stove and the noise summoned their mother to the kitchen.

She saw Miri's face and wasted no time in questioning her. "Why are you crying?" Without waiting for an answer she said, "It's about the move, isn't it?"

Miri could only nod.

"I thought so," her mother said. "Not everyone is keen on leaving Spencer for the unknown, Miri, but we have to make the best of it."

"I don't care about making the best of it, Mother. I hate the whole idea. I can't understand why we're allowing Mr. Lincoln to tell us we have to leave. He's supposed to protect us here."

"Listen to me, Miriam," her mother said. Her left eyelid twitched, an indication she was irritated. "You'd better accept the fact we're going to Haiti and stop whining."

Miri didn't say a word. *There's no sense arguing about it. Nothing will change.*

She got up and went out to stand on the porch. A breeze stirred the hem of her skirt and it danced about her ankles. The crisp evening air cleared her muzzied brain. *Mother's right,* she thought. *I can't stop the move and shouldn't try so hard to resist it. Still, it's a terrible thing to accept.*

A light snowfall began, winter's attempt to linger. Drifting flakes glistened in the twilight. It reminded Miri that she had always loved snow, especially the first snow. A layer of pristine white snow did something magical to the bleak, scarred world. Dead lawns and frostbitten flowerbeds were hidden and bare tree branches reached for a portion of cold beauty to wear like lace.

Spencer's brief, blazing autumn was her other special joy. For a few weeks each year, colors on trees burned across the hills and valleys. The red, yellow and deep orange palette lasted until all the leaves had fallen like flaming butterflies.

She leaned against the bannister, tied to misery by the growing realization she would never experience seasonal changes in Haiti. The island was tropical and warm the entire year.

"Supper's ready," Her mother called from the kitchen.

Miri inhaled a final breath of the night air and went inside feeling hollow but not hungry.

Father wasn't home and they'd eat without him. He was so certain Mr. Lincoln would respond favorably to the letter from the Society, he and a couple of men were making rounds of nearby communities. The goal was to stir up enthusiasm among men of color for enlistment in the army, in the event war erupted.

Days then weeks went by without a word from Mr. Lincoln. Her father's anti-emigration sentiment slowly shifted and he became more and more somber.

Miri stayed close to home and tried to stay occupied rather than dwell on the possibility of an unpleasant answer from Lincoln. She devoted more time to homework assignments and piano practice, and was pleased with the improvements gained.

As a result, Miss Thackerly not only asked her to continue helping Vi, but added several students who were behind in reading to Miri's care. Miss Reed, her piano teacher, complimented her skills and said, "I do believe you are capable of giving beginning level lessons, Miriam."

Teaching was under consideration as a possible career and Miri liked hearing she showed an aptitude for the profession. *I don't want to be a housewife, at least not in the near future, and traditional female occupations of dressmaking, millinery and nanny don't appeal to me. Since Mother and Father both oppose careers for women, I have to wait for the right circumstances to raise the issue.* She took the precious nuggets of praise as secret gifts to open periodically and enjoy and began to think about looking for education and training opportunities on her own.

· · · · ·

Four long weeks passed before a letter from Washington arrived. She followed her father as he took it into the kitchen. He pulled the paper from the envelope and scanned it.

Her mother stopped kneading bread dough and placed a towel over the bowl.

Miri's shoulders rose along with the tension in the room.

Her father scowled, crushed the letter and tossed it onto the table. "Just as I expected," he said bitterly. He wheeled around and snatched his hat from its hook. "Lincoln!" he fumed. "What in thunderation is wrong with that man?"

"Mind your temper, Henry," her mother said as the door slammed.

The sound brought a galloping Georgie to the kitchen. He saw the crumpled letter. "Is that from the President?" he asked.

Miri nodded. Goosebumps skittered along her arms. She smoothed the paper with her palm, already knowing from her father's reaction what the letter contained.

"Let me see it," her mother said.

"We all should know precisely what Mr. Lincoln wrote, Mother. I'll read it."

Dear Sirs,

While I sympathize with your difficulties, there are clear differences between our races, which will never allow your race to live here as equal citizens. This I cannot change even if I desired to. If your race were not among us, there would not be a war.

It is extremely selfish to think that you could live pleasantly here when the needs of your race so clearly point to the need for building a homeland elsewhere. I hope for the good of mankind you will continue plans to become pioneers in establishing a colony in Haiti, or in the central Americas. A more practical solution cannot be found.

As for the question of men of color joining the army, I cannot under the circumstances permit this.

Signed,
Abraham Lincoln, President of the United States

The harshness of the words was shocking. Miri's stomach knotted and her fingers itched to shred the paper. "This is horrible," she said. "I can't understand why Mr. Lincoln is being so mean and unkind to us."

Her mother took the letter. "We must hope things will work out for the best," she sighed.

"Best for who, Mother? Father will not accept living here without equal rights, President Lincoln wants us to disappear, and there's the war. I don't believe moving to Haiti is the best for me but I have no choice, no say in anything."

Furrows creased her mother's forehead. "Would you please stop whining," she said. "Go practice your piano lesson."

Miri flew into a rage. "Why is it that whenever you don't like a comment I make, you tell me to hush. I'm not a child."

"Miriam Rose…,"

Her mother's withering glare brought Miri to her feet. She flounced into the parlor, flipped open her music book to the current lesson and ran through the chords. Unable to focus, her fingers couldn't find the correct keys and she wasn't able to play the entire piece without repeating the same mistakes. She wound the metronome. *Maybe I'll work on a rhythm exercise. It might help me stop fretting about emigration for a moment.* She tapped the arm of the metronome and set it in motion. It sounded like a clock, each tick a reminder that her time in Spencer was drawing to a close. She halted the metronome's sweeping arm, closed the cover over the piano keys and rejoined her mother in the kitchen where, side by side with little conversation, they prepared supper.

Her father returned and announced he had called an emergency meeting for that evening. "I'm fed up with being disregarded by the government," he said, jabbing his fork in the air, "and I am not convinced about this Haiti scheme." He told them he planned to recruit a group of men to go to Washington and request an appointment to speak directly with Mr. Lincoln. The meeting would center on his duty to grant, without further delay, full citizenship and equal rights to all freeborn people of color.

His plan gave new life to Miri's hope of remaining in Spencer. *When Father makes up his mind, he's capable of achieving almost anything.*

"Clear the table as soon as we finish eating, Miri," her mother said. "There's not much time but we need to make something to serve."

The pans of cake had just been taken from the oven when a cluster of men arrived as if lured by the aroma. Philippe and Dr. Stillman were among the group.

In the parlor, the growing crowd waited quietly with tense faces as Miri's father paced in front of the fireplace. Every few minutes he pulled a watch from his vest pocket and checked the time. At seven o'clock sharp, his voice rose above the murmur to call the meeting to order.

Determined to be in the parlor during the meeting, Miri went to the kitchen and quickly sliced up one of the cakes. *Serving refreshments will justify my being in the room.*

The back door opened and Portia walked in with her father. He went straight through to the parlor without greeting Miri or her mother. Portia hung up her coat and Miri handed her a plate of cake slices. "Here, come help me serve," she said.

"Right now?"

"Yes, now," Miri hissed. She glanced at her mother who was busy washing dishes, and hoped she wouldn't notice it was too early to serve refreshments. *If she stops us it will ruin my plan. Why can't Portia simply do as she's told without asking questions?*

Soon they were in the parlor holding empty plates.

Portia tugged Miri's sleeve and said, "Let's go get more cake."

Miri moved, but not toward the kitchen. "Go over there," she whispered, pointing to a space at the rear of a group. "No one will see us and we'll be able to hear better."

Portia shook her head and said, "We'll be in trouble if we stay."

"Suit yourself," Miri said. She positioned herself behind a hefty man in a gray suit.

Her father pounded the mantle as he told the crowd, "We need to make one last attempt to persuade Lincoln to grant us full and equal rights and the protection we are entitled to."

The ensuing debate over the usefulness of a trip to Washington for a meeting with Mr. Lincoln became a noisy exchange of opposing opinions. The back and forth exchange lasted until her father shouted, "Who will stand with me?"

Dr. Stillman, Minister Grady, Mr. Heacock, the undertaker and four other men joined him. He shook hands with each of them and said, "Good. We'll leave on the morning train."

Miri wanted to cheer her father's bravery but, fearing discovery, slipped out of the room instead, unaware Philippe was watching her.

Chapter 5

May 1862

M iri noticed the hush hanging over the house as she hurried to dress. Except for the absence of conversation, the scene in the kitchen was one of normal breakfast activity; Georgie was shoveling oatmeal into his mouth and her father held a steaming cup of coffee. Off to the side her mother sorted and folded laundry. An open suitcase holding some of her father's clothes lay on the counter.

Miri suspected the travel bag was at the root of the silence. Unsure of how to bring up his trip, she rolled and unrolled a pair of socks and debated what to say. In the end she pushed the socks into a corner of the suitcase as a wild string of words spooled from her mouth.

"I know I can't go to Washington with you, Father, but when you meet with Mr. Lincoln please remind him this is our rightful home. We haven't broken any laws and we don't deserve to be exiled like common criminals."

Her father paused, cup midway to his mouth. An eyebrow lifted. "I . . . ," he said attempting to speak but Miri wasn't finished.

"Tell Mr. Lincoln he is duty bound to protect us and must let us stay here," she said. "He must!"

Her father's reply came as a deep, angry growl. "Of course we're not criminals." He got up and closed the suitcase. "Mr. Lincoln is fully aware of that. He simply doesn't consider us worth protecting. We're going to Washington to try to change his opinion."

Her mother reached between them to shift a saucepan from the stove to a trivet on the counter and Miri stepped back to avoid the hot utensil. She said, "I know you'll do your best to persuade him, Father."

"You need to stop your chattering, young lady, and eat your breakfast," her mother said.

Miri didn't dare defy or argue with her mother lest she incur her father's wrath. She closed the conversation by telling him, "I'll miss you, and shall pray for your safety every night."

Though she had no appetite, she stirred a spoonful of honey into the bowl of oatmeal and forced herself to eat. The muffled atmosphere returned, adding to the heaviness of each spoonful, and her shoulders sagged. The quiet was interrupted by the faint squeal of carriage wheels followed by the rap of the door knocker.

Her father went to answer the door and the rest of the family abandoned breakfast and followed him. He invited undertaker Grady and two other men into the parlor, and had almost closed the door when Dr. Stillman's buggy, pulled by a leggy roan, drew up in front of the porch. Philippe jumped down from the passenger seat and tied the horse to the hitching post.

In her haste to dress, Miri had not bothered to fix her hair. Unwilling to be seen by Philippe looking unkempt, she fled to her bedroom. Moments later, properly coiffed, she reentered the parlor to hear Dr. Stillman speaking to her father.

"Again, Henry," he said, "extending the hospitality of your home to Philippe while we're away is a gracious gesture. His uncle, as you know, had to return to Haiti and his medical practice. Had I a wife, Philippe could remain in my house while I'm gone but...."

No need to explain," her father said. "I agree with you. Given we'll be petitioning against emigration to Haiti, it wouldn't be logical to bring him along, and he certainly cannot be left alone to fend for himself." He laid a hand on Philippe's shoulder and said, "I'm sure Georgie won't mind sharing his room with you for a few days, young man."

Miri looked around for Georgie but the soon-to-be host was absent. He had probably snuck off to avoid helping with chores.

Philippe also scanned the parlor and eventually his eyes met Miri's. He smiled, and she noticed a dimple appear near the lower left corner of his mouth. They continued to gaze at each other with curiosity that soon bordered on fascination. For Miri, given her age and upbringing, staring openly at a boy would be considered bold and brazen behavior. Nor was she concerned whether the frank and intense interest Philippe was showing toward her was acceptable in middle class Haitian society. Her common sense was overpowered by new and exhilarating emotions. Goose bumps tingled her arms, and a sensation of weightlessness infused her body. Never had she felt this way... so light that the most delicate of winds could carry her beyond the clouds. The fantasy of drifting across the sky with Philippe caused her to unconsciously move to his side.

The scent he gave off was subtle, more robust than Bay Rum with an intriguing undertone of coffee. She inhaled the unique aroma which seemed to cling to her every fiber. If asked, Miri would have been unable to describe or name what she was experiencing. Others of course would understand. She was enraptured. A yearning to embrace Philippe possessed and pulled so strongly, her arms ached with the need.

An arm encircled her, but it wasn't Philippe's. It was her father's, and over his shoulder she saw the tight mouth and arched neck of her mother, who had come into view. Back from searching for Georgie she had witnessed the exchange between Miri and Philippe.

Tethered once again to reality, Miri was embarrassed. She wondered if her father or any of the other men had noticed her inappropriate behavior. At best she expected a lecture from her mother, at worst more severe punishment. Either way, with Philippe living in her house, sharing meals and conversations for a week or more, she faced a huge test of her resolve. They would be in close proximity with each other, and her mother's eagle eye missed nothing. It was therefore essential she act with the propriety and decorum of her social class.

Her father turned to Georgie and grasped his hand. "Take care of your mother and sister while I'm away, Son," he said, pumping their arms up and down. "And remember, Philippe is our guest, so be civil to him."

Miri dismissed the ridiculous idea of irresponsible Georgie as a protector. At the same time she noted his narrow chest expand as he accepted the assignment. Proudly he said, "You can count on me, Pa."

The men donned hats and coats and moved outside where a light fog dampened the air. The delegation climbed aboard buggies and the quartet on the porch waved them on their way as the horses moved off at a trot.

As the vehicles disappeared into the overcast morning, Miri's mood turned as soggy as the weather. She went back to the kitchen to subject it to a thorough cleaning. If she kept herself busy there wouldn't be opportunity to fret. Soon she had the dishes washed and put away and the cast iron cook pots scraped and oiled. She wiped down the stove, noticed the supply of tinder was low and went to the woodpile. She carried kindling back to the kitchen in the skirt of her apron and dumped it into the bucket. Her final tasks were sweeping and mopping the dirt and crumbs and chips of wood dotting the floor. Pleased with what she had accomplished, she was ready to stop for a cup of tea and a slice of bread.

The mantle clock chimed, and she was surprised to realize it was ten o'clock. She had worked for two hours without any sign of her mother, Georgie, or Philippe.

To catch a breath of fresh air she wandered out to the front porch.

Her mother sat there on a wooden rocking chair, staring out at the empty street. Georgie and Philippe were nowhere to be seen. Miri pulled up the other rocker and sat beside her. The overcast sky had cleared, and flowers on the forsythia bush danced in the breeze like miniature bells of sunshine. "I hope we don't have to move to Haiti," she said. "But if we do, what do suppose it'll be like?"

Her mother shrugged. "I don't know. I know this move is what Mr. Lincoln feels is best for us. I am also not as certain as your father that the President will change his mind."

Miri persisted. "But what do you think is best?"

Her mother shrugged again. "Your father will decide that," she said.

If her mother ever formed an independent opinion, Miri doubted she would voice it. She had read enough about the growing movement for female equality to know that not every woman allowed a man to totally control her life the way her mother did. Her father was a good man, of that she was certain. Considerate of the family, he didn't make rash decisions and would never place them in harm's way. Still, emigration would have a monumental effect on her future and it was Miri's belief she should be able to participate in the decision whether to leave or not.

As she was about to bring up that point, she was summoned to the kitchen by the shriek of the kettle, and went inside to make tea. If her father's ultimate decision was to emigrate, she knew her mother would not dispute it. Her hope that she would never leave Spencer was shattered to the sounds of the snap and pop of burning wood.

While her father was absent, Miri's routine of school, piano lessons and church remained unchanged with one exception. Because he wasn't there it was not proper for her to go to the barbershop. She believed cleaning it should now be Georgie's chore, but she missed being allowed to experience, even briefly, the private world of men.

Ezra kept the shop open, and reported a drop in business. Many of her father's regular customers chose to scrape the stubble from their own chins and pomade their untrimmed hair into place until Mr. Whitfield returned.

Miri marked off the passing of each day he was away with an X on the calendar. Philippe was staying at her house but there weren't many opportunities for them to be alone. Their contact was kept brief by her mother out of a concern for propriety. She discouraged familiarity between the two young people by assigning Philippe a multitude of chores. He chopped wood, weeded the kitchen vegetable garden, fixed the hinge on the gate and painted the tool shed. In addition, he was supposed to keep an eye on Georgie who proved to be a slippery one. Twice he eluded Philippe and joined a group of boys to play stickball.

One day, to thwart Georgie's obvious attempt to avoid work, Mrs. Whitfield decided he, Miri, and Philippe should help collect herbs in the fields along the edge of town. Henbane, dandelion leaves and other plants and flowers she used in remedies for the ill or injured, were at their peak.

The three walked toward open fields while Georgie alternated between dashing ahead and sulking at the rear. As she walked alongside Philippe, Miri estimated him to be about five inches taller than she was. This was the closest she had been to him, and she noticed freckles sprinkled over his ruddy face. The tight curls covering his head had a reddish tint and she wondered if the color was common among Haitians. He was handsome and the attraction she felt made her blush.

"In Haiti we have many *naturopatiques* (natural healers)," he said, using the French form of the word. "And I'd like to learn and compare to see if the herbs they employ are the same or similar to these."

"You're studying with Dr. Stillman. I wonder whether he'd approve of your interest in what he thinks of as folk medicine," she said.

"Many of the poor in Haiti trust natural healers more than someone with formal medical training. They are suspicious of doctors because of the difference in class and education. If I am to work among the poor, and cure the diseases they suffer and die from, I must first understand the medicine they use."

Miri admired Philippe's goal to improve the situation of his less fortunate countrymen. His desire to learn about herbal potions also gained her mother's respect, and Mrs. Whitfield allowed him to assist with grinding seeds and observe the preparation of various concoctions. He twisted and pounded the pestle as Miri cut small rectangles of paper to be used in packaging single doses. She and Philippe talked as they worked, and each realized the other intended to pursue a career before marriage.

"I think women who want to go to college should be allowed to do so," Philippe said, and his sentiment deepened Miri's attraction.

Her mother saw only two young people chatting while busy at a meaningful task.

Eight days later, Miri, her mother, Philippe and Georgie, eager to hear details of the meeting with the President, clustered around her father and Dr. Stillman. Miri looked for a glimmer of brightness in her father's eyes, but saw none. He looked grim as the devil.

"We had two discussions with Mr. Lincoln," he said. "Both times he made it perfectly clear that free people of color are a problem for his administration. He will not grant us full equality. On that he is firm. As far as Mr. Lincoln is concerned, the only solution is for us to leave and establish our own country somewhere else. I never thought I'd speak these words," he said through clenched teeth, "but I agree with him. We will not stay where we are not wanted."

"No," Miri cried as she blinked away tears. "I don't understand. Why won't he protect us, Father?" Suddenly her breath wouldn't come. The world canted, her legs lost strength. About to faint, she clutched the rough tweed sleeve of her father's jacket.

He held her elbow for support and said, "He's not of a mind to, Miri. That leaves us with no choice."

Miri closed her eyes and listened to him pronounce their fate.

"We have to go forward and we will do so with dignity."

Chapter 6

June 1862

Each week the number of crates and boxes increased, and as the stacks grew, any hope Miri had to remain in Spencer shriveled. The decision to emigrate had been made and packing went forward in earnest.

The indignity of being forced to relocate was made even worse by Mrs. Whitfield's insistence on checking the contents of every container over and over again, lest something be overlooked. To aid her at this task, she employed Miri to pore over the list provided by the Emigration Society of food, clothing, household supplies and tools the colonists were advised to take with them. The list was compiled by Mr. Redpath during the year he lived in Haiti, and was published in a thin book, *The Pine and Palm.*

Pencil in hand, her mother read her list. "Honey."

"Yes," Miri answered.

"Molasses."

"Yes."

"Tinned beef."

"Yes."

"Flour."

"Cornmeal."

"Tea and coffee."

Miri barely glanced at the label. Why waste time? Nothing had been unpacked since they last checked.

Her mother continued.

"Yes," Miri replied. "Yes." "Yes."

She waited for the name of the next item. Her mother had gone quiet, gazing at a rectangular box of polished oak sitting on the sideboard. "Bring my medicine case to the table, Miri," she said. "I need to check my supplies. Since I chatted with Philippe, I feel it's important to take along a good quantity of everything. There is no telling what I'll be able to have shipped. Mr. Redpath doesn't say anything about medicinal plants in his book, and I don't suppose he knows much about them, so I believe it's wise to bring my own. Heaven knows what I'll find in Haiti, and it will take time to identify which herbs are the same or similar to these."

Miri unlatched the silver clasp of the case and raised the lid. Inside, bottles were arranged in orderly rows, and tucked into compartments along each side of the case were bags of herbs and small squares of paper. A pouch in the lining on the underside of the lid held her mother's prized book on nursing written by Florence Nightingale. A gift from The Ladies Benevolent Society, it had been presented to her mother in gratitude for her care and assistance to the afflicted during the recent influenza epidemic.

As she removed each bottle Miri tightened the lid. The dried seeds and leaves they contained were familiar to her. As soon as she could walk and carry a basket she had gone out to the fields and bogs around Spencer in the spring and summer with her mother and grandmother collecting plants and flowers.

There was yarrow to treat bleeding, furry, caterpillar-green leaves of horehound to brew for colds and coughing, pennyroyal to fold inside a compress for a sting, sassafras prepared as tea for rheumatism, wild indigo to remedy stoppage in the bowels, and jewel weed to remove warts and cure ringworm. For the discomfort of female ailments there was bitter rue, white pine bark and lobelia.

Seasonal herbs in silk bags, secured by draw-strings, were used to treat the bites, stings, indigestion, congestion and other illnesses resistant to more common concoctions. One bag held colorful little Johnny-jump-ups. The flower was used to make a cough syrup, and the leaves used to make tea to alleviate pain. One bag contained the herb grandmother called "heartsease." Drinking tea brewed made with its flowers was said to mend a broken heart.

The final container in the case held the only item her mother purchased. Miri held the jar up to the light to admire the radiance given off by its contents. Honey was truly a marvel of nature. She liked the sweetness it added to food and drink and especially adored the honey cake they had on special occasions. As a medicine, her mother used honey in various preparations to treat a variety of physical problems from coughs to burns. Bandaged with cloths that had been dipped in honey, all but the most severe burns healed without leaving scars.

Miri assisted with pulverizing and blending herbs and had watched her mother quietly minister to a sick person or a woman in labor. Women in the community, no matter their color, trusted Mrs. Whitfield's skill and sought her assistance to deliver their babies.

The idea of becoming an herbalist and midwife held some appeal for Miri despite published criticism from doctors about the lack of formal training these women practitioners had. With less than a handful of medical schools allowing women to enroll, men dominated the medical field. Yet, most women did not go to male doctors for female afflictions or for help at childbirth. Midwifery and healing were respected female occupations.

For Miri the question was whether she had the stomach to be a midwife. She had accompanied her mother to several deliveries and been assigned to simple tasks. She heated water, gathered clean rags and towels and kept young children from being underfoot. She had yet to witness a human baby enter the world, but had seen the birth of a calf at Portia's. The sight of the cow's bulging eyes as it heaved and strained during labor made her stomach roil, while the stink of blood, urine and manure assaulted her nose. She found the process slimy and foul.

Miri set the bottle of honey beside the case and said, "What is Mrs. Knox going to do after you leave, Mother? Who will take your place as midwife?"

"I've already discussed it with your grandmother and she's agreed to come out of retirement and take on someone to train. I've recommended two upstanding young ladies I believe are good candidates. She returned the bottle of honey to the box. "I'm finished here," she said, and left the room.

Miri put the medicine case back on the sideboard and looked around. The walls were bare. Paintings had been taken down and packed for shipment. She passed a hand across a crate labeled *Pictures.* Inside were tintype photographs and portraits of her grandparents and other relatives who weren't going to Haiti.

She went to the desk, inked a pen, printed *Family* on a label and blotted the ink. When it was dry she turned the label over, spread glue on the back and placed it alongside the other. Satisfied the important cargo was properly identified she gave the label one final pat.

Her mother entered the room and Miri recognized the dresses draped over her arm. They were bought last fall for Miri to wear to school.

Right after classes began she had a growth spurt that added three inches to her height, and as she grew, the skirts rose. Even with the hems let out, they ended above her ankles, too short to be proper. Much to her mother's dismay, it meant the purchase of a new wardrobe, but Miri was delighted. Her legs were stork-like and needed to be hidden. At five feet six inches tall she could look directly into her mother's eyes. The new outfits more suited the young lady she had become.

Her mother folded the outgrown dresses and placed them in a box of donations to go to the church for distribution to the needy. "It's time you sorted through your books, Miri," she said. "There's only space to pack a few, so decide which ones you want to keep."

"All of them, Mother." This was not the first time the conversation had come up, but Miri had postponed the task hoping to find a way to keep her entire library. "I am going to need every single one."

"You know space is limited," her mother said through tight lips.

"But instructions from the Emigration Bureau say we should bring our own books because those in Haiti are mostly in French."

"I'm aware of that, Miriam. The fact is, we do not have room in our baggage. Now, don't be difficult. Stop arguing and go through your books."

"Vi told me she's staying here. I'd be able to keep my things if I lived with her," Miri blurted, regretting what she said almost as soon as it came from her mouth.

Her mother placed a fist on each hip. "Miriam Hazel Rose Whitfield, I am truly surprised at you, she said. "You are part of this family, and you will go to Haiti with us. Do not try my patience further. Go to your room and do as I asked."

Though scalded by her mother's anger, Miri couldn't prevent herself from pleading for more time. "Must I do it right now? I have over fifty books. Can I please wait until Portia comes over after church on Sunday? I'll get it done quicker with her help."

Her mother's eyelids descended like window shades. Miri immediately stopped talking lest she fuel more wrath. There was a long pause before an answer came. "Alright. You can do it on Sunday, but no more arguing or complaining. Is that understood?"

"Yes, Mother." Miri resented Mr. Lincoln's cruel emigration decree more than ever.

Saturday, Portia and her mother arrived to deliver eggs and Miri cornered her cousin in the pantry. "Will you help me go through my books after church tomorrow? I can only bring a few and I really need more. Please do me a favor and take some with you and pack them with your things."

"I'll help you sort," Portia said. "As for packing your books, it depends on how many and how much space they'll use. I have my own belongings to think about, you know. Maybe I can take four or five."

On Sunday, Miri took books from the bookcase in her bedroom. Each one she set aside to be discarded tore at her, a series of sad farewells. She decided to give Portia a set of *McGuffey's Readers, Webster's American Spelling, The Book of Cipher's and Nelly's First Schooldays.*

"Pack these," she told her. "They're the foundation of everything I've learned and I can't bear to part with them." Fortunately the complete set of *McGuffey's Readers* was no larger than a standard novel and Portia was sympathetic.

To bring aboard ship, Miri selected a book of conversational French, one of poems by Henry Wadsworth Longfellow and John Greenleaf Whittier, and a novel. The final book was her prayer missal.

The task completed, Miri and Portia went to the kitchen where their mothers chatted over tea. "You should be pleased now, Mother," Miri interrupted. "I've done what you ordered and reduced the number of my books to almost nothing."

Her mother found her sassy attitude and sharp tongue unwelcome. Instead of the expected praise, Miri was given additional chores. With her smugness snuffed, she stalked from the room.

Chapter 7

June 1862

At the piano, in spite of repeated attempts to play a familiar tune, Miri couldn't get it right, but she didn't care. The fractured melody suited her present sour outlook. During breakfast her mother had announced there would be a trip to the store to purchase more items for their stay in Haiti. Frustrated, she began once more to try to untangle the notes. Suddenly her mother was at her side.

"You can stop now, Miri," she said. "Aunt Rachel and Portia will be here any minute."

"What are we going to buy this time?" Miri asked, closing the cover of the keyboard.

"Something appropriate for the climate in Haiti. We need more lightweight, summery outfits."

Under different circumstances, a shopping trip might be exciting, but Miri didn't want anything for Haiti. She took a look at the list her mother was reading. *"Suitable Attire for a Tropical Climate."* Items recommended included male and female undergarments, trousers and shirts for men and boys, shirt-waists for girls and women, all in either cotton or linen.

It was suggested bonnets and hats be constructed of straw or fiber and have broad brims. A note added such headwear could be purchased in Haiti if need be.

"I've got summer clothes," Miri said.

Her mother folded the list and put it into her purse. "You seem to have forgotten," she said, "I've let the hems out on everything and put longer sleeves on your summer tops. I can't do any more with them so you will need at least a couple of new outfits to carry you until we're settled and I'm able to use the sewing machine. We do need to go shopping so stop trying to find an excuse to get out of it."

Portia and her mother arrived with eggs and milk, and after a quick cup of tea, bonnets and gloves were donned and the group left the house.

Under a bright sun the morning was warm, the air full of scents. Miri smelled baking confections along with a fishy whiff from the markets along the riverfront. Also floating in the air was the stench of horse and pig droppings.

Miri reached out to pinch a cluster of pink blossoms from a rambler rosebush. She wrapped the prickly posy in her handkerchief, held it under her nose and inhaled. The fresh strawberry aroma of the flowers was far more pleasing than the odor of manure.

Stanton's department store was only three short blocks from the house, and the four strolled along the wooden walkways under the shade of elm trees. On Main Street they mingled with people on business errands and those with more casual purposes. The railroad and trolleys brought a few strangers to town and the residents of Spencer took interested, but polite, notice of them.

Several men glanced admiringly at Miri, and two bold ones went so far as to tip their hats to her. She heard her mother's tongue click in displeasure at their behavior. All four of these "ladies of color" were dressed in the latest fashions and at ease in the community.

Miri's group approached a line of horses tethered to iron hitching posts. The restless animals stamped and shifted against their restraints, tails lashing at bothersome clusters of huge, blue-green flies. A black horse was nipped by its neighbor when the women were close, and a commotion erupted. The little Morgan backed away in pain, threw up its head and almost pulled free.

Nearby, a young man noticed the activity, grabbed the reins of the excited animal and retied them. It was Samuel, one of Miri's classmates. He often seemed to appear wherever she was and she thought he might be sweet on her. She was right.

Miri smiled. "Thank you for saving us from being trampled, Samuel."

His face reddened deeply as he smiled in return before he wheeled around and darted into a store.

"Miri?"

Her mother's inquisitive tone prompted Miri to say, "That was Samuel Huntington, Mother. From school."

The answer brought a long searching look and a "Well...," but whatever her mother intended to say went unfinished thanks to Portia.

"He's just a boy in one of our classes, Aunt Sarah," she said lacing her arm through Miri's.

The cousins fell into step in back of their mothers and Portia said,

"I'm so excited. It's not often I get store bought things because what Ma can't sew up she gets from the Sears Roebuck catalogue. With so much work to do on the farm, she don't have time for town shopping and says we can do just as good by mail order. The clothes don't always fit too well, though."

"Really Portia," Miri said. "I don't know why you're so happy. Here we are buying clothes for Haiti, a place I dread going to." She raised her handkerchief and sniffed the flowers. "Everything I truly care about is right here in Spencer, so I would appreciate it, dear cousin, if you would stop blithering."

Portia, silenced and hurt by Miri's sharp tone, moved away to walk alongside her mother and aunt.

Above the trees surrounding the town common Miri saw the white spire of the First Congregational Church. Her church. The sunlight glinted off a brass bell hanging in its narrow tower. Nearby, a row of mature, elegant elms bordered one side of the grassy common, and beneath the trees old men hunched over tables, playing chess and checkers.

Saddened by the realization she would no longer see these familiar sights after she left Spencer, Miri lingered. Her gloomy reverie was ended by a summons. "Come along, Miri," her mother said.

At the corner of First Street the women lifted their skirts to prevent contact with animal waste and crossed the uneven cobbles. Midway along the block, between Duggan's Pharmacy and Major's Boot and Saddlery, they entered Stanton's Department Store where they learned most of the summer clothing had already been sold.

Miri found a robin's egg blue linen blouse in the limited selection. The color was appealing and she thought it was the right size. She held the garment under her chin. "How does this look, Portia?"

"Nice. But shouldn't we get permission before we touch anything?"

Miri smiled at her unsophisticated cousin's concern. "You are such a ninny," she said. "You're supposed to examine clothes and try things on. How else can you find whether they fit or not?"

Again, in less than an instant, Portia's expression slid from cheerful to dejected. This time Miri felt a pinch of guilt for poking fun at her, but before she could think of a way to make up for her unkindness, her mother appeared at her elbow with an armful of clothes.

"Here," she said, handing them to Miri. "Pick out three or four shirtwaists and two or three skirts. That out to be enough to hold you until I can stitch up more."

Reminded of the reason for the shopping excursion, Miri dropped the clothes on a counter without bothering to look at them. "I don't like anything," she fibbed.

"This is not the time to try my patience, Miriam. We need to finish here so I can look at yard goods. We need pillow ticking, denim...," "Don't forget cheesecloth and mosquito netting," Aunt Rachel added.

Miri picked up the blue blouse again and chose two others of white linen. The collar on one was edged with tatted lace and she thought it would be nice for Sundays. She completed her selection with two skirts: a butterscotch colored cotton and one of navy blue twill. Portia had also finished and they placed their garments on the counter.

"Portia and I are going next door to Duggan's to look at the books and magazines," Miri said.

Her mother, preoccupied with the list she must have read at least fifteen times, said, "Fine. Wait for us there. Don't go wandering off."

There were no new books of interest so Miri and Portia paused to watch a game of dominos between two elderly men. One of them smoothed his short gray beard as he kept up a non-stop patter. His free hand slapped tiles down in a blur as he recounted a long, twisted tale with many characters.

Miri found it difficult to follow the story and the game at the same time. The other player seemed to have the same difficulty and the chin whiskers of the winner danced with his gleeful cackle. He raked the tiles into a pile, scrambled them and a new game began.

"Come along, girls," her mother called. "Time we get home and begin supper."

Portia and Miri joined the women and were told everything on the list had been purchased.

"All that's needed now," her mother said, "Are perishables, and they can be purchased a day or two before we sail."

Miri didn't think she could tolerate buying anything more for Haiti. She had to find some way to avoid future shopping trips. Her new clothes were left in their wrappers and the package dropped on the floor of her armoire. Out of sight but not out of mind.

Over the weeks her interest in eavesdropping on the Society meetings waned and she left the parlor as soon as she served refreshments. Discussions now were always about plans and preparations for emigration and she had no desire for more details.

Chapter 8

July 1862

The next morning as she tasted her oatmeal and stirred another dollop of honey into the bowl, her mother scolded, "Miri, please don't dawdle. Eat your breakfast and get dressed. And don't forget your grandparents are expecting you after services."

The plan to visit her grandparents had slipped Miri's mind. It would be one of her last opportunities to spend time with them before sailing off to "that place" as she now referred to Haiti. "I wish they were coming with us," she said. She frowned and pushed the cereal bowl away. "Not hungry," she explained.

"There's no reason for them to leave," her mother said. "They're up in years and have lived in Spencer a long time. There's an excellent chance they won't run into any problems. Now, please go get dressed or we're going to be late."

When she was dressed, Miri went to the special hidden drawer in her dresser, took out a necklace and fastened it carefully around her neck. The small, oval, blue sapphire beads alternated with round beads of embossed silver on a delicate silver chain. The cool sheen of silver highlighted the cobalt blue sapphires which were said to symbolize heaven, and were said to protect the wearer from harm. The necklace was a birthday gift from her grandmother and one of Miri's most prized possessions.

She thought of asking permission to live with her grandparents. If she could, there would be no need to lose her friends or give away her piano and books.

Her mother called. "What on earth are you doing, Miri?"

Daydream interrupted, she put on a bonnet, hurried down the stairs and the family was off to church.

At church her attention drifted again as Minister Grady's voice droned on. All the reasons she didn't want to go to Haiti swirled about in her mind. She began to fidget at the unfairness and received a nudge from her mother.

Refocused on the sermon, she listened to Minister Gray say, "God will see us through difficulties and dark times if we call on Him, just as He did when Moses asked His help when the Israelites were being driven from Egypt."

Far from calming, Minister Grady's words raised the image of people trapped in an unlit maze, and Miri was beset by new fears. *What if something like that happens to us? What if we are lost in Haiti and ask God to lead us into sunlight and He doesn't? What if He forgets us?*

She pushed away the idea of God abandoning them, looked around for Clarice and saw her seated several rows away. Not wanting to leave Spencer on poor terms with her best friend, she waved and caught Clarice's attention.

Since the spat, Miri had come to realize that Clarice's only connection with the emigration project was her opinion, and she was entitled to that. Unsure of how Clarice felt toward her, Miri smiled. It was relief to see Clarice smile back. Tomorrow they would eat lunch together as if nothing happened between them.

The last "Amen" of the closing hymn was sung, services concluded, and the short ride to Chestnut Street and her grandparent's house began. As they approached, Miri took a long look at the familiar, white-trimmed red brick house and her chest constricted. She might never see her grandparents or this house again.

As she stepped onto the veranda her nose caught the yeasty aroma of baking bread. Inside, she placed her hat and gloves on the round, copper-topped table in the hallway and walked into the parlor.

As usual, her grandfather was in his chair. Victor, an ancient black and white collie, lay nearby. Victor knew exactly how close he could place himself to his master and still be safe from the curved rockers. Grandfather's gnarled hand reached down and absent mindedly stroked the fur along the old dog's back. Victor's tail rose and fell, each caress and tail thump timed to the motion of the chair.

Miri gripped the back of the rocker to stop it, and stooped to kiss a bare spot between the feathery hairs on the top of the old man's head. "Hello, Grandfather," she said.

"Hello yourself, girlie," he chuckled. "How are ya?"

"I'm fine, Grandfather. And you?"

He looked at her, his beaky nose tilted toward the ceiling. After a deep breath he said, "I been thinking that whatever's going on in that kitchen has got my mouth to watering."

"It does smell good doesn't it?" Miri said. "It's probably supper, and I think I'll go help Grandmother get it ready."

She left her grandfather and Victor to resume their duet.

Two fat brown loaves of bread were cooling on the sill of an open window as her grandmother bustled about the kitchen, hovering here and there for a moment like a bumblebee. Her short, stout body was captured in a corset, and a white-as-snow apron covered the front of her navy-blue dress. She hummed while sifting spices into a mixing bowl. Atop her head a spiral of gleaming braids sat like an ebony crown, so securely anchored with hairpins and combs, it was impossible to find one stray hair.

Miri took in the scene, storing it among the memories she would take to hated Haiti.

Her grandmother noticed her, and the wooden spoon stopped its circular motion. "Ah, Button," she said, using Miri's childhood nickname and smiling with the light of a sunrise, "Here you are at last. Come here."

Enfolded in a tight embrace of lilac and spices, Miri's wish to stay with her grandparents returned. If it happened, she'd never complain about having the living daylights squeezed out of her. She'd even put up with being forever called 'Button.'

"Well now," her grandmother said, taking an apron off a hook, "Put this on and let's go find some apples."

Miri followed her down into the dim cellar. Spider webs hung from thick wooden beams in the shadowy basement and the air was musty. She could hear small creatures scurry away as she neared nooks and crannies where they were hiding. This cellar was unlike the one under her house. This one was spooky and not someplace she would venture into alone.

Her grandmother lifted the cover off a wooden barrel and thrust an arm into the straw. Miri shuddered. Spiders and other crawly things might be in the straw. "There are plenty of apples, Button," her grandmother said. "Come help me dig them out and we'll make an Apple Crisp."

Though her blouse had long sleeves, Miri feared being bitten by some insect in the barrel. At the same time she didn't want to appear childish to her grandmother who had the ability to ignore insects and could tame half-wild critters. At various times a fox kit, raccoon and even a litter of pups from a coyote/dog mating enjoyed her care. Grandfather often bragged the reason he married Nell Talbot was because she had the most gumption of any woman he'd ever met.

From her reading, Miri knew a wide variety of insects, snakes and lizards lived in Haiti, and because tropical winters were warm, animals did not hibernate. *If I'm going to survive in Haiti, I need to develop some gumption, like grandmother.* She told herself to stop thinking and plunged an arm deep into the barrel. Her fingers searched, touched the silky skin of an apple and she pulled it out, trying to ignore the straw that scratched and poked her hand. Nothing attacked her and with growing courage and confidence, she made an effort to keep pace with her grandmother. Soon the bowl was brimming with rosy globes of Northern Spies and she carried it upstairs.

"Start washing off the dust and straw," her grandma said, "and I'll fire up the stove again. By the time the apples are peeled and sliced and the topping made, the oven should be good and hot."

As the stove heated, the two women stood side by side at the sink paring and slicing apples. "Did you know the peel of an apple can tell the initial of your true love, Button?"

The glint in her grandmother's eye and the turned-up corner of her mouth made Miri suspect her grandmother was about to spin a tale. Miri didn't believe an apple skin could predict the future, and in particular something so important as the initial of a sweetheart, but she went along with her grandmother's playful mood and asked, "How can an apple peel do that?"

"Carefully remove the apple skin in a single unbroken strip. Then toss it over your shoulder. When it lands on the floor, it'll be in the shape of a letter, the initial of your true love's first name."

"Did that happen to you, Grandmother?"

"It did. Your grandfather's given name is Jacob, and J was the letter I saw."

The idea of learning the initial of her true love's name didn't interest Miri in the least. It was the challenge of peeling an entire apple in one unbroken strip which caught her. Fruit in hand, she began to pare it, but the strip of skin snapped before she completed even one circle. She was more careful with the knife on the next try, and things went well until she neared the stem. The skin frayed into a thin thread, broke away and she was left holding an apple wearing a red cap. She decided to make a last try and slid the knife around the third apple with extra care, pausing every couple of inches, scarcely daring to breathe. Bit by bit the skin lifted off until finally she held up a ruby colored ribbon.

"Success!" Miri exclaimed.

Her grandmother clapped. "Wonderful! Now, close your eyes, spin around three times and drop it over your left shoulder."

Helped by her grandmother's hands, Miri's spun rapidly, and her eyes opened to a whirling room. As she waited for the spinning to stop, Victor wandered into the kitchen seeking overlooked crumbs. He sniffed the peel.

"No, Victor," Miri said, but she was too dizzy to stop him from snagging the skin and dragging his prize behind the stove.

It shouldn't have mattered much, yet she was curious, wondering if the letter she had briefly glimpsed before the dog got it, was a "P".

"Did you see what the letter was, Grandmother?"

"I didn't get a clear look, Button, but don't fret. You still have a couple of years before you need worry about a sweetheart. Come on let's finish making the Crisp."

Her grandmother sliced the apples and Miri rubbed butter on the bottom and sides of the baking pan. She layered the apple slices in the pan and sprinkled the top with a mixture of brown sugar, vanilla extract, cinnamon, and oats. All the while she thought about her grandmother's comment.

She's right. I don't really care what letter it was. Peeling the skin without breaking it was what I wanted to accomplish. She handed the pan to her grandmother, and watched her slide it into the oven. Then they went in the other room as they waited for the Apple Crisp to finish baking.

Cooking at her grandparent's was enjoyable. It never seemed like a chore because grandmother was always in a good mood. While they waited for the Crisp to finish baking, Miri remarked, "Mother would say stories like the one about the apple peel are old wives tales."

"I know that, Button. They may not be true, but sometimes it's fun to pretend. Your mother has always taken everything very seriously. It's her nature. But there are times when such deep seriousness can make life a hard burden."

"Oh, yes," Miri said. "Without pleasure, life would be a misery." She realized she was going to miss her grandparents' funny stories and laughter, and made up her mind to treasure every happy memory.

A mouthwatering aroma signaled the Apple Crisp was done. Back in the kitchen her grandmother attended to the main supper dish, Brunswick Stew. She dropped a spoonful of dough into a simmering pot and pointed at a loaf of bread with the spoon. "Well, let's get back to more practical things. The bread needs to be sliced, the table set and your grandfather called for dinner."

Miri ate with zest, savoring the fluffy dumplings and tasty chicken and vegetables of the stew. Conversation at the table was light and pleasant until it turned to the subject of Haiti.

Miri voiced her misgivings about moving, and her grandmother said, "Your parents want the best for you and Georgie. That's a big part of why they're willing to take part in the venture. Creating a society where there is complete equality is something they believe they can accomplish in Haiti."

"I know, but it's going to be so very difficult to leave Spencer."

"You'll do alright, girlie," her Grandfather said with a pat to her shoulder. "You take after your grandma; you've got spunk. 'Twas a fine dineer, Mrs. Minifee," he added, winking at her. "Now, excuse me ladies, whilst I take meself back to the parlor."

Miri knew she'd miss her grandfather's odd Dutch-German pronunciation of certain words. No one else in the family sounded like him.

She swallowed back tears and headed toward the kitchen. "I'll wash the dishes," she said. Staying busy would prevent her mood from sinking and ruining the afternoon.

"I'll give you a hand, but first clear a space on the counter," her grandmother said. "The Crisp has cooled down enough to eat."

Miri took a generous helping of Apple Crisp smothered in cream and a mug of tea to her grandfather.

"Ahh, thank you, Meeri" he said. "I've been looking forward to this ever since I smelled it cooking."

The kitchen was warm, so she and her grandmother took their dessert and tea to the screened-in back porch.

Somewhere in the early summer evening a dog was barking. A mother called her children home and a cricket chirped under the house. Bliss filled Miri's heart. Joy was sitting with her grandmother as the sun disappeared at the close of a delightful day.

"Quick, Button," her grandmother said. She pointed to the first star visible in the darkening sky. "Make a wish."

Without a thought that wishing on a star was childish, Miri wished her father would not come to take her home.

Chapter 9

July 1862

"Three gray geese sat on the green grass grazing. A big, black bear blood bled." Miri sighed and rinsed the soap from a dish. In two days she had to recite the articulation drill in front of the class. "Three gray geese sat on the green grass grazing. A big, black bear bled blood," she said and repeated the phrases twice more. Again, for good measure. "Three gray geese…"

Georgie came into the kitchen, drew the dipper from the water crock and gulped the liquid down in one long, noisy swallow. He swiped the back of a hand across his mouth and grinned. "Guess what," he said. "Tomorrow, me and Pa are going to a bee farm to get hives to take to Haiti."

Her concentration on drills interrupted, Miri corrected him. "Pa and *I*, Georgie, and why would we need hives?" Hives were on the list of supplies, along with milking stools and plows, but she had assumed they were included as a reminder for farmers like Uncle Will.

Georgie's smile grew to a Jack-o-lantern grin. Miri was annoyed with Georgie's gloating. He knew something she didn't. She scooped a handful of suds and was on the verge of hurling them at him when he added, "Pa says we'll have to make our own sweetening 'cause they only make sour gum in Haiti, not honey or refined sugar."

"Sour gum? Oh, sorghum." *The conditions in Haiti are so primitive,* Miri thought. *No school, no church, at least not a one of Protestant denomination, and no books in English.* Now, as well, there was a lack of honey and sugar. The idea of emigration and colonization sounded drearier and drearier. Still, the idea of visiting a bee farm intrigued her. It would be a lot less boring than shopping for clothes and household goods.

"I'm going with you," she decided.

Georgie laughed. "No you ain't. You can't come 'cuz you're a girl. I'm going to the shop in the morning with Pa and in the afternoon me and him are goin' to the bee farm."

He skipped out of range as Miri snapped the dishtowel at his hind end. "You're only saying that to be mean," she said. "I'm going to ask Father if I can go. I can come to the shop at noon when he closes for lunch."

"Bet he'll say no," Georgie said, dodging another flick of the towel.

He could very well be right. There were many differences between the activities and places males and females were allowed to participate in or attend. It was proper for Miri to clean the barbershop after hours, but not when customers were present. Bars and other public drinking establishments were other unsuitable places for ladies.

Despite the likelihood she would be denied, Miri decided to ask permission to go to the bee farm. Georgie nosed about the parlor as she approached her father's chair.

Mr. Whitfield was reading the newspaper. "The war is now full-blown, Sarah," he said. "And it's not going as Mr. Lincoln expected. The losses are far more than anticipated. The President attributes it to a lack of ability and fortitude in his generals. He feels the rebel victory last month at Bull Run proves the Army lacks competent leadership."

Miri coughed and he looked up at her. "Is it true you're going to buy bee hives tomorrow, Father?" she asked.

"Yes. Before we sail I have to learn how to care for them and how to gather honey. The only way I see to do that is by getting my hives now."

This was her chance and Miri said, "I'd very much like to see what a bee farm looks like. Please let me to go with you."

Her mother stopped knitting and sat still, alert for what would happen next.

Miri waited as her father closed the paper and regarded her with dark eyes. She feared he was angered by her bold request.

"Very well, Miriam," he said. "You may ride along."

"Thank you, Father," Miri said, delighted to have gotten the desired answer.

Georgie scowled, stuck his tongue out at her and left the room. Her mother resumed knitting, the click of the needles echoing her "tsk, tsk" of disapproval.

"I plan to leave the shop at three," Mr. Whitfield said. "First we'll stop at the hardware store then head out to the countryside. We should reach the farm at about the right time to move the hives."

"There's a certain time for them to be moved?"

He nodded. "I've been told honey bees get angry if the hive is disturbed while they're gathering pollen. Disrupt their routine and you run a high risk of being stung. They say it's easier to move hives at twilight after the bees have settled for the evening."

The bumblebees Miri was familiar with did not behave that way. In the spring and summer the large, plump insects frequented the backyard, drawn to the beebalm plants. Nectar from the purple flowers made the gentle pollen gatherers even more placid, flying in slow, drowsy loops. There was no need to fear them since they almost never stung. For years she and Georgie had contests to see who could capture more bees. With bare hands they'd pluck bumblers from flowers and drop them into jars. The winner was the person who caught the most.

That night, Miri didn't sleep well due to the anticipation of visiting a bee farm. She rose early the next morning, but chores had to be done before she left for the shop, and as soon as breakfast was over she got busy at them. After changing bed linens, she washed and put away the dishes, swept the kitchen floor, back steps and porch. She filled the laundry bucket, put the sheets to soak and joined her mother for mid-morning tea and a biscuit.

At noon, her mother came to the parlor door while Miri was dusting and polishing the furniture. "You need to eat now, Miri," she said. "And mind your time so you can get things done and leave for the shop by two-thirty."

Miri gathered up the feather duster, tin of butcher's wax, and polishing cloths and returned them to the cabinet. A prompt lunch and reminder to keep track of the time meant her mother acknowledged the outing was important, so she said, "Thank you. I appreciate you didn't object to my going with Father."

"You're welcome, Miri. Remember to act like the proper young lady you are and don't forget your papers."

With her thoughts fixed on bees, Miri ate in a hurry, put her dish in the sink and went back to the remainder of her chores. She was off to the shop before the clock read two thirty.

In the wagon, seated between her father and brother, she listened to the clicking of the wheels and the clop of Jubal's hooves along the cobblestoned streets.

"Whoa there, Jubal," her father said as he pulled up the reins. The wagon halted in front of the hardware store and he got off. Miri stepped down to the walkway behind him. He extended the reins toward Georgie and turned to Miri with pinched eyes and mouth. "What do you think you're doing?" he asked. "Get back in the wagon."

Miri glanced around and remained on the walkway. "I must go inside, Father," she whispered quickly. "You cannot leave me out here alone for some slave hunter to kidnap."

He shook his head and uttered a few words under his breath. Then, with a hand on her elbow, he ushered her into the store.

Arranged on a line along the counter were boxes of square-headed nails and screws of various sizes. A world of tools and implements hung from hooks. More tools were strewn along thick shelves and stood upright on the scuffed floor. Although she could not identify most of what she saw, Miri was fascinated.

All the store's customers were men. Conversations between them were few, as they handled harnesses, equipment, and plows, selected hammers or axes and measured lengths of rope. The heavy odors of sweat, leather, oil and tobacco assaulted Miri's nose and reminded her she was in a man's domain. She stayed close to her father while he completed his purchases.

The journey to the farm resumed and at the edge of town Jubal was guided onto a narrow lane that forked off to the left. The wagon bounced along a washboard surface beneath rows of trees that lined the sides. The trees formed a magnificent canopy and turned the area into a translucent green world.

The wagon stopped in front of a whitewashed, wooden gate set into a fence of round, gray stones. A rectangular yellow sign with black lettering hung from the gate:

Wild Thyme & Sweet Clover Apiary,
Finest Honey in the Catskills,

M. Carleton, Owner

Miri whispered, "apiary," a word she had seen on jars of honey her mother bought. As a curious and inquisitive child, Miri had long ago looked up the meaning and remembered it was the proper name for a beekeeping establishment.

Georgie jumped down, opened the gate and clambered back aboard the wagon.

They rounded a bend. Atop a slight rise a short distance from them was a large house, the same egg yolk yellow as the sign on the gate.

Black shutters framed its windows. A man in tan overalls watched their arrival from the veranda. His straw colored hair ruffled in the breeze.

"Good afternoon, sir," Mr. Whitfield said, touching the edge of his hat brim in greeting. "My name is Henry Whitfield, and this young man," he said, placing a hand on Georgie's shoulder, "is my son, George." He nodded in Miri's direction, "That's my daughter."

"Miriam," Miri said, annoyed he didn't tell the man her name.

"Micah Carlton," the man responded. He approached the wagon and shook her father's hand. Once the purpose of their visit was defined, Mr. Carleton and her father occupied the wagon seat while she and Georgie sat in the wagon bed.

A flick of the reins on Jubal's rump and the vehicle swayed on the uneven dirt lane as it was pulled to the crest of a low hill. They stopped at the edge of a broad field filled with row upon row of rose bushes. A line of pine trees stood, like sentinels, along the right side and back edge of the field.

Her father and Mr. Carleton talked about the method of wrapping hives for transport by ship as they walked into the field. She and Georgie followed and Miri envied the ease of movement that pants afforded the men, even Georgie in his sailor pants. She was forced to deal with a voluminous skirt, lifting and twisting it to avoid getting snagged on a plant or dragging through dirt.

Around her, hives were scattered among the rose bushes in irregular groups of twos and threes and she stopped, entranced. Splashes of paint decorated the side of many hives. The field was a kaleidoscope of colors.

"Georgie, isn't this extraordinary? How many hives do you think there are?"

"I don't know. Maybe twenty-five?"

"Looks like more to me. One, two, three . . ."

"Count to yourself," Georgie said, pinching her.

"That hurt," she said, rubbing her arm. "You're still in a pout because Father let me come, and you don't have him all to yourself. Not so special after all, are you?"

"I'm not in a pout. I just don't want to listen to your chatter."

"George Benjamin Whitfield, I'm your sister," Miri said wagging a finger at him. "And I'm older. You'd better be respectful and stop being mean to me or I'll tell Father,"

"Tattle-tale."

64

The tiff stopped when their father and Mr. Carleton arrived, carrying a hive on a pallet. They put the pallet next to the wagon and brought a second one from the field. Before loading the hives into the wagon, each one was topped with a lid and wrapped in burlap.

"There," Mr. Carleton said. "The bees'll stay quiet for the ride to your place. Uncover them once they're situated."

Though she could have ridden in the front after Mr. Carleton was dropped off at his house, Miri chose to remain in the wagon bed. As twilight descended she dozed to the muffled hum of a lullaby emanating from the hives.

Chapter 10

August 1862

M iri shut her eyes against the sight of the rolling, shimmering ocean, and gripped the railing tighter as icy threads slid down her back. Another wave broke against the side of the vessel and drenched her with frigid seawater. Fluid surged up her throat and she leaned over the railing to vomit. Her stomach, without solid food for days could only surrender a yellow-green liquid that left a hot, sour taste in her mouth.

"We've been sailing for a week now," Portia said, handing Miri a handkerchief. You should be done with your seasickness. Mine lasted only a few days."

Weak and listless from seasickness and lack of food, Miri wiped her mouth. Tears mixed with sea-spray ran down her face. "Help me, Lord," she prayed. "Don't let me be miserable for the entire voyage."

"I'm sure you'll feel better soon," Portia comforted.

"My stomach might, but I won't ever get over leaving Spencer. My soul aches to return." Portia's arm encircled her. "I always thought you were strong and brave," she said. "It hurts me to see you like this, Miri. Please stop crying."

"I can't help it. I miss my grandparents, Clarice and the rest of my friends. I even miss Vi and Ezra. I'm ashamed to admit it terrifies me to think of what might happen to us in Haiti. I have nightmares, yet I'd sooner sew my lips together than let anyone know. I'd be mortified, and you'd better not say a word."

"Don't worry, I won't. Anyway, we'll be safe in Haiti with our parents and others. Think how much courage Vi and her mother had."

"I know. They escaped from their owner in the middle of the night and ran through swamps and woods chased by dogs, and men with guns. They had only each other. I know it was far more dangerous and frightful than this. I should be thankful that at least I have family, even my pesky brother. Still, leaving Spencer for who knows what, worries me."

"Things will be fine," Portia said. "You'll see."

The ocean calmed over the next few days and with quieter waters, the churning in Miri's stomach stopped. Now she could sit on deck and look at the blue sky and blue sea, a blank, sapphire world. Haiti lay south of the States. With no roads, trees, hills and valleys to use as guides, the Captain relied on instruments to navigate.

She closed her eyes and pretended they were sailing toward Spencer.

"I'm hungry," Portia said, interrupting Miri's fantasy. "Let's see if it's time for lunch."

Miri was happy to return to the cabin to freshen up for lunch. No matter how bright the sun, sea air always felt chilly to her. The cold rinse water didn't help. She rubbed each finger dry with the towel and flexed them to bring up circulation again. In the dining galley she accepted a mug of hot tea from her mother.

Eating was a problem. Most meals were soups and stews. To Miri, the chunks of meat, potatoes, carrots and such, floating in brown liquid, resembled vomit. She pushed the bowl away.

"This is nourishing food," her mother said, lifting a forkful of meat. "And you should be giving thanks for it."

"I know, Mother, but my stomach is still not settled and the food is so unappealing."

"Here then," her mother said unwrapping a package. "Some pemmican will soothe your stomach and provide nourishment."

Miri smeared honey on the leathery strip of dry, chopped meat and fruit and bit off a chunk. She savored the salty-sweet taste as she walked back to the deckchair. Eventually the gripe in her gut subsided.

Portia arrived to ask if she felt better and Miri nodded. "Then let's go find some of the other girls to chat with."

"You go," Miri told her. "I'll stay here and read. I'm not interested in silly gossip."

In less than an hour Portia returned. "That was so disappointing. There's nothing new, and I'm bored." She pouted for a moment. "Guess I'll take a nap," she said, and settled into the chair with a blanket.

"I swear I don't know how you manage to sleep," Miri said. "I can't get used to the constant pitch and roll of the ship."

"Is that why you're awake half the night?"

"I get enough sleep," Miri muttered, the lie constricting her throat.

"Don't be upset with me," Portia said. "Remember, we share a room so I'm aware how you toss and turn."

"I do not toss and turn," Miri snapped. She picked up her book. "If you don't mind, I'd like to continue reading, so stop yammering and take your nap."

Portia sighed, curled into the chair like a cat. Soon she was asleep. Miri's mood was gloomy as she thought about the journey to a strange, new world. She worried about surviving in a country where language, religion and Lord knows what else was foreign. To have any chance at a decent life in Haiti, she'd need to conquer her fears and she wasn't sure how best to accomplish that.

Before the family left Spencer, she had spoken to her father about school. Education was important for her and Georgie, and in Haiti schools all classes were taught in French.

"Several teachers are planning to emigrate," he said. "A school will be built and your lessons, in English, will resume as soon as possible." After his meeting with the President he was quicker to flare up at the smallest thing. "I'm sorry, Miriam, but your objections will not change my mind. Mr. Lincoln's position is to continue to deny citizenship and full rights to us. Given that and the present status of the war, our future in the States is uncertain."

Miri was stymied. Her mother was no ally. She held onto beliefs Miri thought old fashioned and went along with whatever decisions her husband made. "Men should rightfully control things outside of the home," her mother said, "and provide security and protection for wives and family."

"What's going to happen with the shop, Father? Will you sell it?"

"It shouldn't concern you, Miri. However, since you ask, I plan to let Ezra have it. Not to own, at least not yet. He'll rent it and take on an apprentice. I think he's ready."

There was nothing more to say.

With a book tucked under her arm, and Portia asleep, she left and walked along the deck. Her father was bent over a trunk, busy performing some sort of task with a tray of glass jars. Each stubby jar was filled with water. He added two heaping spoonsful of sugar to a jar and stirred until they dissolved.

"What are you making, Father?" she asked.

"Sugar water for the bees. It'll keep them alive until we reach Haiti. Once I have a place to set out the hives they'll find flowers and begin to make honey."

Since the evening she had ridden home sitting next to the hives, the hum of bees lured Miri like a song. "I can help you prepare the sugar water." she said, and was thrilled when her father gave her the wooden spoon.

"Be sure the sugar is completely dissolved before you put the lids on," he said, and turned his attention to jars on a second tray.

Having received permission to participate in caring for the bees, Miri did as instructed, stirring until no crystals of sugar were visible. She screwed on lids pierced with small, scattered holes. "How can the bees get sugar water through these tiny openings?" she asked.

"They'll get enough to stay alive," her father said. He took her tray and stacked it on top of his.

"Can I help you feed the bees, Father?"

"No," he said shaking his head. "This is men's work."

Disappointed, Miri watched him disappear down the stairs to the interior of the ship. She returned to the deck chair and read until the sun was low on the horizon.

By the end of evening prayer service the ocean was still as glass, dusk darkened the skies, and mothers began to take little ones off to bed. Soon most of the people on deck had drifted inside and Miri found peace in the silence. An hour later the chill air drove her to the cabin where she discovered Portia already tucked under the blankets.

In her nightdress, Miri sat at the narrow vanity and unpinned her braid. She brushed, counting the one hundred strokes said to guarantee strong hair. "I'll try not to spoil your sleep," she said as she slipped into her bunk.

"Don't be a sourpuss," came from beneath the blankets.

Miri closed her eyes. But instead of soothing sleep, she experienced a nightmare. Devilish goblins and ghostly fiends surrounded her. They recited ugly, vivid scenes of lost children and horrible sickness. Their voices rose to a maddening din she couldn't quiet. She tried to shout. The words stuck in her throat. Her unvoiced scream woke her, still shaking with fear. Her eyes never closed for the rest of the night, and she blessed the arrival of day.

"My dream was so real! There were horrible disasters, even a shipwreck," she said over breakfast. "Do you suppose it's an omen, Mother?"

"We're as safe onboard as anywhere," her mother said. She held out a sheet of paper and a pencil. "Here, check the food cartons and when you're done, come help me in the cabin. Keep busy, Miri and your mind will be too busy to imagine things."

Miri quickly finished the inventory and went to the cabin to return the list to her mother. "What do you think Haiti will be like?" she asked.

"How many times are you going to ask the same thing?" her mother said. "You probably know more than most of us do about the place. Haven't you read everything you found about Haiti in geography and history books and the information we received from the Emigration Society?"

"Yes, but I still wonder what establishing our settlement will be like."

"No one can know for certain how it will be. Nobody can predict the future. I suspect we'll do fairly well with the assistance Mr. Lincoln promised."

"I hope the people will be friendly," Miri said. "I'm trying to improve my French so I can speak with them."

A rare smile brightened the maple color of her mother's cheeks. "Then hadn't you better get to your studies, *Mademoiselle?*"

Miri left the cabin with her French textbook to search for Portia and found her in sitting on deck. "*Bon jour, Mademoiselle,*" Miri said. "That's French for 'Good morning, Miss.' Try to say it."

"Bone jur," Portia said. Miri grimaced.

Twice more Portia attempted to pronounce the phrase correctly then threw up her hands. "It's no use," she said. "I quit."

Unable to convince Portia of the value of speaking French, Miri spent the next hour in solitary study expanding her French vocabulary. She found teaching oneself a foreign language was not a simple task, and closed the book.

At the far end of the deck her father was making sugar water. She watched, biding time as he filled the jars. He took the trays and disappeared below deck. She clutched her skirt with a hand to avoid tripping on it and hurried after him.

His back was to her and the trays were on the table. She ducked into a shadowy niche as he opened a porthole and put on a wide brimmed straw hat with a full veil that fell to his shoulders. He sprinkled water over pieces of rope heaped on an old pie tin, lit a match with his thumbnail and touched it to the rope. The damp fibers didn't flame but gave off spirals of smoke that tickled Miri's throat. She covered her mouth to stifle a cough.

Wearing leather gloves, her father held the smoking pie tin over one of the hives, and blew on the smoldering pile. As more smoke arose and encircled the hive, he put the tin down. After a brief wait he slowly lifted the top to reveal hundreds of bees on the rim of the hive.

Miri's eyes widened at the sight of the humming, vibrating mass. She took a sharp breath, recoiled in terror and retreated deeper into the darkness. Her father heard the sound and hesitated, his expression hidden by the veil. The additional clouds of smoke he raised forced the bees to move deep into their hive.

Next he pulled out a flat, wooden square covered with honey, and laid it on the table. In the same fluid motion he placed a tray of sugar water atop the hive, sealing the bees within.

He repeated the entire procedure with the second hive, and by the time it was over, Miri's fears about being stung had eased. She felt calmer until her father said, "Come over here." He was probably angered by her spying, but whatever punishment he gave, Miri felt was worth it to watch him work with the hives.

"Since you're so determined to be involved with the bees, you might as well do something useful," he said.

Keen to help but still afraid, Miri quivered.

Her father broke a piece off the honeycomb with a jab from a knife and laid it in her palm. "Here," he said with a grin. "You're the official taster."

Miri's mouth closed around the morsel and sunshine melted on her tongue.

Chapter 11

September 1862

With both hands occupied balancing a tray full of jars, Miri wasn't able to hold her skirt out of the way, so she negotiated the stairs with extreme care. She put the sugar water on the table and waited for her arms to stop trembling before going up for the other tray.

Her father was allowing her to help care for the bees, and though pleased with the responsibility, it was a challenge to stay calm near uncovered hives. Determined not to show fear, she took a deep breath.

After her father smoked the hive and removed its top, she placed a tray over the opening with care so as not to agitate the occupants. Her task completed, she went for a stroll along the deck.

Other than the brief satisfaction she got from assisting her father, Miri chafed with boredom. Tired of practicing French and reading the same few books, her restlessness could take her no farther than the length and width of the ship. Every day was monotonous, and although she dreaded their destination, she longed for the voyage to end.

She yearned to walk on solid ground, hear birds sing and see trees, grass and flowers again. In idle moments she stared at the heaving ocean and tried to imagine life in Haiti. Despite her mother's reassurances it worried her that there had already been a number of attempts to establish a settlement in Haiti, and all had failed. Immigrants found few opportunities on the island to earn money. They caught unknown diseases for which they had no resistance and no treatment. Discouraged, many left.

She wondered if any survivors from those colonies still lived in Haiti. If so, perhaps they could provide helpful advice to her group. She also wondered if there would be opportunities in Haiti to continue with her education. And what of social functions? Were there parks where she and other girls her age could attend band concerts, play croquet and have appropriate interactions with young men? She wondered if Philippe and his uncle would visit the colony. More to the point would he seek her out? It would be nice to see him again. She missed his easy companionship and their conversations.

A familiar, annoying voice interrupted her musing. "Isn't it splendid out here, Miri? You can see all the way to the end of the world."

Irritated by the intrusion, she said, "Not everyone loves all this water, Georgie."

"I've been talking to the crew," he said. "A lot of the places they've been to sound exciting. I'd give anything to see them."

"Hmmph. Chatting up deck hands, were you? No wonder Father complains he can never find you."

"Don't tattle on me, please, Miri. Pa will make me stop if he finds I'm hanging around listening to stories about working on a ship."

"I really don't care where any of the crew has been, Splinter. Leave me be," she said, "and I'll keep your little secret."

There simply wasn't enough for her to do to stay busy and stave off the doldrums. As the days wore on, Miri's mood sank even more, and the only meal she ate was breakfast. Oatmeal was oatmeal. With fresh food stores exhausted, lunch and supper had become repugnant. She couldn't dredge up an appetite for sawdust- brown meat and chalky biscuits.

Twenty-seven days after they departed from New York, the Captain entered the dining area during lunch. "Ladies and Gentlemen," he announced, "Haiti can be seen on the horizon."

Miri was one of the first to hurry out to the railing. Showered by a briny mist thrown up by the waves, she gazed across the sea to spot a dark speck where ocean met land. Haiti! The journey would soon be over.

People around her congregated and chattered, their voices brisk and bright with excitement. As the ship drew closer to the island she saw its greenness gradually separate into pea-green grass and the deeper, spinach color of tree leaves. Portia maneuvered through a cluster of women and stood next to her. "Look," Miri said, pointing to a sickle shaped area in the shoreline. "Isn't that a lovely sight? The sand on the beach is so white it looks like salt. I know I didn't want to come here, but it will be a blessed relief to stand on something that doesn't sway."

"I agree," Portia said and started to walk away.

"Where are you going?"

"To pack."

Miri continued to lean on the rail and stare at the island. The crowd thinned as people left the open air for their cabins. White clouds darkened to gunmetal gray over molten fiery red-orange as twilight temporarily took the sky. Full dark descended like a window shade, and a lunar crescent rose in the ink-black world and reflected in the sand. After admiring the scene for hours, Miri returned to her cabin and went to bed.

The next morning a gentle rocking motion woke her. She shook Portia. "Wake up," she said. "I think we've arrived."

They dressed in a rush, went topside and found the ship was anchored a short distance from a row of piers, and the deck clogged by passengers and a bustling crew.

Miri's mother found them. "Come have breakfast," she said. "We'll be going ashore soon."

At the table Miri waved her bowl of oatmeal away.

"Stop acting finicky," her father said. "It's going to be a busy day. At least have some tea and a biscuit."

"What will we be busy at?" she asked.

"First we must get information about housing. Someone from the Emigration Society is going to escort us to the office in Port-au-Prince. Once we know where we'll be living the next task will be to transport our belongings to our new home."

· · · · ·

Under a golden sun they climbed into small boats and were ferried ashore. When Miri's feet touched solid ground she took several steps to reassure herself the earth beneath her was stationary. She caught a whiff of something sweet carried on a light breeze and looked around but couldn't locate the source.

A variety of vessels were in the harbor. Giant ships, sleek steamers and smaller fishing boats draped with nets, creaked and pulled against their anchors.

A cacophony of sounds surrounded her. Overhead, exotic birds in a rainbow of colors swooped and soared. Their chirps and twitters added to the shouts and chatter of foreigners and Haitians milling about the dock.

Nearby, some women haggled with a fruit vendor, and Miri realized she could not understand them. They were speaking *patois*. Philippe had told her about *patois* when he helped her practice French. He said most Haitians spoke *patois*, a mixture of words from various African languages combined with French. Most could also understand and speak passable French.

Miri was glad for that information because the dialect she heard was unlike the Parisian French she had studied and practiced.

So far, everything on the island fascinated and amazed her. Never had she imagined so many people with such a range of skin colors in one place. They went from light caramel to medium brown through sable to cinder black.

She saw flashes of white petticoats but could tell the Haitian women weren't wearing hoops under their long, full skirts. The subdued blues, grays and brown tones of her group appeared drab alongside their brilliant yellow, green and vivid red attire. The heads of many women were wrapped in bright cloth turbans that matched their skirts.

The group moved from the dock, following a representative from the Emigration Society. On the streets Portia linked an arm with Miri and said, "This is no place to get separated."

Miri watched Georgie go into an office of the Haitian government with her father and thought, *I should be there, too.*

She looked through the window and saw her father speak to a man seated at a desk. The man shook his head, and her father placed a fist on the desk. He leaned and said something that drew a shrug. Then he motioned to Georgie and they exited the building.

The scowl on his face prompted Miri to ask, "What's wrong, Father?"

"Yes, what's wrong?" her mother echoed, lines of concern creasing her forehead.

"The temporary housing the Haitian government is so generously providing are cottages," her father told them. "And," he said throwing up a hand, "each cottage must be shared by two or more families."

"They aren't going to charge us for the first month," he said. "After that we're expected to go to the interior, claim our land allotments and begin farming. If we stay in Port-au-Prince we'll have to pay rent." He was seething with anger and the scowl deepened.

"Tomorrow I'll begin looking for a shop. The sooner I start working, the better," he said. "Then we can look for permanent housing here in the city."

We've been here only a few hours, Miri thought *and already there are problems. I hope this is not a sign that the shabby treatment we received from Mr. Lincoln has followed us.*

"Will Uncle Will, Aunt Rachel and Portia be in a cottage with us?"

she asked. Sharing space with family was more appealing than the idea of living with strangers.

"Yes. I told them Aunt Rachel and your mother are sisters and was at least able to get the agent's agreement to allow our family to remain together."

Miri pulled Portia off to the side and whispered, "Living with each other will be good. We'll be able to slip off and explore the city."

Portia shook her head. "We can't go gypsying around here alone, Miri. Why do you want to be so bold? What are you thinking?"

"I'm thinking this is our home now, and as long as we're stuck here we may as well learn about it. There must be something interesting to see, a library or a museum and shops. It won't be dangerous if we stay together and don't venture too far."

"You don't know that, Miri. Your mother's right. You have a mind to do what ladies ought not to. Let's just get settled in the house."

"Fine," Miri said. "I'll find someone who isn't such a nervous Nellie or maybe explore on my own."

"I don't want trouble," Portia said. "If we're caught sneaking out unescorted, it'll be the devil to pay."

"My dear cousin, I think we're clever enough not to get caught. The most important thing is not letting Georgie suspect what we're up to. Come on, Portia. It'll be such a lark to adventure about."

"Perhaps," Portia said, her face a map of wide-eyed anxiety. "I'll go with you but I still don't think it's a good idea."

As they walked, the agent stopped and pointed to compact structures along a narrow semi-circular street. The cottages resembled the small, country farmhouses around Spencer. Like the clothing worn by the Haitians the cottages were painted in bright hues of green, blue and yellow. Her father opted for one of the least garish blue cottages. With its white trim it looked like a confection.

The wagon arrived with their belongings and Miri helped unpack small household items and stock the pantry while her father and uncle brought the sofas and other furniture inside. Two sets of everything crowded all of the rooms.

To Miri's dismay, her bed was left unassembled which meant sharing a bed with Portia. Even worse, they would have no real privacy. A curtain was hung to divide the room and Georgie would sleep on the other side.

To allow space to move about, a bed frame and mattress, one of the sofas, a writing table and two armoires were stacked against the rear wall of the parlor.

Her father placed his barbering equipment on the writing table and went to see to the tools and hives.

As the day wore on, the temperature rose until the interior of the cottage was hot and humid. The heat irritated and exhausted Miri, but despite fatigue she worked along with her mother, aunt and Portia to put things in order.

Georgie was seemingly always underfoot and a nuisance. He was repeatedly shooed away until Miri at last located the box with his beloved soldiers. With a honey-smeared biscuit in one hand and treasured army in the other, he went outside to play.

At sundown a light breeze feathered and rustled leafy tops on the odd, branchless palm trees. Welcome coolness floated through the house and the women stopped their work.

Darkness descended and brought hordes of biting, stinging insects. No amount of fanning and swatting deterred them. Mrs. Whitfield said, "Come along and help me drape mosquito netting over the bedposts, Miri. We need to make canopies to keep the pests away while we sleep."

Miri's passed a fitful first night in Haiti listening to the sizzle and vibration of bugs outside of her gauze fortress.

Chapter 12

December 1862

Miri wiped crumbs off the table, swept the floor and went outside, her mind fixed on the one chore she didn't find tedious. The hives sat in the far corner of the backyard where their inhabitants could forage among a variety of abundant wildflowers. Because the bees no longer required sugar water, her responsibility was to keep the area around the hives free of grass and weeds. With nearly a month in close proximity to the hives behind her, she was more at ease around the buzzing activity, and enjoyed sitting on a stump near the hives to observe their comings and goings.

The production of honey was well underway and she wondered when it would be time to collect it, and if her father would allow her to help with harvesting. She feared he wouldn't. He saw beekeeping as a man's job and was trying to get Georgie, who avoided work whenever possible, interested and involved.

I'll point out to Father that I'm the reliable one, she thought. *Perhaps it'll persuade him to let me help.*

She yanked at a handful of weeds and recalled some advice her Grandmother had given her when she expressed fears that emigration would be unable to provide her with prospects for a decent future.

Her grandmother said, "It's best not fret about things that haven't happened, Button. You can't predict or control the future."

Even so, Miri thought she might be able to influence a small portion of what happens by speaking up. *I may not be as brave as grandmother but I'm more confident than I used to be. I'll write Grandmother of my plan to ask Father to allow me to help with harvesting.* She had been omitting the unpleasant aspects of Haiti out of her letters to her grandmother and focusing on the pleasure she got caring for the hives. She pulled the last weed, added it to the compost pile and went back to the house.

A note from her mother was on the kitchen table; she had gone to deliver a baby. For the first time Miri had the house all to herself. Portia and her parents had left on some errand right after breakfast. Father was out looking for a suitable place to rent for a barbershop, and Georgie was with him. He thought having Georgie along was an advantage.

"He's proof I'm a family man attempting to earn a living." And to Georgie's chagrin he added, "Who can resist a child?" The disappointed expression on her father's face every evening proved Georgie hadn't charmed anyone so far.

At the moment, Miri reveled in the almost forgotten luxuries of peace and quiet. She made tea, took it to the table and picked up the newspaper. Articles and reports about the war covered the entire front page.

The Federal army, touted as large, strong and robust, was losing battle after battle. The defeats were frustrating to President Lincoln and he had dismissed another commanding General. The number of soldiers listed as killed, missing and wounded was staggering. She scanned the long list of names and cities of dead soldiers and was thankful not to find any from Spencer. Somberly she turned the page.

NEW YORK CITY
GROUP EMIGRATION TO HAITI

The steamer, *Janet Kedstone*, under Captain William Clark left port several weeks ago for Port-au-Prince, Haiti. The *Kedstone*, a ship of two hundred tons is fitted with comfortable cabins for passengers.

The emigrants, free persons of color, seeking new opportunities, went out under the sponsorship of the New York Bureau of Emigration, recently organized by Mr. James Redpath of Boston.

The two hundred and twenty passengers originated from New York, Massachusetts, Pennsylvania, and Canada. Families took farm tools and household supplies with them. Those who could not afford these items received them from Mr. Redpath.

On arrival in Haiti, that government will provide each emigrant sixteen acres of land to farm.

Father had brought his barbering equipment, a few household tools and others he needed for the hives, but she was unaware of any farm implements.

The quiet was broken by the slam of the screen door. She frowned, lowered the paper and saw Portia who slid into a chair across from Miri, fanned herself with her hat and said, "My parents and I traipsed over one plot of land after another this morning. They brought me back to milk the cow while they look at another location. I hope my father chooses one of the sections we've already seen so I don't have to look at any more." She peered around. "Where is everybody?"

"Father's off looking for a shop again. Georgie's with him and Mother's at a birthing."

"And you've been lazing about reading the paper?"

"I'll have you know I only just sat down before you came in," Miri snapped. "I made the beds, dusted everything, cleaned the entire kitchen, and tended the hives." She raised the paper, blocking Portia from her sight.

Ignoring her cousin's rudeness, Portia poked a finger at the barrier. "What are you reading that's so interesting?"

"An article about us leaving New York."

"Really? Let me see."

"I'll read it to you," Miri said. She reread the entire article and reached the paragraph she hadn't finished.

"The emigrants seem to have intelligence and other qualities which will make them valuable additions to the Haitian Republic. They will have an open road to success.

"Prior to sailing, the passengers assembled on deck where prayers were offered for their safety and success by Reverend S. Garnett."

A highly regarded Methodist minister, Reverend Garnett, petitioned the Almighty to watch over those embarking on the journey. Initially opposed to emigration, he eventually came to endorse the prospect of colonization.

The closing line of the article read:

The vessel was towed out to sea amid the cheers and good wishes of their families and friends.

Tears filled Miri's eyes at the irony of the statement. Her perception of the wretched experience was of being torn from her home and the people she loved.

As Portia leaned over to see the article, Miri fanned away the odors of animal and manure rising from her cousin's clothes. "Do you know what I hope, Portia? I hope our families find places soon. I'm tired of being crammed into this pocket-sized house. When we first moved in and stayed up half the night talking, I thought it was fun, but I want my own bed and room now. I miss the privacy I had at home."

Miri didn't notice the happy-go-lucky expression disappear from Portia's face. "I thought you liked sharing a room with me," Portia said. "I should have known better. I'm crowded too, but you don't hear me complain. You are spoiled, Miri. All you ever think about is yourself. Anyway, my parents are determined to begin farming as soon as possible so you won't have to put up with me much longer."

Portia's outburst surprised Miri. "You misunderstood me," she said. "I didn't mean you're a problem, it's just this house is uncomfortably small for two families."

"Oh, I understand perfectly well, Miri. You need more room."

"We both do, Portia."

In silence they glared at each other. Their raised voices drew Portia's mother from the parlor as Miri's mother came through the back door. In unison, they asked, "Why were you girls shouting?" and received a jumbled explanation of the disagreement.

"Enough childish bickering," Miri's mother said. "We've got to make something for the meeting."

"What meeting?" Miri asked.

"Some of the men are coming here this evening to talk about land allotments, the soil, and what crops are suitable." She placed two large bowls on the table, selected several spices and said, "I need a jar of honey and the tin of raisins, Miri. Then while Aunt Rachel and I mix batter for the cakes, you and Portia can fire up the oven and prepare the baking pans."

Miri measured out portions of clear amber honey for each cake and licked the spoon. She savored the silky sweetness coating her tongue and thought about the bees. Why had simple insects been given the ability to create something so marvelous? Bees seem to have been born with an understanding of their purpose and how to accomplish it.

Humans, on the other hand had to spend years studying and practicing a skill to gain mastery. Either an apprenticeship or further education followed the decision as to which trade or profession to pursue. Miri knew apprenticeship and college were for the most part male concerns but she had not given up the hope of having a career.

Professions currently open to women were limited to teaching primary grade students, dressmaking and millinery, and none required more than basic education or training. Midwifery and herbal medicine, necessary and valued skills, were seldom spoken of outside female circles. Dissatisfaction with their status as chattel, prevented from higher education, with no voice or vote in politics because of gender, women had started to talk about their capabilities and seek the same opportunities available to men.

"Miri," her mother said, "pay attention. I've asked you twice to flour the raisins. Portia's already stacked wood in the stove while you've been lollygagging."

Their cross words again on her mind, Miri said, "Portia said she's moving soon. Is that true?"

A glance flew between her mother and aunt, wooden spoons clacked against the sides of the bowls. No one answered.

Miri dusted the raisins with flour, gave them to her mother and rubbed lard on a cake pan. "Will someone please answer my question?"

The spoon in her mother's hand stopped half way around the bowl. "Nothing is certain yet," she said. She lifted the spoon and watched as batter dripped from its tip. Satisfied, she poured a ribbon of cream-colored batter into one of the pans.

"The fact is," she continued, "many families will go to an area called Artibonite to take ownership of the free land offered by the Haitian government."

"Are we going?" Miri asked. She liked what she'd seen of Port-au-Prince so far. On one adventure into the city she and Portia had come upon a neighborhood of large, stately homes with gingerbread trim and long verandas. Other than their bright, lively paint colors, they were similar to houses in Spencer. Trees along their streets resembled the shady oaks and elms native to the northeastern states.

Another attraction for Miri in Port-au-Prince was Philippe. He lived somewhere in the city, and though she wouldn't seek him out, she hoped for a chance encounter. She had enjoyed talking with him when he and his uncle joined Doctor Stillman each week for supper at her house in Spencer. The two doctors discussed medical concerns, and the Haitian doctor always brought his nephew along to translate.

To Miri's relief her mother said, "No, we're going to stay here because your father has work, such as it is."

True. With only two barbers in the colony, he had plenty of customers. Still, her mother was exasperated because her kitchen was also his barbershop. Haircuts and shaves interfered with the cooking schedule but she never complained to him. Her displeasure expressed itself among the women in the house. If Miri or Portia overlooked even a single hair when they cleaned, she was quick to scold them and demand they redouble their efforts.

In Spencer, Miri hadn't been allowed in the barbershop when customers were present, but things were different here. She was free to watch her father sharpen a razor to a keen edge. The "thrip, thrip" sound of metal drawing across the leather strop would be a memory forever bound in the marrow of her bones.

"Is that why people are moving?" she said. "Because they can't find work in Port-au-Prince?"

Again a look was exchanged between the sisters, and Aunt Rachel nodded. She remained silent as Miri's mother said, "You and Portia are old enough to be told the truth. Lack of employment and dwindling funds are the main reasons people are relocating. Men who have never held a hoe have decided to give farming a try. They hope to raise enough crops to at least feed their families and perhaps have some to sell."

"Our menfolk probably haven't been able to find work because they don't speak French like the people from Louisiana," Miri said. "Those others are getting jobs because they can talk with the Haitians. Why don't men in our group learn French from the men in the Louisiana group?"

Portia was impressed by Miri's boldness, but from the tone of Aunt Sarah's voice, knew she was not pleased.

"Miriam," she said, "people from Louisiana also belong to the Church of Rome and your father believes good Congregationalists should not associate with those who've pledged to follow the pope. On that point he, Minister Grady and the majority of the men are firm. They would not consider ever asking help from Catholics, even if they are people of color."

"But doesn't Minister Grady also say it is wrong for us to hold ourselves high and mighty and believe we are more righteous than others?"

The rebuke was swift. "You'd best mind your tongue in speaking of your elders, Miriam Rose. The men are doing what they deem best."

The idea of her small community shrinking further sounded terrible to Miri. She had observed the Haitians staring in an unfriendly way as the colonists in her group went about their daily activities. With fewer colonists to watch, the eyes of the Haitians would miss nothing.

Chapter 13

January 1863

Portia's snoring woke Miri often, and the desire for a room of her own grew each time she struggled to get back to sleep. It would be a blessing to hear nothing at night louder than the flutter of insect wings and the chirrup of crickets.

Georgie caught her trying to stifle a yawn at breakfast. Not one to miss an opportunity to needle, he said, "Good morning, Sleepyhead. Did thinking about a certain boy keep you awake last night?"

Across the table her father lowered the paper and peered over the top; her mother turned from the stove and her aunt, uncle and Portia waited for her answer.

"Don't talk nonsense, Georgie," she said. "What I had were nightmares about pranks my pesky little brother plays on me."

Georgie dug a spoon into his oatmeal, his interest renewed by fear Miri might be asked for details about his escapades.

With her brother's trouble-making squelched, Miri greeted the rest of the family. Further conversation was stopped by the sound of boots and shoes on the back porch.

Her father opened the door to a group of men from the colony. She could hear murmurs of conversation but nothing clearly. *Why they had come to her house at this hour of the morning?* Her father and uncle went outside and Miri was irked to see Georgie follow them.

"Finish up, Miri," her mother said. "I'm expecting company and need you to lend me a hand." She refilled the teakettle, set it on the stove and left the kitchen.

Miri took her bowl to the sink and couldn't resist pulling the curtain open a crack to see what was happening on the porch. Her father was standing in the center of a cluster of men, reading aloud from a newspaper. The men paid rapt attention. A crackling intensity rippled within the group and she knew something significant had happened.

Shortly after, her father folded the newspaper and came inside, wearing an expression Miri had never seen. Sourness twisted his mouth, a frown merged his brows, and coal black eyes smoldered over the bridge of his nose. Men surged through the door behind him in a babble of deep-voiced conversations.

She felt someone nudge her. It was Portia. "Come on, Miri," she whispered, "we should be in the parlor with the women."

Miri hadn't heard her come in because of the noise level in the kitchen, but nothing blocked her mother's voice. "Miri," she called. "You can serve the tea now."

Why are women visiting so early in the day? Miri wondered. *Likely they're here for the same reason as the men.*

She found her aunt, Mrs. Clement the midwife, and Mrs. Grady the minister's wife, perched side-by-side on the sofa. The wing-back chairs were occupied by her mother and Mrs. Barkley, who clutched a newspaper against her ample bosom.

Portia admitted several more ladies into the house while Miri served tea. She went to the kitchen to refill the teapot and returned to the *tink* of her mother's spoon tapping against a glass. The silence was immediate.

Mrs. Barkley unfolded the newspaper. In a strong contralto she read the front page of *The Liberator:*

SLAVERY ABOLISHED. THREE MILLION SLAVES SET FREE
January 1, 1863
GLORY HALLELUJAH!

The women clapped and cheered. Mrs. Barkley waited for the hubbub to subside to continue:

> Mr. Lincoln has set slaves in those States in rebellion free. He pronounced it an act of justice, reasonable under the Constitution and necessary for the preservation of the Union. People freed will be protected by the military.
>
> Further, former slaves and other persons of color will be accepted for enlistment into the Federal Army under General Order 143.

Mrs. Grady was usually the first to comment. "So President Lincoln has at last unbound the shackles of those poor unfortunate creatures. It's a blessing, to be sure."

Miri couldn't take her mind off the order that authorized the formation of colored regiments. She was certain her father would want to enlist. She froze at the thought of him in the thick of the conflict.

Father is a middle-aged barber with a wife and children. He has a rifle, but I've never known him to shoot it. How can he change from family man into someone who is capable of killing another human?

Mrs. Barkley raised her voice above the women's happy din and read the article below the headline.

"'President Lincoln has signed a decree to free slaves in the District of Columbia. The decree shall become law in ninety days. Slaves in the hundreds are fleeing owners. They follow Federal troops seeking protection, and ask soldiers for food and shelter. The Army has declared the runaways 'contraband of war' and refuses to turn them over to anyone claiming ownership.

"The Army is employing able-bodied males as laborers, and women to work as cooks and nurses, but supplies and resources are strained.

The number of runaways congregating around the President's home is increasing and several Abolitionist groups have pledged to assist newly emancipated people find housing and employment.'"

The room was hushed for a moment after Mrs. Barkley stopped reading. Then Miri's mother said, "So the true destruction of slavery at last begins. Let us pray it brings equality and unity to all of us." Her comment served to spark another animated discussion.

Had she continued listening, Miri would have heard sentiments similar to her mother's from most of the other women. Her mind drifted back to the reaction her father displayed after he read the article. She was certain his dander was up, because what he had longed and argued for had come too late. If they were living in Spencer he could join the army even if it wasn't as a soldier. The idea of him as a soldier woke a dreadful realization.

The names of men who were wounded or died in battle were printed in the papers. Without doubt those lists would soon include names of soldiers in colored regiments. Her worst fears would be realized if she found her father's name among those in the black-bordered columns. She shuddered at the thought and bit her lip to hold back the tears.

She refused to cry in front of a room full of women. Instead she listened to them express gratitude and profound admiration for Lincoln. Unable to summon a similar level of adoration, she said nothing, and using the teapot as an excuse, went to the kitchen to find out what the men were saying.

The crowd was thinning. Men were taking leave, muttering about

86

neglected errands and chores. Her father had a customer in the chair. "The way I see it," he said as he lathered the man's chin, "The degree of equality a person is accorded is determined by the color of his skin. As people of color we are not perceived as equal to a white man. The only thing Lincoln is giving us with his decree is the privilege to become unarmed participants in a war he's losing. "

"But, Henry," Uncle Will said, "this is what you wanted. If our men show Lincoln we are eager to join the Army, I'm certain he'll recognize our willingness to fight."

"Oh, I think not. He has said nothing about equality for us in the courts, granting us the right to vote or to be real soldiers. Though our blood is the same color as our white brethren, the only equality Lincoln is offering us is to die. Still, you do have a valid point about demonstrating willingness."

The potholder Miri was holding fell onto the hot stovetop at the mention of death. She grabbed it, burning her fingertips and fled from the kitchen. A moment later she returned for the forgotten teapot.

Her emotions swung like a pendulum. She was proud her family had risked its own freedom to aid runaways like Vi Sparks and her mother from slavery, and elated they would soon be legally free. She also sympathized with her father and his anger and frustration with Lincoln's failure to entirely erase racial inequality.

"This will be enormous," she told Portia later. "Freedom for runaway slaves, and the Army now officially able to hire colored men will change everything. I know my father is itching to go back to Spencer and sign on with the army. I want to go home too, but not if he's going to be sent to a battlefield. I'd be terrified he got injured, or worse."

By midmorning Lincoln's decree and the subject of emancipation had been explored from many points of view. Interest in continuing to chew on it was waning, and the number of people in the kitchen and parlor dwindled. Conversations drifted into general topics spaced by longer periods of silence. The noon bell of the Catholic church reminded the remaining women to go home, fix lunches, and catch up on neglected housework.

Miri's noon meal was accompanied by more complaints about Lincoln from her father.

"I don't believe he was honest with us when we met," he said. "I suspect freeing the slaves was something he already intended to carry out."

Her mother said, "The important thing, Henry, is that he has at last begun to do what is right. We are in Haiti now and must focus on our new life."

"Granting freedom to runaways is the logical thing to do, Sarah, but if Lincoln had acted on emancipation sooner we would be at the level of equality we deserve, and thousands of us could have enlisted to help win this war." He pounded the table, "We would certainly not be here."

"All the anger on earth toward the President won't change a thing," her mother said.

While she cleared the dishes, Miri listened to her father continue to sputter. For the first time, she felt a strange relief to be in Haiti and far from the war. Distance prevented her father from enlisting and putting himself in danger.

She took Georgie's bowl from him and blocked his path to the backdoor. "I finally found one good thing about moving here," she said.

"What?"

"Father can't go off and join the army. He's safe here."

"Girl's don't know beans about war," Georgie said, reaching around her for the doorknob. "Men don't stand around whining about being safe. Soldiers are strong and brave and fight for what they believe in, and that's what Pa wants to do."

Georgie had no idea of the horrible reality of war. Miri wanted to shake some sense into him. "Soldiering is dangerous, George Benjamin Whitfield," she said. "It isn't playing with tin soldiers. Real, live soldiers can be wounded and many die. Father can't even join the Army as a regular soldier. He'd be a laborer and issued a shovel, not a gun. And another thing, Georgie, don't you dare call me 'whiney'. I may not be allowed to become a soldier because I'm not a man, but at least I'm not an ornery brat like you."

Mrs. Whitfield appeared in the doorway. "Are you two squabbling again?" she said. "What's the fuss about this time?"

Miri glared at Georgie to silence him. There was no purpose in revisiting the topic of war. She said, "We disagree about who is the best at dominoes, Mother."

"It's hard to believe the nonsense you bicker over." She looked from one to the other of them and asked. "When will you two learn to grow up?"

"Speaking of learning," Miri said, "when do you think a school will open?"

"At the moment, schooling isn't as important as the need for employment for the men, and decent housing. Those things must come first." She took an envelope from her apron pocket. "I almost forgot," she said. "This came for you."

Georgie took advantage of the diversion to slip out.

Miri recognized the awkward handwriting and unfolded Vi's letter.

December 12, 1862
Dear Miri,

I am writing to let you know how Mam and me are fareing. Mam has got more ladies to work for now that so many washerwomen went to Hayti. I was thinking to quit from school and get my own washing jobs but Mam sayed NO. She don't want me to be working hard always like her and I must stick to learning.

Spencer is quiet and I am more easy and less scared walking out but Mama and me are still careful. I don't talk to them I don't know and ALWAYS keep my ~~regti~~ registration paper with me.

Clarice and them girls that is your friends talk and act nice to me. But I cant visit with them because of school work and helping Mam with customers.

Maybe you can write me some about Hayti. I would like that.

Your friend, Viola Starks

Miri refolded the letter and returned it to the envelope. Answering could wait.

The next morning as her father was out preparing for the first harvest, Miri propped the broom against the wall, impatient to get to the field before he got started. The extra care she had taken with sweeping was worth the time. Her mother approved her efforts and she was permitted to leave.

The hives were still closed and she suspected her father had waited for her. He handed her a pair of gloves and a hat with a veil. "Put these on," he said, "and fill the tin."

The hat and gloves didn't fit well but would protect her hands and face from being stung. She gathered dry pine needles and fresh grass in the pie tin and sprinkled them with water.

Her father put a match to the damp pile. It raised a flame that blazed for an instant before subsiding into a plume of light gray smoke. "Ready?" he asked.

She nodded, carried the smoldering tin close to one of the hives and blew smoke across it, taking care to aim the smoke directly at the hive. The sound of humming grew quieter as the bees reacted and settled down.

"Well done, daughter," her father said.

Because of the veil her triumphant smile wasn't visible.

She and her father still disagreed about whether or not beekeeping was a suitable activity for a female. "Father, I have a genuine interest in caring for the hives and learning how to harvest honey. Georgie doesn't. Besides, there's no proof women lack the capability to carry out such tasks," she said.

She was proud of the fact her father had allowed her to smoke the hive at this first harvest, and how well she had done it. Now she stepped back as he inserted a knife and sliced into the wax along the edge of the hive cover.

He lifted the top off and a few guard bees drifted out to circle his head. He ignored the hovering insects as he removed two frames filled with honey and placed them in the wheelbarrow. He inserted the empty frames into the vacant slots and replaced the hive cover.

Miri followed as the sweet cargo was trundled to the shed. Along the way she took off her gloves and lifted the veil to enjoy the cool, cloud-free morning in the company of her father.

He cleared his throat. It was something he did before a rare reprimand to Georgie or making an important pronouncement. "We'll be moving soon, Miri," he said. "I've decided to go to Artibonite."

"Moving?"

"Yes, Miri, we're moving."

"But why leave Port-au-Prince, Father? It's a city. Artibonite is farm land."

"You have to understand, since most of our men moved to Artibonite there's little need for a barber here. I can't earn enough to feed us, so I'm going to try farming."

Miri held her tongue. Artibonite had no appeal, but they faced hardship if they stayed in Port-au-Prince, and returning to Spencer would give her father an opportunity to enlist. The idea of her father in the army was more frightful than the thought of relocating to Artibonite. Casualties were high in the war between North and South. Armed with only a pick and shovel, he would be defenseless against bullets.

Her happy mood evaporated faster than a puddle on a hot summer day.

Chapter 14
April 1863

Though at first Miri accepted her father's reasons for relocating to Artibonite, over the next week she argued and even pleaded with him to stay in Port-au-Prince.

Tired of revisiting the topic, he said, "Miriam, we must move in order to survive."

"Yes," her mother said. "Your father wants to make sure the family is provided for. And we will have another mouth to feed later this year."

"What do you mean 'another mouth to feed'?" Miri asked.

Her father answered, "We will have an addition to the family, Miri. Your mother is expecting. The decision to move is final. There will be no further discussion on the matter."

"Mother's expecting?" Miri was in disbelief. There had been a time when she wished for a little sister, but years passed without one arriving and her hope evaporated. Now with such a huge gap in their ages she was likely to be more a second mother than a sister to the newcomer.

Her parents smiled and nodded and Georgie grinned.

She didn't want to put a damper on the celebration, and quashed her misgivings about bringing a newborn into such an unsettled situation.

Eight days later she looked out at a wide, flat field from the back door of a small, unpainted wooden house. Through a mist of clouds in the distance, mountains bordered the shallow, bowl shaped depression called Artibonite.

Wild grass covered much of the family plot, and waved lazily in a hot breeze. Along its borders tightly spaced trees formed a natural barrier. Cows grazed near a barn in the middle of the field, and in a fenced enclosure several mules and horses were bunched under the shade of a solitary tree. Chickens, ducks and geese ran about freely in front of a coop.

The land, from house to barn, was her father's allotment. Land on the other side of the barn belonged to Uncle Will. The brothers-in-law agreed to a partnership in owning the livestock, with care primarily under the oversight of Uncle Will. His management of the animals was a boon for her father who would need advice and hard work to become a farmer.

The house, like others in the colony, sat along an unpaved road not much wider than a path. At the rear of each dwelling a peaked roofed outhouse stood like a sentry. The hard-packed, dirt streets formed a pattern resembling spokes on a wheel, each spoke terminating at a circular clearing. A short road led out from the rim of the wheel to a small, box-like wooden church. Port-au-Prince was inferior to her beloved Spencer, but compared to Artibonite it was a model of modern living.

She and her mother unpacked and hung curtains and a few pictures, and placed knickknacks on the copper-topped calling card table whose glowing amber surface provided a bit of brightness. But in spite of decorations, the house did not feel like home.

Materials necessary to construct the school failed to arrive, and with no studies to occupy her time, Miri was assigned additional chores. A large part of her day was taken up by drudgework. Her least favorite job was the weekly laundry. She loathed wrestling with heavy, wet sheets and tackled them last of all. The lye in the laundry soap irritated her hands and arms and soon they felt rough as sandpaper. Every item had to be rinsed several times, and by the time everything was wrung out, her hands were lilac colored from the bluing solution added to the last rinse that assured white items wouldn't look dingy and yellow.

Miri pushed a pillowcase back beneath the rinse water with the wooden laundry paddle and reflected on her circumstances. *I've been doing these same horrid chores for weeks now. I don't want this circle of dullness to become my life, but unless conditions improve, the future is sure to be bleak.* Dispirited, she had no appetite and wasn't inclined to join the women.

Her mother was minding a group of the younger children off to the side on the grass. She had been given the task because persistent back pain prevented her from doing heavy chores. Her agility waxed and waned, and at times she was unable to tend to infants in cradles and chase after toddlers who could crawl and walk. This morning was particularly taxing to her with three cranky, teething babies in the group.

She wiped spittle from the chin of one and said, "This can't go on. We're having a hard time with so much more work on our shoulders. Without stores and farmers' markets, everything we eat has to be planted, grown, slaughtered, skinned or plucked before it can be cooked. We can't go to a butcher, fishmonger, fruit peddler or buy eggs, milk and butter.

In addition to laundry, ironing and sewing, raising herb gardens, keeping track of children and minding our homes and husbands, we're expected to hoe and weed huge gardens, tend to livestock, make butter, bake, and on and on. The work never ends."

"I agree, Sarah," Mrs. Everett said. "But what can we do?"

Miri paused from wringing a towel.

"I don't know the answer," her mother said, "but we need to think of something. With a baby on the way, and after months of working like a mule, I'm plain tuckered out."

Miri worried about her mother's weariness. Pregnancy had heightened her sensitivity to heat and she often complained of not sleeping well. There was no vigor in her voice and her body sagged with fatigue. A trio of lines appeared between her eyebrows.

"Well, dearie," Mrs. Everett said, dipping her pillowcase-sized drawers in and out of a bucket of suds, "If you do find a solution, be sure to tell the rest of us."

Laughter danced around the pavilion. Mrs. Whitfield's face grew red. She looked and felt like a scolded child.

Miri twisted the wet towel in her hands so hard her wrist ached. She wanted to wring the neck of snotty Mrs. Everett. Instead, she tossed the towel into the basket, balanced its load on her hip and trudged up the hill, pinned wet laundry to the clothesline and mulled over her mother's complaint. There must be something she could do to help.

Midway through hanging the towels, the answer to the problem struck her. With a new infusion of enthusiasm, she hurriedly hung the rest of the laundry and presented the suggestion to her mother.

"I can watch the little ones," she told her, "and you can take on something easier like darning and mending. I can teach the alphabet, basic reading, simple arithmetic and spelling, and use the slates, chalk and books intended to supply the school we don't have. Portia can help me, and Georgie can take over her work in the garden. It'll answer Father's concern about Splinter not having enough chores."

"Well, it sounds fine to me," her mother said, "but let me find out how the rest of the ladies feel about the idea."

At suppertime Miri was told a few women had concerns because of her lack of experience in childcare. "Nevertheless, we agreed to allow a one week trial beginning tomorrow," her mother said. "I must say, I'm proud of you, Miri. This idea shows you're maturing."

Miri smiled and accepted the rare praise with a simple, "Thank you, Mother."

"The nursing mothers prefer their infants remain under my care, so you and Portia will be responsible for the Warner twins, Molly, David, and Gideon Jones, the Cooper boys and that tribe of Nunnallys."

Miri counted twelve. The five Nunnally children would be a challenge. They had a reputation for unruly behavior and absence of manners, but with Portia's help Miri felt confident they could be contained. David Jones was another story. He was fifteen and should be working, but was being coddled because he'd been kicked in the back by a mule.

After lunch Miri found Portia in the garden, weeding the pole beans. Portia listened to the plan and gave Miri a quizzical look. "I never took care of children in Spencer. Why do you think I would I want to be bothered watching the noisy little things here?"

"Because either we watch them or be forever stuck doing laundry and other backbreaking chores. I'm exhausted when I get done with the washing, and cleaning smelly diapers is worse than mucking out filthy stalls."

Portia nodded. "Minding kids might be better than laundry and shoveling manure," she said, "but who's going to do those things if we don't?"

"I've already suggested Georgie take over in the garden," Miri said. "And I'm also going to propose he haul water from the well for the women on laundry day. It's time he stopped loafing around so much. Meet me at the barn after breakfast tomorrow so we can get an early start on our new job."

Portia pounded the tip of the hoe into the ground and said, "Alright. But for now weeding is my responsibility and I'd better get back to it."

The following day, they kept their lively charges occupied for several hours with games. After tag, they played crack the whip, a favorite of the boys, especially David. He darted about in delight, pulling girls off balance until their skirts became tangled and they tripped. Miri cautioned him not to play so roughly. He laughed, yanked the hand he was holding and the girl fell.

The boys always won crack the whip because one of them was always the last one standing. Revenge came to the girls in the game of statues where impatience prevented the boys from holding a pose for very long.

In the second round of games David said, "I quit. Me, the twins and some of the other boys are gonna go find bugs for our collections." And in a blink they were gone.

Miri had no chance to stop them. "Be careful!" she shouted to the fading screech of renegades galloping into the waving grass. She prayed David wouldn't put them in danger and turned her attention back to the remaining children. Portia was playing marbles with the little boys so Miri took the girls to collect flowers and pine needles and showed them how to link needles and flower stems together to create living jewelry. Soon everyone, including the boys, were bedecked like royalty in colorful, aromatic coronets, necklaces and bracelets.

Playtime ended when the sun reached its highest point. Miri spread a cloth beneath a tree. She and Portia laid out a cold lunch, holding a portion of meat, bread and dried apples aside for the marauders.

Miri recognized that most children were polite, curious, and eager to learn. She also found the process of teaching fascinating. A good teacher can pass an amazing amount of knowledge to her students. It made her think once more of making this a possible career. Her tenth grade education more than satisfied the required qualifications for a teaching certificate.

The noise and dust of a galloping, whooping horde signaled the return of the boys. Most of them proudly carried captive insects tied inside handkerchiefs, and led by David, behaved like hooligans. They ran among the girls and tormented them waving the buzzing, wriggling bundles around. Chaos ruled until the boys collapsed in a gleeful heap and Miri quieted the shrieking girls.

Molly was the first to speak after calm was restored. "Cousin Miri, can we play hide and seek?"

"Yes, we can, Molly," Miri said. The game would provide an opportunity to reestablish her authority and control over the boys. "Stay close to the clearing," she told them. "Don't go too far into the woods. You could get bitten by a snake or stolen by the bogeyman."

David said, "That's nonse...."

"Rules are rules," she said, cutting him off.

The game lasted until sweaty faces alerted Miri to stop the game and settle the group into a cooler, quiet activity. She gathered them under the trees, opened a *McGuffey's Reader* and said, "Let's do some lessons."

"I don't want to study," David grumbled shaking his head. "Why can't we play marbles or checkers?"

Molly picked up his sour attitude. She pouted and crossed her arms. "No fair, Davy," she said. "You choosed games I don't know how to pway."

Everyone looked from David to Molly.

Eventually all eyes landed on Miri whose head was awhirl. She needed to prove to them and herself that she had the skill to solve a problem named David.

She was in no mood to tolerate any more of his defiance but had to take care in how she corralled it. The boys admired David. If she lost control of him she ran the risk of losing control of them all.

"David," she said, "We will work on lessons until Molly's ready for her nap. Then as long as you do it quietly, you can play checkers."

He glared at her.

She refused to back down and they locked eyes.

"I like to pway tiddowy-winks," Molly said.

David smiled at his sister's fractured pronunciation, kicked the ground, and slumped against a tree. The standoff was broken.

Miri captured the attention of the boys with her knowledge about the insects they had caught, and Portia chanted ABC's and nursery rhymes with the younger children. David came to the edge of Miri's group with questions about the snakes and lizards native to Haiti.

As she detailed the habitat of a lizard, Molly squirmed into her lap and yawned. "Pwease tell me a story, cousin Miri. Pwease, pwease," she said and stuffed a pudgy thumb into her mouth.

Miri looked around. The boys were looking at David and she waited for his reaction to Molly's request. He nodded, and Miri realized he could be kind and considerate, given the right circumstance. The rest of the boys went along with him and for the first time that day, an agreement had been reached without bickering.

Miri's story was pure fantasy set in the future, but she hoped the events would happen as described.

"The war between North and South is over," she began. "The North was victorious and peace united the states again. There are no slaves, no slave hunters, and no one is required to carry registration papers. President Lincoln has acknowledged his shabby treatment of people of color who were free before his Proclamation. He is especially apologetic to those of us in emigrant settlements in Canada and Haiti. New laws have been enacted to guarantee and protect our right to work and travel without restrictions, and the President invites us to come home."

"Aw, that's nothing but a fairy tale," David said, scrambling to his feet and stomping off.

Miri sighed. She now realized the job of watching children was not easier than doing laundry. Dirty clothes didn't sass or argue.

"Should I go after him?" Portia asked.

"No, leave him alone. He'll only get more irritated."

David returned, said hardly a word to anyone and spent the rest of the afternoon playing checkers.

Children were reunited with mothers at suppertime and Miri was thankful the day was done. She went to bed early to rest up for the challenges tomorrow was sure to bring.

Chapter 15

Late Spring/Early Summer 1863

An envelope with Miri's name in familiar handwriting lay on the table. She hadn't heard from Clarice in months.

Dear Miri,

I hope you are well and find your new location in Artibonite pleasant. The vast farmlands you described and the area surrounding it sound splendid and exotic. I found a book in the library with illustrations of the birds and flowers you wrote about and I envy you. I would give anything to actually see pink flamingos with legs like stilts and rainbow colored parrots. Such creatures are wonders of nature and I don't understand why you complain of missing the drab little chickadees and sparrows here in Spencer.

It must be amazing to have orchids grow around you in wild abundance. Are you allowed to pick them? What kind of plant is a yucca?

Remember, during the winter in Spencer, to have fresh fruit other than an apple is a rare treat. Now you have the luxury of indulging in an orange or grapefruit whenever you please. Your description of a lime raised the picture of a green lemon in my mind. Do they taste similar?

You were never one to shy away from a challenge, Miri, and you have achieved many things. Though farming might be difficult to learn, I know you will do whatever is necessary to master it.

As for my news, there is talk circulating about a possible Rebel attack on New York City. We hear they are plotting to skirmish along the entire coastline as far north as New York. Father is concerned for the safety of Mother and me and insists we womenfolk leave Spencer and be out of harm's way. We sail for England in two days and will stay with relatives.

I don't expect the trip to be pleasant. Mother and I are at great odds over my wish to go to college and I suspect she will use our time abroad to mount a protracted effort to dissuade me. She is eager for me to attend Miss Porter's Female Finishing School. Mother's paramount desire is that I possess the skills to make a suitable marriage, but my mind is firm. Next term I plan to send applications to several colleges for women.

Enough about me, I don't mean to vex you with my complaints and I apologize. Dearest friend, I think of you often and am anxious to hear from you before I sail, so please answer this letter as soon as possible. With fondest regard,

Your friend always, Clarice

P.S. I will be staying at 18 Fair Huntington, Worcester, NW England through the end of July and perhaps early August.

Painting such a lovely picture of Haiti had been a mistake. Clarice thought Haiti was paradise. The next letter to her would have descriptions of the lizards that roamed the fields, the crocodiles in the river, the million kinds of insects and the unrelenting heat . . . each one a degree of counterbalance to the false image.

Because Miri, too, aspired to a career, she had contended with the objections of her own mother, and understood Clarice's conflict. To spend years learning the art of home management, needlepoint, and steps required to be a proper hostess in preparation to attract a husband was a waste of intelligence.

Yet given the present circumstances she knew all too well she had little chance of ever attending college. But marriage to one of the unappealing young men in the colony was not acceptable either. It seemed she was destined to be a spinster.

After supper she walked to the clearing with her family. Her parents joined the group assembling under the pavilion for a community meeting, and Georgie ran off to play with a group of boys.

A short distance from the pavilion, a half dozen or so young men strutted like peacocks near a cluster of giggling girls who cast flirtatious looks over fluttering fans. Portia was in that circle, but Miri had no interest in it and beckoned to her cousin. They chatted and agreed to organize a sing-along, an event that held high appeal for unattached young adults. It was a social function both sexes could engage in without chaperones, and the absence of adult supervision provided an opportunity to position yourself next to someone you were sweet on.

The impromptu chorus came together and sang several songs with enthusiasm, but sounded off-key and ragged to Miri. She missed her piano that might have unified the voices and kept them on pitch. All she had now were memories of her hours of practice on the beloved Steinway, the lemony smell of the polish her mother used on the wood, the squeaky hinge on the piano bench when she opened it, and the mirror-like sheen of slick, black keys. Her most treasured and painful memories were those of compositions that had stirred her. No longer could she bring forth with her hands what was so dear to her heart. The piano counted among precious things she lost because of the move to Haiti.

She saw three girls slip off into the shadows, one after the other. A boy followed each of them. Though it was dark, one furtive figure was easy to identify. Maude Nunnally stood a full head taller than any girl in the colony. Dismayed by the rash behavior of girls who had been enticed into who-knew-what, and disappointed with the quality of singing, she called a halt to the informal concert.

"I'm going to find out what they're talking about in the meeting," she said to Portia. "Come with me."

"I'm not interested in snooping, and likely it's boring anyway," Portia said.

"It is not snooping," Miri said. "Whatever they discuss usually affects us so we have a right to know."

Portia preferred to catch up with the other girls so Miri went to the pavilion alone, arriving as the debate finished discussing when to start a school session and shifted to rumors of unrest in Port-au-Prince.

Anger against President Geffrand was growing among the Haitians, who blamed him for an ineffective government and increasing poverty within the general population. Concerns and questions arose about the possibility of small uprisings or outright war and the impact on the settlement. The majority opinion to wait and see how the situation evolved was adopted and the meeting ended on an unsettled tone.

She could not believe her ears. They came to Haiti because of a Civil War at home and here they sat, at risk of becoming caught in another. Was there no place on earth where they could live in peace? On the walk home she was plagued by troubled thoughts.

Her father was waiting when she arrived. "Miri, Georgie," her father said, "We approved lessons to be taught in the open. Mrs. Barkley isn't pleased with the idea, but there is a genuine concern that you children are falling behind in your studies."

Miri said, "I'm a young woman, Father, not a child, and I overheard Mrs. Barkley say a proper school ought to have been built by now. That's the likely reason she's upset."

"Miriam Hazel Rose," her mother said, "you certainly have better things to do than eavesdrop. And mind how you speak to your father. Except for Mondays when we need the pavilion for laundry, Mrs. Barkley and other teachers can hold classes there. It'll provide some protection from sun and rain."

The promise of school rekindled Miri's intent to focus on a career. She would also no longer need to babysit. Relieved, she was unbothered by the scolding.

· · · · ·

Two months later she waited for Portia at the corner of the barn. The animals were mooing and bleating and she pinched her nose in reaction to a whiff of manure. *I'll never get used to this,* she thought. *I hope Portia gets here soon so I don't have to endure this stink and noise much longer.* Her wish was answered.

Portia emerged from the barn and they walked into a field to gather wildflowers to place on the altar for today's service. Their modest church had been constructed of local wood but its interior walls, still unfinished, would need more than flowers to improve its appearance.

The same could be said for every house, barn and outhouse in the settlement. Not one scrap of the promised lumber or supplies had arrived from the mainland. All the buildings were assembled from rough boards cut by the colonists with tools they'd brought to Haiti.

She found a cluster of orchids in the shadow of taller flowers. She clipped one with her scissors and was shocked to see Portia yank an entire plant, roots and all from the ground. Now she understood why Aunt Rachel complained Portia had become more uncouth since they moved to Artibonite.

Miri took a deep breath. She thought of how best to instruct her cousin on the proper way to gather flowers and decided on a simple chat. "You know, Portia," she said, "Thanks to you, I've learned to gather eggs without getting pecked too often." She didn't mention her aversion to putting her hand under angry hens as she probed for eggs.

Portia grinned. "I do know a bit about chickens and cows and..."

"I know," Miri interjected. "You know almost everything there is to know about farming, but now it's my turn to show you something. Cutting flowers is not the same as weeding. Don't pull plants out of the ground. Leave them rooted and they'll bloom again. Look for stems with flowers and buds and use scissors to clip them. When they're in a vase of water, the buds open over two to three days and the blooms lasts longer."

Portia took the instruction in good humor and Miri was grateful she hadn't reacted to her as a bossy know-it-all.

They carried armloads of flowers to a table beside Portia's house, snipped off unnecessary leaves and tucked the trimmed flowers into vases. The four tall bouquets were taken to the church where two were placed at each end of a linen covered altar.

Miri ran a fingertip lightly across a petal and inhaled. "This tropical climate produces flowers with such sweet fragrances and rich colors," she said. "And though this church can't compare to any in Spencer, look how these arrangements make a homely place beautiful." She did a last fluffing and adjustment to the flowers before they went home to clean up.

When she returned, early arrivals were already assembling in front of the closed door. Georgie was one of a quartet of gangly boys fidgeting and scuffing at the dirt while men stood stiff-legged or milled around in tight circles. Jackets were unbuttoned and hands felt for watch chains, pulled at suspenders, or hooked thumbs into vest pockets. In chalk-white shirts, somber brown, gray and black trousers and jackets, old and young men resembled sparrows and chickadees.

The outfits on women were a great contrast to the plain attire of the men. Everyday chores set aside, the ladies were on display in their Sunday finery. They dipped and swayed, greeting and chatting with one another and created a dancing bouquet of colors that rivaled the flowers.

Mr. Richmond, the Sexton, moved through the crowd ringing a bell to signal the start of services. Jackets were buttoned and people moved inside the church. Conversations ceased or dropped to low whispers. Miri went in and sat with her parents and Georgie. Minister Grady entered the sanctuary from a side door and announced the opening hymn as the last stragglers hurried to their pews.

As she sang, Miri recalled her grandmother's words. "Your father is resolved to establish a homeland where you will be free and equal to everyone else in every respect."

In spite of the uncivilized location and its crushing heat, hordes of insects, lizards, snakes and lurking crocodiles, an attempt to achieve that goal was underway, and Miri's admiration for her parents reached a new level. She had to find the gumption to help make the dream become reality, and a new vigor fueled by determination infused her singing and prayers.

After services, women spread cloths over tables of rough—cut boards in the churchyard for the weekly community lunch. Men brought hampers and baskets of food from wagons and buggies, and four boys were sent to retrieve jars of lemonade and tea from the river. The men clustered in groups to chat and watch several games of horseshoes while ham, chicken, cheese, cold baked beans, biscuits, quick breads, jam, honey and butter was laid out by the women.

Miri handed her father a glass of tea and he looked closely at her.

"My goodness, Miri," he said. "You're near as brown as maple syrup."

Portia snickered and was speared by Miri's scowl. Displeasure evident, she said, "I can't help that the sun in this backwater is making me dark, Father. I can't stay indoors."

His eyes looked straight into hers. "Don't be sassy, young lady," he said.

The table fell silent at the tone of their exchange.

A chastened Miri smeared butter on a biscuit, drizzled it with honey and ate in peeved silence. She rose to collect dishes to be washed and was again surprised by her father.

"I need you to work in the garden today, Miri."

"But it's Sunday, Father. I was planning to enjoy an afternoon down by the river with Portia."

"Miri," her mother said. "Didn't your father tell you a minute ago to mind your tongue? You will not go to the river if he needs your help."

"If I must work on the Sabbath, Father, why of all places must it be in the garden? You just told me I'm getting darker."

"All the rain has caused the pole beans to shoot up and weeds are running rampant," he told her. "The bean stalks need staking and tying and if the weeds aren't pulled every edible thing will be choked. The faster you get at the work the quicker it'll get done and you might salvage some time to spend at the river." He turned to Georgie. "And you are coming with me, young man," he said. "I've got a job for you too."

"Wear a sunbonnet," said Miri's mother.

"Hats are a nuisance," Miri grumbled.

"I don't want to hear another word from you, Miss." There was no mistaking the tight lipped, razor-sharp tone. Miri knew better than to say more. Her mother had laid down the law and it wouldn't take much more for her to completely lose her temper. Worn down by the heat and an advancing pregnancy that made it difficult for her to lie down comfortably, it was no wonder she was crabby.

Though it was nearly impossible for anyone to sleep at night due to the constant buzz of insects, Mrs. Whitfield had received netting from Dr. Stillman to drape over her bed as protection from bites and stings. Alarmed by the high number and severity of insect attacks, he had collected most of the mosquito netting, and allotted portions to families with babies and children under five, the frail and elderly and to pregnant women. The remainder he kept on hand for people who became sick or bedridden.

Miri was among the healthy and young without netting to defend against mosquitos and other nocturnal bugs. Lack of restful sleep brought her to the point of bad temper and she was so drained of energy her legs felt as if they were moving through sludge.

Portia's voice broke through her distraction.

"I'll help, Aunt Sarah," she said. "I can teach Miri how to wind the beanstalks without breaking them. I know the difference between seedling and weed and I can teach her that, too. We can go to the river some other day."

Miri was against working on Sunday but had lost the argument. She gave her cousin a look hot enough to fry bacon. In the garden she rebuffed Portia's attempts at conversation and pounded and poked at the ground in fury. Before long her vise-like grip on the hoe raised blisters on both palms and several fingers. She silently lamented the ruin of her hands while pulling at a thick tangle of scrubby weeds.

Household chores and childcare are hard, but fieldwork will make my hands unfit to play piano again. This is not the type of labor I anticipated doing. Not ever.

A sudden gust scattered the weeds she had piled at the edge of the row and the day began to turn twilight gray. Overhead, enormous, sooty clouds clumped together and crows floated on the wind like cinders of coal.

"It's going to rain again," she said. Rain was a common event. Almost daily, soft sheets of water cascaded onto the island and left pathways and dirt roads mucky and full of puddles.

Now she saw the sky growing darker and more fearsome. The velocity of the wind increased. It roared in her ears, slapped away her breath and pushed or pulled her with each shift of direction. Huge drops of rain hurtled out of the murk as if flung from a gigantic waterwheel. In an instant she was drenched.

From behind came a loud "CRAAAAACK." She swiveled in time to see the top sheared off a tree.

Chapter 16

July 1863

The sound of the wind became a baleful shriek of destruction. Miri dropped the hoe and yelled, "We've got to get inside!"

Skirts and petticoats billowing like sails, she and Portia ran, leaning into the turbulence, fighting to stay on their feet. In the distance was the dim outline of her house, and with a tight grip on Portia's hand, Miri continued to struggle toward shelter and safety in fits and starts. A tree toppled near the chicken coop blocking their path. The crashing timber galvanized her. She scrambled over the trunk, pulled Portia over and dashed the last few feet to the front door.

It took their combined strength to shut the door against the force of the wind.

Safely inside, Miri shivered and sighed with relief. The parlor was dim. The shutters were closed against the storm and the only light came from a solitary lamp. She began to relight the candles blown out when the door was opened. Her mother took the matchbox away.

"You two get out of those wet clothes," she said, "before you catch your death of a cold."

In Miri's bedroom, Portia and Miri draped their damp clothes over a rack to dry, and Miri loaned Portia a petticoat and dress. They were a snug fit on her large frame but she didn't complain and they went back to the parlor.

Calmer and more composed, Miri realized her father wasn't in the house but still out somewhere in the monstrous storm. She peeked through a narrow opening in a shutter, worried for his safety. At that moment, the wind tore part of the barn roof off. Like a tailless wooden kite, it wobbled higher and higher and disappeared.

A figure approached the house out of the dark. She recognized her father's silhouette and opened the door. He staggered in, water dripping from his clothes and running in rivulets from the edge of his hat. When he removed it, more water cascaded from its brim.

Mrs. Whitfield handed him a towel and began mopping the puddle at his feet with a rag.

"Whew," he said, wiping his face and hair. "This has got to be a hurricane. You girls did well to get inside. For just this instance I might be grateful to Mr. Lincoln," he added, with a wry grin.

"Why?" Miri asked.

"He never sent us those pre-constructed walls and such to build with, and that works to our advantage. I'll wager these houses we were forced to notch and plaster together ourselves are holding up better than the material he promised."

The bedlam of the storm abruptly stopped. Miri was almost as unsettled by the eerie silence as she had been by the noise. Her ears ached and she wondered if her hearing was damaged.

"The eye of the storm is above us," her father said. "We're not out of danger yet. This is only a lull."

Georgie looked up from his army of tin soldiers. "The storm has an eye?"

Miri had learned about hurricanes by reading about the climate of Haiti. She said, "Hurricane wind moves in a circle, Georgie and the 'eye' is the calm area in the center of the circle. The backside of the storm will follow the 'eye' and has to pass before it'll be safe for us to go outside again."

Satisfied with the explanation, Georgie's attention returned to his soldiers and he moved their skirmish underneath the table. For amusement Portia and Miri played cat's cradle, while listening to the *click-click* of her mother's knitting needles.

The sounds of wind and rain returned and increased in intensity with each minute. Shutters rattled against windows and a large object thudded against the side of the house like a giant fist. Drafts slid through chinks and crevices around windows and beneath the door. They teased candle flames into a frenzied, flickering death and pulled spirals of smoke from lamp wicks. The storm had ferocious strength, and hammered the settlement. Concern for the welfare of her family and the community compelled Miri to pray for the second time.

Hours later the pelting rain and wailing winds eased and, with the end of the storm, she began to relax. She raised a window, pushed the shutter aside and saw a sunbeam emerge from the clouds like a beacon. She also saw tree branches scattered about the yard, tilted bushes, and missing flowers.

"Let's go to the field. I want to see what happened to the bees," she said. "I doubt they or the hives survived out there in the open."

"I'd better get home," Portia said. "My parents are probably worried sick about me."

"I'll go with you," Miri's father said. "I need to assess the damage in the garden and help your father with the animals."

"I'll check the bees," Miri said.

"If they survived it wouldn't be a good idea to get near the hives now," her father said. "The bees will still be angry and upset. Leave them 'til tomorrow. Right now we have work to do in the garden."

Though disappointed, Miri didn't argue with him. He knew more about the behavior of bees than she did.

He summoned Georgie from under the table. "Let's go. Work is waiting for you too, Son."

Miri and Portia had to lift their skirts and petticoats above puddles, and exercise care not to get snagged on branches and debris. At the barn Portia took the path toward her house while Miri continued toward the garden with Georgie and her father.

The scene in the garden was shocking. Plants, snapped into pieces or ripped out of the ground, were scattered everywhere. Not one bean-pole or stalk of corn stood upright. The entire garden was in chaos and the destruction was painful to see.

All the weeks of backbreaking work they had put into creating the garden, fighting weeds and bugs as seedlings were coaxed to grow, were erased. Miri especially ached at losing the immature corn. It was her favorite for its sweet and buttery taste, and the young ears had not yet produced silk.

Cries and bleating came from the barn as the damage in the garden was being assessed. "Can we save anything, Father?" she asked.

"First things first," he said. "The animals are frightened. The garden has to wait until they've been tended to. While I help Uncle Will, you and Georgie see about the chickens."

Though its door was suspended at an angle by one hinge, by some miracle the chicken coop was upright. Miri rounded up a half dozen squawk-ing hens while Georgie watched. His only contribution was telling her, "Be careful and don't scare them, Miri, 'cuz if you do they won't lay no eggs."

"*Any* eggs," she said, counting birds as she shooed them inside and propped the door across the opening. Two hens were missing, a speckled biddy and the big Rhode Island Red, their best layer.

"The chickens are flighty because of the storm, Mister Lazybones," she said. "And you should help me find the Red and the spotted hen."

She hunted under fallen branches and leaves and found them trapped inside a tangle of grass and twigs, eyes closed, necks twisted. She picked up the still warm bodies and took them to the barn. "Come on, Georgie," she said. "Let's find Father. He could use you since you don't want to help me."

On the way she saw her uncle milking one of the cows while the other, udder bulging, bellowed and stamped in discomfort. She followed the sound of a hammer and found her father working on Jubal's stall. Jubal had kicked off the door of his stall and it lay broken on the floor. Miri left the dead hens on a piece of the wood. There was no need to linger. Her father would remove their heads and she didn't want to watch. At least these hens were already dead. Worse were the headless chickens running about with blood spurting everywhere.

In the coop the hens had quieted. Miri filled their water pans, removed old bedding and started to spread clean straw. Nestled in a pile of leaves beneath the roost, she found three warm eggs.

Georgie poked his head in and said, "Pa wants you."

"Alright. But while I see what he wants, make yourself useful in here." She ignored his scowl and went back to the barn.

"Here," her father said, handing her the two dead chickens she had found. "Tell mother to give one to Minister Grady and use the other for supper."

Drops of blood oozed from the headless carcasses and landed at Miri's feet. Repulsed, she held the chickens by their bony legs and carried them at arm's length. Mother was going to expect her to help with plucking them, and she hated tugging away at the feathers. On the other hand, she might be allowed to keep some, and her pillow could benefit from additional stuffing.

She met Portia coming down the path and told her about the ruckus the cows were making.

"It hurts them not getting milked when they're supposed to," Portia said. "I'm on the way to help Pa do it now. Where are you taking those chickens?"

"Home," Miri told her. "One will be supper and the other's for Minister Grady."

In the kitchen with her mother, she pleaded the importance of working in the garden. Her ploy succeeded. She did not have to pluck or clean, and the request for some feathers was granted. She went to the garden in good humor and began removing fallen branches and broken plants. Her spirits fell as more bare ground was exposed.

Her father arrived, lines of worry etched in his face.

"We can replant, can't we?" she asked.

"I'll have to talk over the possibility with the other men," he said. "I don't think there's much seed left. Even with luck and no more hurricanes, the harvest is sure to be scant."

She shivered. It was a feeling she'd had before. Grandmother told her it was a dark omen caused by a person walking across the grave of someone you loved.

The pile of cornstalks rustled as Portia clambered over them.

"Mercy!" she said. "It looks like the end of the world here. I hope we never have another storm like that one."

"So do I," Miri said, bending to lift a broad, flat leaf and then a second. "Look," she said in surprise, "melons." Under leaves on another vine she discovered a squash.

The pinch on her father's face relaxed a little and they spent the next couple of hours removing debris and straightening the remaining healthy plants and vines.

Working helped Miri erase the memory of the shrill, howling wind, and a morning of physical activity stirred her appetite. Prompted by hunger, she said, "I'll go get some sandwiches and lemonade for our lunch."

The uncooked chicken lay on the cutting board.

"Good you're back," her mother said. "Wash up and give me a hand. I've got to go deliver a baby." She took a knife and in two swift motions cut the feet off the bird and made a slit between the legs. "Here, remove the innards and rinse the carcass while I mix some dough for dumplings."

Miri grimaced. "But Father and Portia are waiting for me to bring lunch."

"Alright. Be quick about it. Fix something, and take it to them. Tell your father I've been called out, then come straight back. I'll wait and help you get supper started."

Miri walked back from the garden dreading the ordeal she faced. Cleaning a chicken was even more disgusting than plucking it.

"For heaven's sake, get a move on," her mother said. "You know what to do. Reach in, grab, and pull until you see daylight."

Miri never imagined life in Haiti would come to be long days full of disgusting chores. *I'm living a deprived existence and forced to do work I hate. That's slavery,* she thought. Secretly, she wanted the colony to fail and prompt a return to Spencer where she could resume a proper, civilized life.

She reached inside the chicken and tugged, bringing out a tangle of dripping guts. She threw them into the garbage pail and proceeded to cut up the chicken.

"This delivery is a first baby," her mother said. "Labor might take a while, so I don't know how long I'll be." She took her medicine satchel from the shelf and left.

Miri rinsed chicken pieces and dropped them into the stew pot.

Chapter 17

Late Summer, 1863

The dumplings in the fricassee were light and fluffy, equal to her mother's and something to be proud of. Miri was pleased. The broth had to be at the right temperature to make good dumplings. Tablespoons of dough should be dropped in when the liquid reached a slow boil. The dumplings would expand and float as they cooked and form a white cloud on top of the chicken and vegetables.

She filled a bowl and placed it in front of her father.

He shook his napkin and draped it across his knees. "Tomorrow I'm going with a couple of the men to repair a house and barn. You'll have to see to the hives without me, Miri."

He was giving her complete responsibility for the hives. The idea excited her but also raised some worries. She was uncertain of her ability to perform the tasks as well as he did, and reviewed the steps with him. Also, some household chores would need to be done before she went to the field. That meant she would have to wake up early, so when she went to her bedroom for the night she left the window shutters open. She yawned, bone weary, and soon dropped into a dreamless sleep.

She woke when the first light of dawn hit her face, and by mid-morning was in the shed stirring sugar water. Most of the flowers had been destroyed. The bees needed to be sustained until new blooms appeared and they could forage again.

Puffs of cottony clouds hung in the bright blue sky but with so many birds killed, a strange quiet lay over the fields. Veiled and gloved, Miri carefully balanced the tray of bottles and made her way along the path of scrambled debris. Walking was difficult but she reached the hives without dropping the tray and set it down on a nearby stump.

One hive lay on its side, half hidden in the grass. Two feet away, the other stood upright, a solitary sentinel guarding its fallen partner. She removed the top of the standing hive, set the sugar water over the opening and went back for the second tray. It took every ounce of her strength to right the fallen hive and wrestle it back onto its foundation. While she jostled the hive, a few scouts emerged and flew around her head. She told herself to breathe slowly and remain calm. Once the tray was in place, the guardians were lured back inside by the odor of sugar.

The hum of the colony feeding was balm to her discontent. Impressed with the bees' ability to endure and persevere, she left the field with new resolve. *If the bees can survive the calamity of a hurricane, I can do the same.*

That evening she went to the emergency meeting in the church and took the seat next to her father. He made no comment and she ignored her mother's raised eyebrow. Reports on the extent of hurricane damage were chronicled, and needed repairs were discussed.

Most chicken coops had been blown apart and they were first on the list of items to rebuild. Chickens were a vital food source and those that survived the storm needed immediate shelter and protection. Livestock was being hobbled or tied to prevent them from wandering, making it essential to erect pens and enclosures as soon as possible.

An entire roof had been ripped from one house and several others required partial restorations. Shattered windows and fear of another violent storm gave urgency to rehang dangling shutters and replace missing ones. Every family described losing most of their crops. All gardens would have to be tilled and replanted. Finally, the pavilion was gone and construction of the school would be abandoned again. The announcement dismayed Miri, but she understood the reasons.

The men sorted themselves into crews, each group choosing a project to work on. Her father decided to tackle putting up fences. "I can take my son with me," he said. "About time Georgie got a taste of what real work is. It'll be a good lesson for him."

Seeding, planting, and tending gardens were delegated to the women. Mrs. Whitfield's pregnancy ruled out strenuous tasks like digging and hoeing, and Miri took full responsibility for the family garden.

In the following weeks she paid diligent attention to the newly seeded ground. Not a weed escaped her eye, and when sprouts started to appear they were scrutinized every day for pests. Any bug unlucky enough to be discovered received a generous squirt of soapy water pumped from the sprayer. Most flying and crawling insects retreated or died under a deluge of smothering suds, but a few grubs and cutworms managed to survive. She assigned the job of picking them off the plants to Georgie, but he proved to be ham-fisted and often broke tender stalks. He was more harm than help, so to ensure there would be a crop to harvest, she had no choice but to take over the unpleasant, but necessary task. Spraying was then turned over to Georgie, and it melded perfectly with his soldiering fantasy. Insects became his enemy in a war to protect the garden.

In addition to the garden, Miri insisted she could also continue caring for the hives. Much to her surprise, her father agreed. Her routine now was to rise before sunrise, breakfast with Georgie and her father, tend the garden then go straight on to the hives. She would clean and tidy the house after washing up and having lunch.

It made sense to complete outside chores during cooler morning hours. The normal weather pattern had returned and once again oppressive heat and humidity followed afternoon showers.

Rain, added to water from the hurricane, lingered in depressions, furrows and wagon ruts. Bogs developed in rotting vegetation, and in the stagnant sludge mosquitoes multiplied into the millions. Day and night hordes of winged stingers tormented the colony.

Dr. Stillman advised extra precautions to prevent the spread of disease. Drinking water had to be boiled, chamber pots emptied frequently, and soiled diapers laundered as soon as possible. Despite his recommendations, a week later many adults and children suffered fevers and vomiting, reducing the number of men fit to work.

As the condition of those who were sick worsened, their skin took on a sallow tint and their eyes yellowed. Soon the affliction was being referred to as "the yellow sickness."

Repair and construction slowed to a near halt as the sickness spread. Soon the ranks of healthy women thinned, and for many, weeding and hoeing became too exhausting and was abandoned.

Mr. Whitfield summarized the situation. "It's a shame," he said, "There are hardly any able bodied men left. We're struggling to complete essential repairs, so it's going to be quite some time before we can even think about building a school."

Miri accepted the disappointing information but couldn't resist adding her opinion. "Mrs. Barkley says we'll become savage heathens without a proper education. She says we didn't pay attention to lessons in the pavilion because there were too many distractions. I don't think her mouth will relax until we have a school with walls."

Her mother sighed. "You best have a care, Miriam," she said. "You shouldn't be repeating gossip, and that is certainly no way to speak of an elder. It's rude and disrespectful."

"But it's the truth, Mother. Mrs. Barkley's a pinched-face sourpuss. You said so yourself."

Her mother grimaced and caressed the growing bump of her belly. Though pregnant, she still made rounds among the sick with her box of herbs. She and Dr. Stillman were kept busy tending to those with yellow fever and providing advice to others about their various ailments.

"Shush and eat," she said. "I'm too tired to argue."

A week later, Miri shook the sprinkling bottle, dampened a shirt, rolled the garment and added it to items stacked in the laundry basket.

Her mother still insisted everything they wore be pressed. She said, "I don't care how warm it is, we will not be seen in wrinkled clothes." Shirts, skirts, slips, and trousers were to be ironed. Drawers and chemises, not visible to the world, were the only exemptions.

Miri set the irons on the stove to heat, brought chairs from the dining area to the parlor and placed them between the sofa and armchairs forming a half circle.

Her mother was hosting the stitching group and they would be arriving soon. To escape scorching late afternoon heat, the ladies had changed the meeting time to just after lunch.

Miri lifted an iron from the stove, touched a wet fingertip to it. The sizzle she heard told her it was hot enough and she went to work on the clothes. When the ironing was finished she would be free to go to the river. As she straightened and aligned pleats on a skirt and applied the iron, the sound of Mrs. Barkley's irritating falsetto voice came from the parlor. It was hard to understand how or why Mother tolerated her. The woman was just plain unpleasant to be around.

"Miri," her mother said from the doorway, "Please put the kettle on and come join us."

Had she heard correctly? "But I'm not done with the ironing," she said, "and I don't belong to the sewing group."

"Leave the ironing for now," her mother told her. "You're a young woman, and its time you learned to tat and quilt."

Miri filled the kettle. "I've only darned socks, hemmed and done some simple mending, Mother. I don't know how to do fancy needlework."

"I'm well aware of your skills, Miriam." The stony expression on her mother's face was a warning.

In the parlor her Aunt Rachel said, "Nice to have you join us, Miri.

You're old enough, and might even get married in a few years. It's high time to think about making things for your hope chest."

Miri was not considering marriage, and didn't care about a hope chest. "My birthday is today," she said changing the focus of the conversation, "And I'd like to celebrate it…"

Her mother interrupted. "We aren't going to talk about your birthday now.

This is a sewing session and we're starting an album quilt about Haiti."

She handed Miri a square of white cotton, about the size of a man's handkerchief. "Each of us will design and work up a square and embroider our name on it. Wouldn't you like to see 'Miriam Whitfield' on the finished quilt?"

"I recall you embroidered an alphabet sampler that was quite nice," Mrs. Barkley said. "It showed you have a delicate hand with stitchery." She patted a chair and said, "Come sit next to me."

Mrs. Barkley's squat, round body encased in black, along with the gleam in her eye, reminded Miri of a poem she memorized in third grade. *"'Will you walk into my parlor?' said the spider to the fly…"* Mrs. Barkley was the very image of a spider, and Miri, unable to find a way to escape from the sewing group, understood the desperation of a trapped insect.

From a jumble of fabric on the table, she chose a piece of butter colored chintz with a pattern of dainty red flowers and deep green leaves. The warm yellow background reminded her of the wallpaper in her bedroom back in Spencer. Another swatch caught her eye. With her finger she traced the loops and curls of vines scrolling across cool green taffeta. She placed the taffeta beside the chintz and for her final selection opted for a small triangle in the same shade of pink as the rose bush by the Spencer porch. Though the proposed quilt was to be about Haiti every one of her choices evoked a cherished memory of Spencer. She had created a dilemma. Instead of using Haiti for inspiration, she decided to illustrate the strong pull of her family bonds and applique a Tree of Life on her square.

As instructed, she sewed cotton to each piece of fabric to provide reinforcement. She basted outlines of a tree, leaves, yellow sun and pink flowers, and leaving a half-inch border around each shape, cut them out. It didn't take long to attach them to the background with a blanket stitch.

She held the square up and looked around. "Finished," she said.

The corners of Mrs. Barkley's lips turned up in a smirk. Other mouths wore similar expressions. It was clear they didn't think much of her skill. She was embarrassed.

Her mother took the square and secured it on an embroidery hoop. "It's not quite done," she said. "Watch carefully. I'll show you how to do a quilting stitch."

Miri tried to place the needle exactly as her mother did. She concentrated and worked slowly but the stitches from her fingers were neither small nor evenly spaced. Thankful when the tedious handwork halted for a refreshment break, she listened to the chatter of the women.

After an exchange of recipes the conversation shifted to concern over the growing number of people beset by fever, and moved on to the status of the war and the terrible impact a shipping blockade was having on supplies. The women were united; the situation was grim. They prayed the blockage would be lifted. Delivery of food and medicine from the states needed to resume without delay.

When teatime was over, the ladies returned to their needlework for another hour. Then, clucking and fluttering like a bevy of hens, they gathered their belongings and departed.

Miri removed her thimble and placed her square in the sewing basket. "Can I go to down the river now, Mother?"

"Not *can I*, Miri. The proper grammar is *may I*. You are an educated young woman so please pay attention to how you speak. As for your question, yes, you may go to the river but don't stay too long. There is still the ironing and other things I need your help with."

Miri's face burned at the rebuke. Lately nothing she did seemed to satisfy her mother. She slammed the door and trotted down the path to find Portia prowling about under heavy-leafed trees along the riverbank.

"Where've you been? I didn't think you were coming."

"I was almost finished with ironing," she said trying to catch her breath, "and my mother made me join the sewing group. She said I'm old enough and it's time I learned how to do stitch work she calls fancy and I think of as fussy. She expects me to keep attending the meetings. Today they started a quilt and now I'm stuck making a square."

She found a flat, smooth stone and cast it sidearm at the river. It skimmed across the water in three shallow arcs before disappearing with a *sploop*. The distance it traveled brought a smile to her face. She had learned the fine art of skipping stones from Portia, and in a short time had become as good at it as her teacher.

Portia slung her stone carelessly toward the river. It made contact with the water and without a single bounce, was gone. "Drat, dash it and swamp doodle!" she muttered.

Miri said, "I'm glad Mother can't hear you. Your language would prove to her we girls are uncouth and rough mannered. I say if we are, it's because there aren't any cultural or social events to attend. How can we possibly be civilized in such a wilderness? There's no place to hold ice cream socials or a decent dance. All we have is a church barely large enough for services."

"I don't care about ice cream socials," Portia said. "But a place to dance would be nice."

"I know why you'd like to have dances. So you could be around Josiah, that young man you're all moony-eyed over."

"Not true. It's because I enjoy dancing."

Miri didn't believe her cousin for one second. "Portia and Josiah sitting in a tree, k-i-s-s-i-n-g," she sang.

"Oh, you're horrible!" Portia said, and stomped away.

"Wait! Wait!" Miri called, feeling contrite. She hurried to catch up with Portia. "Sorry, I didn't mean it," she said, putting her arm around her cousin's shoulder. "Come on, let's go back to the river. I have a feeling we won't get many more chances to laze about."

Portia's nod let her know their friendship was mended.

After lunch, Miri went to the garden, disappointed no one had even mentioned her birthday. Though she knew the reasons a party would have been frivolous, it was discouraging to have her parents act as if it were an ordinary day, something she might expect from Georgie, who rarely thought of anyone other than himself. Disappointment put her into a sulky mood. A forgotten birthday, the insult of working on a Sunday added to the annoying task of weeding.

Portia said, "Let's go get some water."

Glad for the suggested break Miri nodded. She didn't trust what might come out of her mouth.

The water crock was empty. "I'll bet this is Georgie's doing," she said. "He never refills the crock."

"Forget Georgie," Portia said. "We can fill it at my house."

A chant of "Happy birthday to you" greeted Miri when she stepped into Portia's kitchen. Her parents, aunt and uncle, and Georgie surrounded the table. In the center was a frosted layer cake, a pitcher of lemonade and two packages wrapped in white paper. Her birthday hadn't been forgotten after all. She smiled, took a package from Portia and began to unwrap it.

The smile grew when her aunt said, "I made honey cake, Miri. I know it's your favorite."

Portia's gift was a small, round, lidded box woven out of palm leaves. The tight, straight lines and walnut sized handle on the cover indicated a high degree of care had been used in its construction.

"Portia, this is lovely," she said. "Perfect for my trinkets. Thank you."

"Once I cut the leaves into narrow strips, the rest was easy," Portia told her.

"It was the same as doing one of those reed baskets Grandma taught us how to make."

Georgie pushed a card into her hand. On the front he had drawn a boy holding a rake. Inside he had written *I promiss to weed the garden for two weeks. Happy birthday from Georgie.*

She ignored the misspelled word and hugged him. He squirmed away and she turned her attention to the other package. The box contained a quilt square comprised of pieces from an old vest of her father's, a jacket Georgie had outgrown, and bits of a blue dress her mother had worn on Sundays.

"That's the first square of your memory quilt," her mother said, and Miri knew the gift was a prompt. She was expected to complete a memory quilt for her hope chest.

Elated by the birthday celebration, Miri thanked her mother and didn't dwell on the implication of the square. She unwrapped the brown butcher paper from a second item in the box and slipped on a pair of canvas and leather gloves. They were a smaller version of the ones her father wore around the hives.

"These are perfect, Father," she said. "Now my hands won't feel awkward and clumsy when I handle frames. Thank you."

She appreciated the thoughtfulness of her family for planning the surprise party. She got as much pleasure from the modest celebration as she did from more elaborate parties in Spencer. "Thank you all," she said. "Now let's cut the cake before Georgie fidgets to death."

Chapter 18

August / September 1863

The shade and cool air was a blessed relief from the searing heat of the fields and the river was away from the anxious expressions of the adults. Miri dangled her feet in the water and enjoyed the feeling of the water flowing between her toes. "It's been two weeks since the meeting," she said. "Dr. Stillman was over to supper last night and he said the yellow fever is spreading."

"I wish . . . ," Portia paused, as a group of young men splashed into view. "I wish I knew if Josiah Jennings has feelings for me," she said, trying to find him among the swimmers.

"Josiah?" Miri asked. "You're looking for a serious beau?"

"Well, I think it's time to consider who might make a suitable husband," Portia said. "There aren't many young bachelors, and I don't want to settle for an old husband, or a widower with a bunch of children."

"I'm not interested in marrying," Miri said. "I want more education and to have a career, maybe as a teacher or a doctor." She broke off a thick blade of grass and placed it lengthwise between her thumbs. "Is marriage, a husband and children what you really want, Portia? Or are you saying this because it's something we women are expected to do?"

"A wife is what I think I'll be best at, Miri. I know farming, cooking, how to manage a house and a bit about babies. Book learning has never been my strong point."

Miri stretched the blade of grass taut as a piano wire. "Being Mrs. Somebody might be fine for you," she said. "As for me, it isn't that I never want to get married or have children. I also want to make a contribution to society through teaching or caring for the sick. Speaking of which, Dr. Stillman's going to turn the church into an infirmary. He says he'll be better able to see people with the fever if they're together, and maybe isolating them will keep the fever from spreading."

She lifted her hands and blew on the grass causing it to vibrate. Its non-musical duck-like squawk raised the bittersweet memory of learning to make "Indian horns" from her grandmother. She longed for a pillow-soft hug from her grandmother but knew there was no sense dwelling on the impossible. She let the green sliver fall from her fingers.

"My mother has volunteered to provide care to patients in the infirmary even though Dr. Stillman warned her about risks to both her and the baby," Miri said. And, as if I didn't already have enough to do, I'm to help with laundry and changing beds."

"My ma's making me do the same," Portia said. "Just thinking about handling the bedclothes and sheets of those sick and dying people scares the bejaspers out of me. I'm afraid I'll catch the disease."

Miri didn't want to think about that possibility and pushed it from her mind. She twirled her feet in the sunlit river. Lacey patterns danced around her toes, lingered for an instant then spun away and dissolved into shimmering light. The watery designs and happiness in her life were similar. Both were fragile and neither existed long enough to be firmly etched in her memory.

"I heard that out of the two hundred and twenty people who sailed with us fifty-six have died so far," Portia said.

The statistic reawakened Miri's concerns about contracting the fever and its high rate of death. She left the riverbank filled with morbid thoughts. How many more would die? What if her mother or father or both of them became ill? Distracted, she didn't hear Georgie pounding down the path, and he nearly bowled her over.

"Pa's goin' to Port-au-Prince tomorrow," he said, prancing in a circle. "Him, Ma, Uncle Will and some other people are gonna ask the Haitian gov'ment to help us with food and stuff."

Portia said, "If they all go, Miri, we can come to the river after our chores are done."

"Yeah, and I get to come, too," Georgie said.

Miri asked, "Are you sure Mother is going?" In her condition the long ride to Port-au-Prince would be especially tiring.

Georgie stopped hopping and nodded. "Yep. She said they're leaving early to get to the city before the hottest part of the day."

"Alright then, Master Georgie, if you want to come with Portia and me, you will have to pitch in and help with chores. Father won't be here and you cannot be your usual lazy self."

"Don't worry. I'll work hard. You'll see," he said.

During supper an anxious discussion took place between her parents about the colony's desperate need for aid with every form of sustenance. The stock of medications was especially low.

The state of the settlement is appalling and appears ready to fail, so why is there no thought being given to going home? Miri wondered. Back in the States, the war was being fought in the south. Living in New York, far from the battlefields, could not be worse than living here. Their colony would be defenseless if conflict erupted in Haiti, and even now it was reduced to petitioning a foreign government for help.

Deep sorrow descended upon her. The fork grew heavy in her hands and she could not summon enough strength to lift it. No matter. She had lost her appetite.

"No need for such a somber expression," her father said. "Don't put too much mind to this conversation. I'm confident the Haitian government will help us and things will improve."

Reluctant to let him know the depth of her worries, she said, "I'm tired, Father. There were more weeds than usual in the garden, and I try not let them get ahead of me."

She cleaned the kitchen and prepared for bed under the light of a half-moon suspended in a star sprinkled sky. To her sincere and fervent prayer on behalf of the colony she also asked the Almighty to grant her wish to return home. Spencer held salvation and hope for a decent future. Her grandparents, best friend and the opportunity to pursue an education were there. Here she faced the horrid likelihood of ending up either a spinster or wed to some plodding farmer.

She settled under the sheet and remembered hearing Mrs. Barkley say, "Haitians don't think their Catholic god and our Protestant one are the same." How Mrs. Barkley came upon this fact and whether it was true Miri didn't know, but she did wonder if her Congregationalist prayers would be heeded if she said them in French.

Before the sun had fully risen, she, Splinter and Portia waved goodbye as the wagon with their parents joined others on the road. The early morning warmth promised a sullen, sweltering day, and the girls immediately tackled and finished household tasks. They resented the meager amount of work a grudging Georgie performed in the barn and garden despite his earlier promise.

They returned to Miri's to wash up. She and Portia packed a lunch of bread, cheese and fruit, ordered Georgie to fill the crock with water, then rushed off for a carefree afternoon along the river. They returned to the house at twilight, tired but happy. Animals were fed and Portia milked the cows while Miri made biscuits and warmed leftover stew for supper.

Georgie finished two helpings and sprawled on the floor with his soldiers. Portia claimed the rocker and Miri lit the lamps before getting comfortable in her father's wing chair.

Footsteps woke her. In the shadowy lamplight the faces of her parents, aunt and uncle looked gray. Was that an omen? Anxious, but urged by curiosity, she asked, "What did the Governor decide?"

"The meeting didn't accomplish much," her father said. "The Haitian authorities don't feel responsible for our welfare. They're reluctant to become involved in our problems since we aren't Haitian citizens."

Her mother said, "However, Dr. Stillman was successful in achieving his goal. He gave a detailed description of the level of illness in our group and the Haitians agreed to extend humanitarian aid. A group of doctors will arrive the day after tomorrow to evaluate our medical situation."

There's a good chance Dr. Lazarre will be one of the doctors, Miri thought. *If he comes, Philippe will be with him.* She hadn't seen Philippe since she moved to Artibonite, and missed their weekly conversations. The possibility of seeing him excited her. She said, "We must make some refreshments, Mother. A pound cake perhaps, and some tea. I can pick mint for garnish, and Georgie can put the crock of tea to cool in the river."

"Those are good ideas, Miri. Now, if everyone will excuse me, I'll say goodnight. I'm worn out and need to rest."

Miri's worry worm twisted. Her mother didn't readily admit to being tired, so she must have been exhausted. Miri resolved to keep closer watch on her.

· · · · ·

The Haitian delegation arrived, composed of a government representative, three women and three physicians, one of whom was Dr. Lazarre.

Miri smiled at Philippe and looked at the women. Two had light amber complexions and she could tell they were mixed race descendants of former Haitian landowners from France and slave women. They were wives of the doctors, elegantly outfitted in ruffled, formal visiting dresses and hats trimmed with snowflake-white lace and silk flowers. The third woman was a black nun.

Miri had seen Irish nuns, teachers at Spencer's Catholic school, as they floated along the town walkways in voluminous black habits accented by pristine white bibs and wimples. In contrast to those, every item of clothing on this black nun was white, including her bib and wimple. Her ebony face expressed inner peace and an angelic air of calmness.

"This is Sister Marielle of the Sisters of Mercy," Dr. Stillman said. "The mission of her Order is to care for the sick. Sister Marielle received her nurse's training in Europe and she will advise and assist our women with bedside care."

After introductions were made all around, Dr. Stillman led everyone to the infirmary. A survey of the church kitchen revealed how little food was in the pantry. Patients able to eat received an oatmeal breakfast and only one other meal per day.

In the sick ward, the doctors' wives murmured to one other from behind perfumed hankies their gloved hands held to noses.

The tour finished with Dr. Stillman describing his depleted medical supplies in detail, and voicing his frustration at being unable to replenish them.

As Miri served refreshments she listened to the men discuss the situation. Her understanding of French was good enough to know what decision the delegation arrived at before it was revealed in English. In two weeks one doctor, medicines, several nuns from the Sisters of Mercy and a supply of food would arrive at the colony.

The purpose of the visit completed, the Haitian men departed, wives following in a flurry, the smell of elegance and dismissal drifting behind them.

"You and the representative had a private conversation, Henry. What was it about?" Uncle Will asked.

"He's going to contact President Geffrand and recommend our plight be officially communicated to President Lincoln, and request he come to our aid. In the meantime I've half a mind to abandon this backwater and return to Port-au-Prince. At least things are somewhat civilized there."

"I don't condone the idea of moving, Henry," her mother told him. "Miri and I are working in the infirmary and it would be sinful to desert the sick." Her brow knitted. "Another concern is that my term is coming near, and I want Dr. Stillman to attend the birth."

Miri spoke up eagerly. "We should go back to the city, Mother. You won't have to work so hard there, the climate is cooler and no doubt you can find a French doctor..."

"Miri, Dr. Stillman speaks English, and at such a private time I don't want care from someone I cannot communicate with."

Her father, persuaded by her wish for Dr. Stillman, decided the family would remain in Artibonite.

Despite a galloping fear of catching yellow fever, Miri's pride would not allow her to shirk responsibilities in the infirmary. She sponged fever-ish brows, provided dry bedclothes and changed sweat soaked beds. Soon the tasks were a familiar routine and she found that talking while she ministered to patients often soothed their delirium and calmed their thrashing about. The topic didn't matter. Most often she described things she missed about Spencer. She talked of the town common and old men playing checkers under the elms, the lion-headed drinking fountain and the rich, clear peal of the bell in the church spire. She spoke of gentle, caressing colors. Buttercream wallpaper in her bedroom, a haze of lilac flowers below the window and the blush pink rambler rose.

Her grandparents, the twins, and Clarice were subjects only on occasion, and caused a wealth of pent-up emotions to pour forth. Remembering she could not visit her twin brothers' graves stirred a deep sorrow within and nearly brought her to tears. An effective nurse could not cry while she was on duty.

She dabbed a patient's face with a damp cloth. He babbled and his gnarled fingers clutched her wrist as he sucked and expelled air with the rattle of a dry gourd. His body shuddered convulsively, the blanket ceased to rise and fall and he lay still as a board, his mouth agape.

The look of death was familiar. She beckoned her mother and said, "I think Mr. Ackerly has passed."

Her mother lifted his withered wrist and found no pulse. She took a small mirror from her apron pocket and held it to Mr. Ackerly's open mouth. No breath fogged the glass. "He's gone," she said, confirming what Miri already knew.

Once, the thought of witnessing a death frightened Miri. She imagined it as scary, not the same as seeing a ghost, but strange and out of the ordinary. Now she felt a sense of relief knowing old Mr. Ackerly's suffering was over. He was reunited with loved ones waiting for him on the other side.

A grimace contorted her mother's mouth. She was pale and her hand rubbed the dome of her belly.

"Are you alright, Mother?"

"I'm fine, Miri. It was just a twinge. Please bring me a basin of water and tell Mrs. Barkley I need her assistance. Oh, and I'll need a shroud as well."

"I'll help you, Mother," Miri said. "I tended Mr. Ackerly as he died and I'd like to prepare him for burial."

"Mrs. Barkley and I will do it. You are a young, unmarried woman and it would be improper for you to wash the body of a man."

"For heaven's sakes, Mother. I have a brother. I know what men look like."

"No, Miri."

"I don't understand. You tell me I've reached the age when I must wear a corset and long dress. You call me a young lady but you still treat me like a child. Let me do this. Cover what you don't want me to see."

Her mother sighed. "Stop sputtering. I said no, and that's final. I'll let you help prepare a woman but not children or men."

Pleased with achieving a small victory, Miri went to find Mrs. Barkley.

Chapter 19

September 1863

D r. Stillman had been down with fever three days. His illness was a calamity. The colony was without a doctor.

Mrs. Whitfield had taken responsibility for mixing medications at the infirmary. She would leave home early each morning with her herb case. When she finished her work there, she made visits to expectant mothers and the homebound sick. She often returned home late, and nodded in fatigue over a warmed-up supper.

Four days later to Miri's relief, Dr. Lazarre, Philippe, Sister Marielle and a second nun, Sister Terese arrived.

Doctor Lazarre began examining patients at once. He moved from bed to bed, peered into mouths, listened to each chest with a stethoscope. He tried to communicate with patients, but his thick French accent and limited English made it difficult.

Philippe, able to understand and speak both French and English, stepped in to assist. Although Miri knew his ease with English was the result of the years he lived with relatives in Louisiana, she was impressed with his ability to provide information about symptoms, the stage of illness and treatment.

The Haitian nuns could, of course, converse with Dr. Lazarre, but like him they lacked the ability to understand or speak English, so Philippe also helped by explaining the medications prescribed by his uncle to women from the colony.

Soon, the women united and refused to allow the nuns to administer any medication. Mrs. Whitfield justified the decision. "After all," she told Philippe, "these are our people. We need to explain things to them in English and persuade them to take the medicines prescribed by your uncle."

Philippe passed the decision on to Dr. Lazarre and the nuns. The Haitian entourage nodded in agreement.

Two weeks passed and the death rate did not decline. Lines of sick people continued to come to the doors of the infirmary every day. Beds didn't stay vacant for long. There was always some poor soul waiting for Miri to put clean sheets on a mattress.

One day when Miri went to the storeroom for laundry supplies she overheard several women talking together about their suspicions that Dr. Lazarre might be providing poor care on purpose. They mentioned the general lack of improvement among patients taking his medicines and the persistently high number of deaths. "Some of the women who are helping here say they are going to stop giving Dr. Lazarre's medicine to patients," one of them said.

Miri was stunned. Not for a moment did she believe there was any truth to their speculations. She believed Philippe was a good, honest person and assumed his uncle was, as well.

She told Portia what she overheard. "I wonder why they think Dr. Lazarre is trying to harm us? If Dr. Stillman wasn't able to make headway against the disease why is more expected of Dr. Lazarre? Why don't they trust him?"

Portia threw a pillowcase over the clothesline, jammed clothespins into the corners and picked up her basket.

"Because the colony is a failure," she said. "People think the Haitian government wants to be rid of us. Ma says we'll all die here if we don't leave soon."

"People are dying, but I don't believe the Haitian government is trying to murder us. Disease is killing people and the yellow fever epidemic is still out of control." She placed her empty basket on a shelf. "Look at how low our supply of sheets is. There are fewer and fewer every week. Do you know why?"

"No. I wash sheets," Portia said. "I don't count them."

"It's because there aren't any shrouds left to wrap the dead in, and sheets are used instead. People are still dying, and it's not Dr. Lazarre's fault. He is a trained physician doing his best in a bad situation. Philippe is helping his uncle and is at risk of being painted with the same brush of distrust. I need to find some way to prove the doctor isn't giving out poison or purposely trying to harm anyone."

"How?"

"I'm going to get my hands on a packet of his medicine," she said, "and find out exactly what's in it."

"What! You're not a doctor, Miri."

"Oh, for pity sakes, Portia, I know that. I'll ask my mother to examine the medicines and herbs Dr. Lazarre is using. No one else in the community has her depth of knowledge and she'll be able to reassure the women the medicine packets are safe."

"And you'll get punished for meddling where you've got no business."

Miri dismissed the warning and went to the infirmary. Midmorning rounds were in progress. Dr. Lazarre, Philippe, and volunteer women clustered around a patient's bed. After he finished examining the man, Dr. Lazarre spoke to Philippe who translated the information into English. One of the colony nurses accepted a medicine packet from the doctor, stirred the contents into water and held the glass to the patient's mouth. Rounds continued and the doctor dispensed one or more medication packets for each patient.

Carrying a supply of clean sheets and towels gave Miri freedom to move about the ward and she stayed close to the group. Their final stop was at Dr. Stillman's bed. He seemed to be in deep slumber and didn't respond to his name, or rouse when his eyelids were raised.

Dr. Lazarre watched the immobile form for a moment then listened to Dr. Stillman's chest. Worry creased the French doctor's forehead as he sorted through medicine packets.

"*Monsieur Docteur. Monsieur Docteur. Allez! Allez!*" one of the nuns called urgently. He quickly handed two packets of medicine to a nurse and went to tend a young girl in dire straits. The rest of the group followed him.

Unnoticed in the commotion, a third packet fell to the floor and landed at the nurse's feet. She pivoted as she reached for a glass of water, and her skirt swept the packet under the bed.

Miri didn't waste the opportunity. She laid fresh linen at Dr. Stillman's bedside and "accidentally" dropped her handkerchief. It was retrieved along with the packet, and both items slid into her apron pocket.

That evening she laid the open packet on the kitchen table. "Mother, do you know what herbs these are?" she asked.

"Where did you get that?"

"From the infirmary," Miri said, and explained how she obtained the packet. "I heard some women talking. They said Dr. Lazarre is giving out poison and. . . ."

"What? Pure nonsense! People are dying because of the disease, not because of the doctor. He is not using poison. And, Miriam, you should be ashamed for listening to gossip and for pilfering medicine. It should have immediately been returned. I did not raise you to be a thief."

"I'm sorry Mother. I only took it to prove Dr. Lazarre's innocence. I thought you'd be familiar with the herbs he's using."

"I don't know a great deal about the local plants, Miri, but Philippe probably can help identify them. I personally believe Dr. Lazarre is trustworthy and wouldn't harm anyone."

"So do I, Mother. Will you speak to the women and reassure them?"

"Yes. Lord knows we don't need malicious rumors interfering with the care Dr. Lazarre is providing."

On Monday the laundry area was abuzz with news. A representative from Washington had arrived in Port-au-Prince and was on his way to visit the colony.

Eager to hear Mr. Lincoln's representative; the women were in a scrubbing and washing frenzy.

A boy ran by shouting, "He's here! He's here!"

Aprons were stripped off and unfinished laundry abandoned. Miri and Portia joined the crowd gathering in front of the church. On tiptoe, Miri strained to get a better view of the visitor, then edged her way toward the front of the crowd.

A gray haired man in a suit stood on a wooden crate, shifting from foot to foot. His hands held a round hat across his midsection like a shield. Without any introduction he began to speak. "Good day. My name is Gideon Hughes and as you know I come on behalf of President Lincoln."

He paused as a low rumble pulsed through the throng, then went on. "The President is fully aware of your plight," he said. "The blockade is over, and as I speak several ships are preparing to depart New York."

Applause broke out and some in the crowd shouted, "Hurrah!"

"The steamer Marcia C. Day will arrive first and pick up survivors of the colony on *Isle a Vache*. The Day will then proceed to Port-au-Prince. Those of you wishing to leave may then board."

Miri felt a kernel of hope sprout with the possibility of going home and she squeezed Portia's arm.

"There will be no cost for passage," the representative said, "But you must register for departure in Port-au-Prince. I'll need a tally of those wanting to leave by the end of next week." With that, he stepped off his makeshift podium, went to a waiting carriage and departed.

"We're going home. We're going home," Miri crooned. Portia grinned and sang along, caught up by her cousin's exuberance.

Shouting erupted nearby as opinions split the men into two factions. One group welcomed the prospect of leaving Haiti; the other believed returning to the States while war continued to rage was too risky. Instead of passage back into civil unrest, they wanted to press Lincoln to send the promised supplies and equipment. The opposition said jobs, decent food and medical care were only available in the States.

Miri's spirits, light as a kite, soared on hearing her father advocate for leaving. It offered her the possibility of a brighter future.

The heated argument between the two sides flared into an angry bonfire of words, and the women began to remove themselves. Miri tugged Portia's sleeve. "We'd best go," she said, and they headed back to the laundry.

The issue of leaving affected the women, too, but rather than loud outbursts, it fostered a tense atmosphere and subdued discussions.

Elbow deep in suds, Miri picked up the conversation with Portia. "I'm so glad my father wants to go home," she said. "And I don't care what people think of us for abandoning the colony. It's Lincoln's fault it failed, not ours. I'll be thankful to escape the horrid conditions we've been enduring."

"I hope my father decides to go," Portia said. "I'd hate to be left here by myself."

"Oh, I think he'll join the group that wants to leave," Miri told her. "I feel it in my heart. There couldn't be more than twenty men who want to remain, not really enough to sustain the community. I can't wait to tell Grandmother and Clarice the good news. I'll write them this evening, and if I'm not too tired I might also dash off a brief note to Vi."

·　·　·　·　·

Later that day, Miri returned home to find her mother whipping potatoes with such fury they threatened to erupt over the side of the bowl.

"What's wrong?" Miri asked.

Mrs. Whitfield suspended her assault on the potatoes and set the bowl down. She blew a strand of hair out of her eyes. "You know your father was itching to fight," she said. "Well, he just told me he intends to join the army as soon as we get home. As if his fighting for Mr. Lincoln will matter one whit. It's no secret the North is losing the war, the papers are reporting there are hardly any able-bodied white men left to recruit.

That's the only reason Mr. Lincoln is allowing colored men to enlist."

Miri couldn't rebut her mother's argument and they finished preparing supper with little conversation. Dread that her father would become a soldier choked Miri's hope for a brighter future in Spencer. Her dream of resuming the sort of life she had before coming to Haiti was in danger. There was no acceptable future in Haiti. Life on the island was harsh and not much better than that of a slave, yet returning to New York meant her father would go off to war.

"Mother," she said. "We must convince him not to volunteer."

Her mother sighed. "It's unlikely we'll be able to change his mind. Stubborn is his middle name." She eased around the table, careful not to bump her large belly. "Right after we eat I'm going to check on a woman in labor," she said, "So you'll need to clean up."

A host of confusing thoughts swirled in Miri's head like kites lashed about on gusts of wind. Nothing had gone well for her since the family left Spencer. Now it appeared going back wouldn't be a solution either. Why was there always an obstacle or conflict in the way of a decent life? Was there no place of peace for her family anywhere on earth?

"Georgie," her mother said, "Your father's in the chicken coop. Go tell him supper's ready."

They had been eating the same food for the past week. Boiled eggs, fried corn mush, a cooked vegetable and potatoes. Parts of chicken not considered edible in better times were heaped on a platter.

The prospect of her father soldiering had shrunk Miri's appetite. It was further diminished by the sight of tough gizzards, mealy livers and thick, yellow-clawed chicken feet. She wrinkled her nose in distaste.

"I know our meals have gotten monotonous and aren't to your liking," her mother said, "but I don't have to tell you supplies are low. This is the best we have and you should be grateful and not picky about what's put before you."

The piece of liver Miri swallowed did not easily pass down her throat and she turned to the vegetables.

She decided to approach her father and have a talk about his desire to enlist. What he did affected the entire family. *I'm a woman now and should be free to express my opinion to Father. Mother will try to stifle me, so of course I'll speak to him when she isn't around. And I won't tell Portia because she can't keep a secret.*

Then there were the other concerns about going back to Spencer.

"I'm not the same Miri who left Spencer," she told Portia. "And I wonder how much Clarice and Vi have changed. My biggest worry is what grade I'll be put in after all these months without formal instruction."

Portia, ever the farm girl, said, "I'll have to get used to fall and winter weather again. I hate milking when the temperature is below freezing. It's hard to get the cows to relax enough to release the milk. And we'll need galoshes and winter clothes again. So that means at least one shopping trip."

Miri remembered Portia's delight with their outing to Stanton's department store. "True," she said. "Packing is going to be easy. Most of my clothes are so worn I don't care to take them with me. I'm only packing a couple of dresses and my books."

In spite of her anxiety about the conversation she planned to have with her father, her excitement about leaving Haiti was boundless, and she often dreamt of boarding a ship.

Chapter 20

September 1863

The *skritch, skritch* of chickens scratching below the window woke her. Though Miri would have loved to curl up and sleep a bit longer, it was already bright morning. She sat up in bed, stretched, dressed, and went into the kitchen.

Her father was at the kitchen table with a cup of coffee. He was unshaven and haggard, as though he hadn't slept. She poured coffee for herself, sat across from him and said, "Good morning, Father."

"Morning," he replied. His work-roughened hand rubbed the stubble on his chin.

"Where's Mother?" she asked. "Is she alright?"

"She doesn't feel well and she's resting. I want you to stay here and keep an eye on her. I'll take care of the hives and have Georgie do your garden chores."

He went to the stove and poured a second cup of coffee and Miri began preparing breakfast. She sifted a scant cup of flour with two teaspoons of baking soda for skillet bread that would be more air than substance. There was only half a crock of flour left and she was forced to skimp. No one knew when or if supplies would come from the mainland. To compensate for the poor bread, she made sure the oatmeal was good and thick.

Georgie came to the doorway. He saw her cooking, saw the expression on his father's face and became frightened. "Where's Ma?" he asked Miri.

"Not feeling well, so she's staying in bed." Miri handed him a bowl of cereal and placed a pitcher of milk and a container of honey on the table.

"Do you think Mother is feeling poorly because of the baby, Father?" she asked.

"I'm not sure," he said. "I think she's probably just tired." He reached over and tapped Georgie's shoulder. "Eat hearty, Splinter," he told him. "You're going with me and we'll be working hard all day."

• • • • •

When they left, Miri went to check on her mother. Mrs. Whitfield was asleep, but even in the darkened room Miri could see beads of perspiration on her forehead and upper lip, and a high flush of fever on her face. Miri laid a palm on her mother's forehead and, alarmed by its heat, filled a basin with water from the crock and moistened a towel. She sponged her mother's face, arms, and legs in an effort to cool her down and break the fever.

After rewetting the towel half a dozen times the water was too warm to be useful. She poured it on the flower bed next to the back porch, refilled the basin and resumed sponging until her mother began to grow restless.

She stopped her efforts and put a pot of broth on the stove. While it was heating she took a pail to the rain barrel outside the kitchen. Two pails of water refilled the crock and she made sure to put the top back on the barrel so insects and vermin could not spoil the remaining water.

In the bedroom, the few sips of broth and a mouthful of water she coaxed her mother to swallow were vomited back. It happened so fast there was barely time to grab the basin and catch it.

Anxiously, Miri prayed. *Please don't let Mother have the yellow sickness. The ship will arrive soon to take us out of here. The fever would be dangerous and likely ruin our plans to go home.*

From years of assisting her mother Miri knew herbs that could reduce fever, but fearing they might harm the unborn baby she decided not to use them.

At supper that night Mr. Whitfield was updated on the situation, and decided it would be best for Miri to remain at her mother's bedside. He would sleep in Georgie's room.

Miri caught brief naps on a pallet next to her mother's bed and continued 'round the clock care for the next four days. Her efforts didn't help; the illness would not relax its grip. Her mother's fever still burned, and she now breathed with a raspy wheeze.

On the fifth day Miri and her father stood at Mrs. Whitfield's bedside listening to the results of the midwife's examination. She said, "You know the illness has weakened her. She is not recovering, and she can expect to give birth in a little over a month. If she travels, both she and the baby will be at risk. She should remain here until after the baby is born and she is stronger. Also, remember that Dr. Stillman will not be on the ship."

The assessment and warning worried Miri. The ship was their only chance to leave this awful place.

Her mother began a woeful, wracking wail.

"I'm sorry, Sarah," her father said, raising her hand to his cheek. "But circumstances leave me no choice."

"No choice, Father?" Miri said.

"No. Two days ago rebels attempted to take over the Presidential Palace in Port-au-Prince. If tensions escalate there is a strong possibility the Haitian president will call up men in the colony to support him."

"But he has no right to do that, Father," Miri said. "He doesn't want to help us because we're not Haitian citizens, so how can he ask us to help him?"

"It's not a question whether we want to or not. President Geffrand can enforce a clause in our contract. That clause says it's mandatory for all able-bodied male colonists over the age of fifteen to join the Haitian Army in the event of civil unrest. I, for one, have no intention of being drafted into the Haitian Army. Any fighting I do will be for the purpose of keeping the States united."

Miri's hope died with his words. A roar filled her head and tears rolled down her cheeks. Her father had a responsibility to protect and provide for the family and he intended to abandon them.

"You mustn't cry," he said. "As soon as Mother is better, I'll arrange passage home for all of you."

"But what are we to do if you go, Father? How will we survive without you?"

"This is not an easy decision for me, Miri, but if I don't leave with the rest of the men, there won't be another chance. Georgie thinks like a boy, so you will have the main responsibility to oversee things. You're level headed and capable, and I have confidence in you. Aunt Rachel and Portia will help out when the house is no longer under quarantine."

"But, what about the revolt? Won't we be in danger?"

"The discord between the Haitians has nothing to do with our colony and the fighting will end as soon as President Geffrand or his rival controls the Palace."

· · · · ·

Colonists who were brave enough to venture into Port-au-Prince heard more and more talk of a planned political coup and saw occasional gunfights in the streets. At night Miri could see the fire of burning buildings dance across the far horizon. Worry about forced conscription rose in the colony as men hurried to complete preparations for departure.

The ship sent by Lincoln arrived, and with it the day Miri had to say goodbye to her father. She had a desperate urge to stow away and sail to New York with him, but the duty to care for her ailing mother and Georgie tied her to Haiti.

Over the next three days she wept enough tears to float a canoe, and while she struggled not to fall into bottomless despair, her mother grew stronger. She was now capable of washing and feeding herself, and took to complaining.

"This fever has got to ease soon," she said, "Or I'll be parched to a crisp. If I knew where to get a bit of crushed birch bark or willow, I could bring down my temperature. I asked the midwife but she said there's none to be found."

Miri listened and went on sweeping and dusting. She dare not tell her mother she and the midwife had colluded to withhold herbs that might be harmful to the unborn infant.

Her mother moved onto her other concern. "I wish I could delay the birth of this poor, innocent babe until I'm back home. To be born in Haiti will ensure it a woeful future." The deep regret she held over the decision to leave Spencer had become a daily litany.

Miri silently agreed. Coming to Haiti was a bad idea, but now she had her mother's health and the baby's survival to worry about. Chores could be managed, and she had the skill to make broths and assist with physical care. What she lacked was the ability to remedy the dark mood enfolding her mother like cloak.

"Please don't say such things," she said. "The baby will be healthy and beautiful. You'll see."

At her next visit the midwife reported Dr. Stillman was in critical condition and not expected to survive the night. The lines of sorrow on her mother's face deepened at the news.

Miri saw the midwife out, warmed the bread left from breakfast, and drizzled it with honey. It was a poor substitute for honey cake but she hoped it might bring her mother some comfort. It did not, and her misery deepened because she could not attend Dr. Stillman's funeral.

Chapter 21

September / October 1863

A wrinkled and smudged envelope arrived. It was Father's handwriting and a knot squeezed Miri's stomach. The envelope held three folded papers. One had her name on it. She unfolded the thin sheet with shaking hands and almost tore it.

Dear daughter,

I hope you and Georgie are well when you receive this letter and I also pray Mother is recovering.

I hardly have had an idle moment since arriving in Spencer. During the week I'm at the shop and on weekends work down at the dock, loading ships. Most of them carry supplies for the military to Baltimore and Washington. The pay is good and there are a lot of jobs available what with every able-bodied white man in uniform and off fighting.

I plan to send some money soon. Use it for day-to-day needs and if there is anything left, save it toward what you will need for tickets home.

Ezra sends his regards to you. He has done a fine job with the shop. Customers are genuinely pleased with his barbering talent and he has taken young Samuel Jacobs on as an apprentice.

The war is not going well for the North and Lincoln is fast making preparations for the enlistment and training of Colored soldiers. There is already a recruitment office in New York City where we'll be able to sign up when official approval comes from Washington.

"... we'll be able to sign up." The words left no doubt as to her father's intention. He was filling boats with military supplies. Why couldn't he be content to contribute to the war effort from a safe distance? Too upset to finish the letter, she put it in her pocket and returned the other sheets to the envelope. She bought it to her mother who wept when she read it.

Over the next week the newspaper reported tension and several altercations between discharged soldiers and colored dockworkers in

New York. The current cycle of white versus non-white in New York City began when the draft was instituted. Businesses would not hire white men who were draft eligible and hired colored men instead. Discharged veterans added to the number of unemployed white men, many of whom resorted to mob violence to express their frustration and anger.

In his next letter her father wrote he was no longer working on the dock because the atmosphere was too dangerous.

"I think he's made the right decision," Miri said. "He has a decent income from the barbershop. The last thing we need is for him to be attacked for a few extra dollars."

Her mother sighed. "I agree. But it does affect when we will have enough to pay our passage home."

She helped her mother walk the short distance to a chair in the yard where she could get some fresh air. A few hours of sun each day had given a healthier glow to her mother's skin. As her outlook improved, complaints decreased. Miri saw her smile at a batch of newly hatched, fluffy chicks chasing each other around the yard and thought, *she's almost returned to the parent I used to know.*

Chapter 22

October 1863

Mrs. Whitfield entered the kitchen with a strange look on her face. "Miri, we have another letter from your father," she said. "It is addressed to you. Let us pray it is good news." With trembling hands she passed it to Miri who looked at the familiar handwriting as she tried to quell the nervous flutter in her stomach. She had hoped to be the one to see it first, in case the news was bad. "Mother, would you like me to read it out loud for you?" she asked. Mrs. Whitfield nodded. Miri shook out the thin sheets and read.

My dear daughter,

It will come as no surprise to you to hear I have enlisted, as I have often expressed a desire to fight for the cause of equality for everyone, no matter the color of their skin. My regiment was straightaway sent to Riker's Island Military Camp for training. We learned to march in formation, received instruction in military terms as well as strategy. Most importantly for me was learning about artillery, how to use a pistol and rifle, and loading and firing large weapons.

The Army has provided me with a uniform and necessaries. I have utensils for eating, a bar of serviceable soap, a razor and other supplies for my personal needs. A small book of prayers, paper and pencil are also in our packs and I hope to find a quiet minute or two to put them to use.

Tomorrow the regiment will march down Fifth Avenue be mustered in at a ceremony presided over by a number of dignitaries. I expect each one is likely to give a speech. Our regimental flag and battle flag is to be presented to Colonel William Silliman, our commanding officer. After he accepts the flags we will then officially be recognized as the 26th, Regiment New York, United States Colored Troops.

Since he reluctantly accepted the mandate to abolish slavery, I find it no surprise that Mr. Lincoln chooses to relegate his non-white soldiers a separate equality based on color.

Miri, I have no doubt you are doing a good job looking after your mother and Georgie. At the same time mind your own health and do not become overtired from the amount of work. I pray that you, mother and Georgie are well and will continue to be so.

I shall write again as soon as I am able,
Affectionately, Father

Miri's emotions wavered between pride and terror. Lincoln had recognized the desire of men of color to fight to maintain the Union and her father had taken action and followed up on his word to volunteer. Enlistment was a sign of his valor but doing so guaranteed he would be sent into battle and be at risk for his very life.

His safety wasn't certain. If he did not survive the war, neither would the family. They depended on him for money to live on while they waited for the baby's birth before booking passage to New York.

As expected, news of his enlistment was hard on her mother. Her spirits plummeted and nothing Miri did could lift them. At bedtime, she added an extra prayer for the protection of her father and the wellbeing of her mother and fell into a troubled sleep plagued by nightmares.

In the morning a clear blue sky greeted her and she put the letter in her dress pocket and got busy with chores.

No one had much to say at breakfast and after cleaning the kitchen she went out to the woodpile and stood a section of log on end atop a stump. A few additional pieces ought to be enough to make it through the week. She had taken on the task of chopping wood after imagining Georgie missing the wood and severing a toe. With both hands firm on the axe, she swung it overhead. Her aim was accurate. The axe struck and split the log with a sharp crack.

By midmorning she had put the bedrooms to rights and joined her mother in the kitchen where Mrs. Whitfield sat cutting a frayed sheet into diapers. As Miri set the teakettle on the stove to heat there was knock on the door. It was Dr. Lazarre. He was alone, and declined the offer of tea. The visit was not a social call, he said. He was concerned about her mother's condition and proposed to assist, "*a metre au monde le bébé de Madame.*"

She thought her mother got the gist of his offer to bring her unborn child into the world, but she translated it nonetheless.

"*Maman dit, merci,*" she said, providing her mother's approval in French. "But the birth should be easy and the midwife will assist."

The doctor held the brim on his flat crowned, straw hat and bowed.

"Madam, Mademoiselle," he said in a heavily accented mixture of French and English, "Please. You are call me if you have need. Eh?"

Miri expressed appreciation for his concern and saw him out.

"I prefer the assistance of someone who speaks English," her mother said.

"I doubt he'll come back," Miri said. "There are so many in the infirmary who need his attention."

She saw her mother wipe perspiration from her brow and said, "Leave the sheet for later and go sit in the parlor. It's cooler there."

Her mother napped after lunch and Miri went into the garden to inspect Georgie's work. She reminded him to mound soil around the bean plants to insulate the roots from the heat. From the garden she went to check the hives. Bees were coming and going and she sat on the same boulder she used to while watching her father tend the hives. The humming of the bees was solace, a bit of balm for her aching soul and she sat until the heat of the sun prompted her to move.

She returned to the house, set leftover stew to warm for supper, and made a skillet of pan bread. Afternoon shadows were lengthening by the time she began a letter to her father. Thinking of him again brought images of mangled, bleeding men writhing and howling and dying in pain. Mr. Ackerly's suffering and death seemed almost peaceful by comparison.

She forced the terrible scenes away by picturing her father safe, in a warm tent. It didn't help, so she put the pen aside. The letter would have to wait until her mind was calmer.

"It's unfair," she complained the next day. "Mr. Lincoln originally said he was fighting the war to keep the states united, yet he drove us away. Defeating the south will now keep the union whole and ensure freedom for slaves, but we've lost what we already had."

The hand she pushed under a hen to get an egg received a sound peck on its thumb. It smarted but wasn't bleeding and she went to the last roost. "We're prisoners on this island," she grumbled, "And the colony is reduced to a bunch of old men, women, and children."

"I think so, too," Portia said as they exited the coop. She scythed her free arm through tall grass bordering the path. "Ma cries a lot now."

"At least she's not sick and expecting. I have a ton of work and responsibility, and Georgie has yet to stop his childish ways. I have to keep a sharp eye to make sure he does his work correctly."

Wildflowers dipped and waved in the breeze. Miri stopped to take in the kaleidoscope of colors and listen to the flutter of insects and birds harmonize with the hum of the bees. She wondered if there was enough honey to harvest.

Portia interrupted her thoughts. "It's near lunch time, Miri. We better get home."

That evening Miri answered her father's letter.

Dear Father,

I was overjoyed to receive your letter and proud to learn of your enlistment. Mother is bearing up fairly well. Her health has improved and her strength is slowly returning. I am managing the chores and Georgie is better about helping. I do believe he is on the way to becoming a responsible young man.

Regretfully, many of the people who were in the infirmary when you left have passed on, including Mr. Ackerly. We also deeply mourned the loss of Dr. Stillman. Now those afflicted with the yellow sickness rely on the skill of the Haitian, Dr. Lazarre.

Thankfully, no new patients were admitted this past week and a few cots are empty. Everyone is praying the epidemic has run its course.

The enclosed is a token of my handiwork and the locks of hair in it are Mother's, Georgie's and mine. Tuck the pouch in a pocket and you will have us with you no matter where the war takes you.

Father dearest, I pray for your safety every night and I pray for an end to the conflict soon so our family may be reunited.

Please be careful and write whenever you are able,

Your loving daughter,
Miriam Hazel Rose Whitfield

Chapter 23

November 1863

Miri draped a towel over the pail to protect the milk from leaves and marauding insects, and stepped out of the barn. An early morning rain on this already hot and muggy day was trickling off to a light mist. She had just started pouring the milk into the stoneware crock when her mother called from the bedroom.

"I'll be there in a moment, Mother," she said. The tension in her mother's voice urged her to hurry, but the milk would curdle if it remained in the metal pail. She finished transferring it, placed the lid back on the crock and hurried to the bedroom.

Her mother sat on the edge of a chair, the edges of her lips white with pain. "Get Mrs. Clemons. It's time," she said through clenched teeth, as another spasm caused her to tighten her grip on the arms of the chair.

"A pillow behind your back will make you more comfortable," Miri said, reaching toward the bed.

"No. No pillow, Miri. Find Mrs. Clemons."

Georgie came to the door, saw his mother's distress, and retreated to the kitchen.

Miri left her mother, told Georgie the baby was on the way and to spoon up cereal for himself. He nodded and wolfed down the oatmeal with his usual speed.

She handed him a hastily made sandwich and banana for lunch and sent him off to the garden.

Her pace to Mrs. Clemons' house was brisk enough to make her short of breath by the time she knocked on the door.

A tall, stout woman swung it open. "Who's out here pounding? Oh, it's you, Miri." The midwife's growl softened. "Your mother's labor must've started."

"It has, Mrs. Clemons, and she's in a lot of pain."

"Come in," the midwife gestured. "I'll need a moment to pack my bag and get a clean apron. And don't worry. Labor pain is to be expected in childbirth. The cramps help push the baby out."

Miri couldn't image how the large knife, scissors and thick needle were going to be used and mulled over possible purposes of the implements on the walk to her house. Although she had been at several deliveries with her mother she'd never actually witnessed the process of birth.

At their home, Mrs. Clemons gave the same orders her mother did: heat a pot of water, gather towels and clean rags and finally, stay out of the bedroom.

"But I want to help," Miri said.

Mrs. Clemons twisted her hair into a knot and secured it under a bandana. "You are helping," she said. "Put the knife and scissors in a basin and pour boiling water over them. Take them out when the water cools down and lay them on a towel. I'll let you know when I need them." With that, she closed the bedroom door.

Each time her mother moaned or cried out, Miri's stomach lurched. Hours went by. Something wasn't right. Her mother said the birth would be easy. Eventually the sounds ceased and her anxiety heightened. Mrs. Clemons emerged and softly closed the door.

"Is everything alright?" Miri asked.

"Yes," she said. "I gave your mother something to make her comfortable and at the moment she's sleeping."

Neither of them felt like talking, and while they waited they ate a lunch of cold chicken, pickles and johnnycake. After, Mrs. Clemons returned to the bedroom. To keep from brooding, Miri mopped the floor. She scrubbed every surface and crevice in the kitchen and still there was no baby. She was frightened and tired, struggling not to break down. Suddenly, from the bedroom she heard an infant squall. Tears burst from her eyes.

Mrs. Clemons called. "Bring me the knife and scissors, Miri, and meet your little sister."

The naked newborn lay across her mother's chest, its tightly closed eyes tucked deep into plump, pink cheeks.

Too bad Father isn't here, Miri thought. The baby's lips pursed and yawned, revealing a dimple in her right cheek. A soft moan shifted Miri's attention. Her mother was drowsy from the fatigue of labor and the potion Mrs. Clemons had administered. Dark circles rimmed her eyes.

"Your mother's a bit worn out," the midwife said, "A good night's rest will do her a world of good." She lifted the infant's umbilical cord and severed it with the scissors.

The sound startled Miri, and she became aware of a smell enveloping the room. It was the same organic, metallic odor of blood that accompanied the long ago birth of a calf, a birth she had witnessed with distaste.

Mrs. Clemons pinched the piece of cord attached to the baby with two fingers and picked up a piece of twine with her other hand. "Here, Miri," she said. "Tie the stub off nice and tight, then bring me a fresh basin of warm water and put another potful on to heat."

Coached and assisted by the midwife, Miri gave the baby her first bath. She was dried, diapered and had a bellyband snugged and pinned around her middle to assure the navel would heal without protruding. She slept through being put into a gown and swaddled in a blanket.

Miri placed her sister in a cradle, refilled the basin and was again banished from the bedroom.

"Go clean my instruments while I tend to the afterbirth and your mother's hygiene," Mrs. Clemons told her.

When Mrs. Clemons finally emerged from the bedroom she remarked, "It's been a long day for both of us. I'll stop in tomorrow to check on your mother and the baby. Try to get some rest."

Miri nodded. She was tired, but there was still supper to make and she set about preparing it as soon as the midwife left. The food was almost ready when Georgie returned from the field hungry and curious. He was filthy and she told him he couldn't see the baby until he washed.

A finger to her lips, she opened the door to the bedroom. "Mother's exhausted and she's sleeping, so try to be quiet."

Georgie looked to Miri when he saw how pale his mother was.

"She'll be better in a couple of days," she reassured him.

He peeked into the cradle at the baby and said, "Gosh, she's tiny. Ain't she, Miri?"

Georgie's voice disturbed the baby, who began to fret. Miri gave Georgie a push. "Shoo," she said and ushered him out. She rocked the cradle to settle the baby, ate a stew and biscuit supper and was able to coax her mother to take a few spoons of stew broth. Pleased, she sat in the rocking chair next to the bed and nodded off. The sound of squalling woke her and she saw her mother trying to get the baby to nurse.

Miri improved her mother's position by propping her up with two pillows. Once the baby's hunger was satisfied, Miri burped her, changed her diaper, and returned her to the cradle. Then, tired to the bone, she went to bed and fell into a deep sleep.

In the morning Portia arrived and paced up and down the porch.

Miri opened the back door. "What are you doing here at this hour?" she asked.

Portia stepped into the kitchen. "Georgie was shouting across the field yesterday that your mother was having the baby, and I'm here to see it."

"*It* is a girl," Miri said. She led Portia to the bedroom and picked up the baby.

"Does she have a name yet?"

"Mother chose Lavinia Ruth," Miri whispered. "But I'm calling her Livy." She caressed the infant's doll-sized hand.

"Can I hold her?"

"For a minute. Sit in the rocking chair and I'll hand her to you."

Portia hardly breathed. She cradled the baby like a fragile piece of china. With no siblings of her own, she had always thought of Miri as a sister, and now she had another. Livy was precious and dear, and Portia wanted to hold her forever.

A wet diaper and Livy's hungry wail finally prompted Portia to give her up. Portia's comfort was in tending to animals, not infants, and she made a quick exit for the barn.

Miri put Livy in a dry diaper, handed her to her mother to nurse, and went to make breakfast. She ate and filled Georgie's bowl twice, then ordered him out of the house for his chores.

With some urging her mother ate half a bowl of oatmeal thinned to the consistency of gravy and drank a cup of tea. After, she wanted to bathe, and Miri took it as a good sign. She put a pot of water on the stove to heat and while it warmed, made bread dough and chopped vegetables. With soup on the stove simmering for lunch, she gathered towels, soap, a fresh nightie, sheets and clean "female" cloths. Livy also needed a bath, so she added a gown and bellyband to the stack.

Two days later Dr. Lazarre was at the door with Philippe. "*Bonjour, Mademoiselle*," the doctor said. "I am come because the Madam Clemons she say the *Maman*..." He stopped and turned to Philippe.

"My uncle," Philippe said, "Wishes to examine your mother. Mrs. Clemons told him she is weak and not much out of bed."

"But first, *le bébé*," the doctor said as he and Philippe followed Miri into her mother's bedroom.

"Mother," Miri said. "Mrs. Clemons asked Doctor Lazarre to pay you and Livy a visit."

"I know. She told me."

Unsure of the doctor's skill with infants, Miri paid close attention as he listened to Livy's breathing, looked into her eyes and ears and mouth. He smiled and said, "*Elle est en bonne sante*," and handed her to a relieved Miri.

The baby was healthy.

The doctor murmured to himself as he examined her mother and the sound of her cough made him frown. He took a handful of medicine packets from his bag and spoke rapidly in French to Philippe.

"Your mother has *le catarrah*, um, congestion in the chest," Philippe told her.

Doctor Lazarre selected two brown packets and laid them on the bedside table.

"*Mademoiselle*," he said. "*Vous . . . Ah, je suis desolé*," he said with a troubled expression. He nodded to Philippe for help.

Philippe said, "My uncle said you must be sure to give your mother the medicine. Mix a pinch of it in a glass of water and have her drink one in the morning and another in the evening."

Miri said, "Tell your uncle I'll follow his instructions." She was willing to do whatever necessary to help her mother's health improve, even if it meant administering medicine from a Haitian doctor.

There was no money to pay the doctor so she got a jar of honey from the pantry while he was putting his stethoscope away.

"*Miel* — honey. *Pour vous* — for you," she said handing the jar to him.

He held the container to the light and admired the golden liquid, a pleased smile on his raisin colored face.

"*Ahh, Merci, merci, Mademoiselle* Miri," he said with a courtly bow. He continued speaking but reverted to the local dialect and she didn't understand what he was saying. Her book-acquired Parisian French didn't have much similarity to the French patois spoken by the Haitians.

The doctor and Philippe were delighted with the honey. The depth of their reaction at such a token thank you gift was a surprise. It wasn't until later, when she was cutting out biscuits that she understood the reason why. Honey was an expensive, imported commodity for Haitians, the reason why her father and others in the colony had brought hives with them. For the majority of Haitians, their only sweetener was a locally produced, rough sorghum.

Mrs. Clemons and Dr. Lazarre made weekly visits because her mother had a lingering cough and was slow to regain strength. Miri also suspected the doctor might be frequently returning because he wanted more of the honey she paid him. He always brought Philippe along, so she didn't discourage the visits because they were opportunities for her to talk with Philippe.

Chapter 24

March 1864

Nearly six months had passed. Work was never-ending. Helping with chores had been tiresome enough, now she had full responsibility to make sure everything was done.

Georgie's laziness and inability to follow instructions was exasperating. It might be easier for her to do everything, but that would soon wear her out, so she kept after him to do his share.

Still afraid he would injure himself, she chopped and split the logs, but had him stack the wood into neat piles and collect kindling. Every day she prodded him to feed the chickens and scolded until at last he learned to be careful and collect the eggs without breaking them. At times she thought her back would break under the burden of cooking, cleaning, laundry, ironing and gardening. Yet if they were to have any chance of surviving she had to keep up with it all.

She bathed Livy as Portia chatted with her. The baby cooed and Miri smiled. Livy was blossoming into a cheerful, bright joy in these days of grinding labor and constant weariness.

"I'm working from before sunup to well after dark every blessed day," Miri sighed. "Some jobs require the strength of a man. I wish I could get some relief, but my mother's still not well and I can't whine to her like a child."

"I guess I'm lucky," Portia said. "Even though there's a lot to do at home, at least my Ma isn't sick."

On Wednesday Dr. Lazarre finished the baby's weekly exam and Miri felt his gaze on her as she slipped Livy into a gown. He spoke to Philippe then turned back to her. "*Madamoiselle* Miri," he said. "Philippe, he work. Help you. *Pour le miel.* For the honey. *C'est bon?* Is good?"

Philippe said, "I can do some of the heavy tasks your father did, Miri. I don't know how to milk a cow, but I can learn."

Having Philippe's help sounded heaven-sent. But the decision was not hers to make. "Mother," she said, handing Livy to her, "Dr. Lazarre proposes that Philippe work for us."

"I heard him, Miri. Thank you, Doctor," her mother said, "However, we don't need help."

"But we do, Mother," Miri said. "I need help. I'm always tired. The amount of work I'm doing is taking a toll on me. Philippe is strong and he speaks English." She hadn't intended to argue, certainly not in front of Philippe and his uncle. The words tumbled out before she could stop them. Already in deep water and with nothing to lose, she plunged ahead.

"Philippe can take over the heavier chores and we can pay him with honey. We have shelves full of it, and Haitians value honey more than our dollars."

Miri waited as her mother's gaze passed from the doctor to Philippe.

"Very well," she said after a long minute. "He can work for . . . well, until we depart."

Miri could feel a flood of relief and happiness wash through her. She said, "Thank you, Mother. I'll take Philippe around and explain which chores he'll be responsible for."

Late in the day she sat on a velvety carpet of grass at the river's edge and listened to the water sing its way along to the sea. It was a delight to be able to relax.

Portia leaned against a tree, pulled off her shoe and shook out a pebble. "You're looking happy for once," she said.

Miri told her about Philippe.

"With money so tight how can you afford a hired hand?"

"I'm going to pay him like I do his uncle, with jars of honey," Miri said.

· · · · ·

Once Philippe and his uncle began to work in the settlement, they decided to move into one of the abandoned colony houses. Soon they had an established routine. At dawn they made rounds in the infirmary where Doctor Lazarre stayed to monitor patients and see the ambulatory sick in the clinic. Philippe joined his uncle in making rounds and came every day but Sunday to Miri's house where he discussed tasks of the day with her and went about his chores. He was a diligent worker, and Miri's burden grew lighter.

Because they mostly spoke to each other in French, within weeks her vocabulary and ability to hold a conversation improved. She learned Philippe was seven years old when he was orphaned during a yellow fever epidemic and his uncle became his guardian. Before the war broke out he spent summers with cousins in New Orleans. English was their primary language and the extended visits allowed him to attain fluency.

An added bonus to hiring Philippe was the change it brought about in Georgie, who looked on Philippe as a kind of older brother and trailed after him, imitating his walk and mannerisms. Georgie also became less childish and lazy. He did chores without constant goading and had even picked up some French from Philippe.

Gradually, the long months of tension in Miri's muscles and bones loosened. She reveled in the free moments she had now, and took to wandering the fields and the riverbank. The sounds of birds and insects and small creatures scrabbling in the undergrowth and the ruffling of leaves became familiar again.

She heard coins jingling and turned, for a moment expecting to see her father, but it was only the heat playing tricks with her imagination. There hadn't been a letter from him in months. She supposed he was busy fighting and didn't have time to write, and she said a quick prayer for his safety. She finished weeding the last row of bean plants and heard humming from a clump of flowers nearby. Bees flew among the blossoms.

In the past month, with the arrival of Livy and her mother's slow recovery, the hives had not been much in her mind. Now she decided to examine them.

Activity at both hives was brisk. Bees left to collect nectar and returned slowed by the added weight of their prize. They continued to work despite lack of attention and care. Strands of gold decorated the sides of both hives, as honey oozed from full honeycombs. A crop was ready to harvest, and Father was gone.

"Care and management of hives and collecting honey are jobs for men," her mother told her when Miri mentioned it. "Let Philippe do it."

Miri refused to yield. "Philippe is a good worker but he knows nothing about bees or how to collect honey." The hives and bees were her responsibility. She had cared for them from the beginning. "I don't have the same fear of bees you do, Mother. I am going to continue taking care of the hives, and I will also harvest the honey."

Though she used honey in a number of health products and beauty aids, Mrs. Whitfield never ventured near the hives. The stock of personal care products she had put up before her lying-in was almost exhausted. Due to her breathing problems and long convalescence, she hadn't been able to replenish the supply. Only a few bars of honey-mint soap were left.

"You are stronger, and the worst of the epidemic is over, Mother. So you should know there have been requests for cucumber and honey facial cream and honey-lemon hair rinse. I've told the ladies they'd be available soon but not to expect any more honey-oatmeal soap. They understood and agreed that cereal is precious as food and shouldn't be put into bars of soap."

Her mother didn't answer right away. At last she said, "You're right. I am much better and need to get busy. I can make soap with other ingredients."

"Philippe and Georgie can help by building fires, filling buckets and such," Miri said, happy to dispense with the conflict about the hives.

On her next visit to the field she observed the bees' patterns of flight. She didn't think she'd ever tire of watching them. When a bee alit on her arm, she slowly and gently brushed it off, then moved past the hives to the shed.

Inside, the air was stale and heavy. She opened the shutters, found a broom and swept away dust and spider webs. Her father's overalls dangled from a hook on the back of the door and his veiled hat lay on the workbench next to his gloves. Behind them an assortment of bottles were arranged in rows alongside the smoke pan and a knife.

From the shelf above the workbench she took a small, fawn-colored notebook. *"A Guide to Keeping Bees" Henry Whitfield, 1863"* was written on its cover in her father's neat, cursive hand. She spent a minute browsing through pages of monthly entries on tending the hives before she slipped the journal into her apron pocket.

That night, lying in bed, she opened it again.

NOTES

The shed is finished and the hives set away from the house near the tree line where wildflowers are abundant. A river is not far off and the bees can easily obtain water. Both queens are healthy and robust with plenty of comb for eggs.

CHORES

The following have been unpacked and stored:

[*Here the handwriting changed because he had allowed her to list the tools and supplies*]

• One smoker pan
• Matches — in jars to protect from dampness
• Two scrapers

- Two hive tools
- Six goose feathers
- Two uncapping fork
- Four pails
- One roll of cheesecloth
- Oilcloth, 6 yds.

Fatigue tugged her eyelids. She slid the journal beneath the pillow, doused the lamp and entered a dreamscape.

Father was near the shed wearing his veiled hat and holding the smoker pan.

She called him but he didn't hear her and walked toward the hives. A thick fog rose and before he was completely enveloped, he turned and extended his hand toward her. The journal floated from the mist.

Fragmented images lingered when she rubbed sleep from her eyes and began the new day.

Later at the river, Portia said, "Your mind seems to be somewhere else, Miri. Is everything alright?"

"I'm just enjoying the afternoon. Since Philippe started working for us I've had time to relax." Actually, she was thinking about the dream. She felt it was a sign Father approved her harvesting the honey and she didn't want to discuss it with Portia.

She resumed reading the journal after supper.

- One hat with veil
- One pair elbow length twill gloves
- Jars — 24 pint and 12 half pint
- One knife
- Two stirrers
- Two funnels

That completed the entries. She didn't remember doing the list, yet it was her handwriting. The next page detailed the steps necessary steps for hive care, and for harvesting honey.

Her father's methodical and organized management of the barbershop was evident in his approach to management of the hives. She skipped familiar steps and learned new techniques as she read. Harvesting the honey would be simply a matter of following Father's notes.

She saw herself as Miriam Whitfield, Apiarist. No. That sounded a bit too snobbish. Miriam Whitfield, Beekeeper, was more suitable.

Chapter 25

April 1864

Miri said to Portia, "Abolishing slavery was long overdue. Lincoln didn't author the Proclamation because he's benevolent. If I recall, he said war was necessary to preserve the sanctity of the Union and not out of concern for the plight of slaves."

"Maybe he emancipated them because he developed more sympathy for their circumstances and suffering," Portia replied.

"I'm not convinced of that. For months the newspapers outlined problems I believe drove Lincoln to finally issue the Emancipation Proclamation. There was clamor from abolitionists, and growing pressure from liberals in his administration to do what was humane and right. The generals were also after him to address and clarify the status of runaways. Articles in the paper said there were so many runaways, they clogged roadways and slowed movement of the Army."

"The poor things were only seeking protection from bounty hunters," Portia said. "They felt safe with soldiers. And camping alongside troops assured them some degree of shelter and food. I understand provisions for the soldiers only went so far. Generals had to ask advice from Washington on how to manage the situation. They'd already done the decent thing in declaring runaways contraband of war and refusing to return them to their former owners."

"I know," Miri said. "The Army put healthy male refugees to work. They had them build earthen fortifications, dig trenches and even construct bridges. And because former slaves were both unschooled and unarmed, they followed orders without question. Officers reported they were invaluable. One lieutenant wrote his commanding officer that runaways were so grateful to breathe freedom's air they wouldn't refuse even the most odious task. He said, 'Henceforward, to allow men who are trained soldiers to devote their abilities to that pursuit, I am assigning retrieval of and interment of dead soldiers exclusively to contraband.'"

It had to logically follow, Miri surmised, for Lincoln and his advisors to recognize the value of redirecting the eagerness and loyalty of former slaves toward combat. The unexpected duration and ferocity of the war had taken a terrible toll on Federal forces, and the number of soldiers lost was catastrophic. With fewer and fewer able-bodied replacements, neither the draft nor volunteers could fully replenish the ranks of fighting men. The General Order approving recruitment of colored soldiers into the Federal Army had arisen out of desperation, and proved to her that Lincoln was less than heroic.

No one had better reason than former slaves to fight against those who had once been their oppressors. Colored regiments mustered by the states of Massachusetts, Connecticut and Rhode Island in defiance of Lincoln, had already demonstrated the willingness of black men to fight and sacrifice their lives in battle. The President had refused to allow their recognition as Federal troops. General Order 143 rectified that denial and satisfied the petitions from free men of color who sought the right to enlist as soldiers in the Federal Army.

Portia said, "There is nothing for us to do but put our faith in God and pray He'll protect our fathers and the other men."

"I wish I could adopt your attitude," Miri said, "But that recruitment order ensured the failure of our colony. We're floundering without enough able-bodied men to work the land, a shortage of supplies and another wave of yellow fever. We need money for aid and supplies to sustain us until we can leave. That money was supposed to come from the men who went home. No telling when the Army will begin paying them."

Father's enlistment could alter the plan to leave Haiti when Mother and the baby were able to travel. Their departure depended on receiving money from her father to purchase passage.

After Portia and her mother left, Miri prepared lunch and called Georgie. He put a basket of vegetables on the counter, washed up, glanced at Livy and took a seat. Ravenous, he wasted no time emptying his bowl and sopping up a puddle of broth with a hunk of bread. To Miri's astonishment he said, "Thanks. That was good. Miri's a good cook, ain't she, Ma?"

His mother nodded but said nothing.

Miri rewarded her brother with a generous slice of cake. He took it from the plate, bit off a chunk and saluted the women. "I'll eat this on my way back to the garden," he told them and was gone.

His abrupt exit didn't concern Miri. She was worried about her mother, who hadn't said a word, looked pale and listless and was staring at her food with pinched lips and a drawn face. The small health improvements she had made over the past few weeks seemed to have vanished.

"Eat your stew, Mother. You need to eat to keep up your strength," Miri urged.

"I don't have an appetite today," her mother said, poking at a piece of potato.

"I know you're fretting about Father, but you have to stay strong for the sake of the baby." She took her mother's bowl to the stove and dumped its contents back into the pot. "You must not give up. Father would tell you the same if he were here."

She looked out the window. "I'll reheat your stew. The sky is clear. Let's sit outside for a while and enjoy the afternoon. Maybe you can do a little needlework while I snap beans."

"I'll snap beans, too," her mother said. "I want to do something useful."

"Fine. If you eat, you can help with the beans."

Fast as a bolt of lightning, both mother and daughter realized their relationship had changed. Miri's new authority, and its acceptance by her mother had erased the old child-to-parent power struggle, and had become more like a union of equals.

Chapter 26

May 1864

Miri was paying Dr. Lazarre and Philippe with honey, and her supply of liquid gold was running low. Less than half a shelf of jars remained. But the honeycombs in the hives were full, and without space to store nectar the bees would abandon the hives and start new colonies elsewhere. The honey had to be harvested. Miri closed her father's journal. "I should get some sleep," she said.

She fell asleep preoccupied with collecting the honey. Tomorrow, after chores she would assemble the necessary clothes and tools.

When Portia arrived, Miri said, "Both of my father's hives. . . . No. *My* hives are full of honey and it's time to harvest. Will you help?"

Portia threw up her hands. "Not me. Just because your father let you help doesn't mean you know how to work with bees. Mess with them and you'll get stung to bits."

Hoping Portia didn't notice how nervous she was, Miri said, "For your information, my father kept a journal about beekeeping, and I've been studying it. Everything I need to know is there. And I'm not foolish. I plan to be very, very careful to avoid riling the bees, and I won't get stung."

She started down the path and called over her shoulder, "With or without your help I'm going to organize everything and harvest the honey."

Portia stayed on the porch. "I can't help," she said. "I'm afraid."

Miri stopped in her tracks. "For heaven's sake, I'm from the city. You're a farm girl. You shouldn't be afraid of bees."

Portia hurried to catch up with her. "Bees are always around the fields, Miri," she said, "but I stay away from them and their hives. I expect there must be millions of bees in a hive," she said with a shiver.

"Well the honey has to be harvested, and my father isn't here. I could use a hand, and you are my choice because Georgie would be more trouble than help. Trust me, Portia. I'll thoroughly smoke the hives to make the bees good and drowsy before we do anything."

"I suppose...."

"Don't start whining. I told you...I'll make it safe." They reached the edge of the field and Miri paused to listen. Bees flew around the hives and the hum created by hundreds of beating wings was like the vibration of a B flat piano key. The air trembled with the presence of so many bees and she felt goose bumps of excitement when one hovered close to her ear.

She went into the shed, removed her skirt and petticoat and stepped into her father's coveralls as Portia watched, open mouthed. "Oh, Miri, it is very bold of you to wear men's clothing," she said.

Miri ignored the remark and rolled the sleeves and pant-legs of the coverall to shorten them. She strode back and forth, testing the fit.

"Men's clothes are more practical for working around hives," she said. "There's no flapping skirt to agitate the bees, snag, or interfere with moving." As she spoke, confidence grew in her ability to achieve a harvest. She put on her father's hat, but it fell so low over her brow she couldn't see. She took it off and set it on Portia's head where it found a better fit.

"But now you don't have anything to protect you, Miri," Portia said. "Maybe it's a sign you should leave the hives alone."

"Nonsense. I'll make a hat. I can create something suitable."

Portia grinned. "You're twisting your braid. Admit it...you're afraid."

"I am not afraid, but I've got more important things to do than stand here and argue with you." Miri reviewed the equipment and got things ready to harvest on the next day. For now the bees were left to forage in peace.

That evening she sewed the sleeves on Livy's new dress and turned a generous hem on it to adjust for growth. She put a button on the back of the neck, snipped loose threads and added the garment to the pile of ironing.

Her mother said, "You did a fine job on your sister's frock."

"Thank you."

"That kind of sewing serves a wife well."

Miri stifled a sigh and began removing the veil from the first of two old hats that had seen better days.

"What are you doing?" Her mother asked. Her voice rose shrilly, and drew a wail from Livy.

"Father's bee hat is too big for me, so I'm making my own. I'll be collecting honey tomorrow and need to protect my face." She removed the second veil, carefully folded and basted the raw edges of both, and blanket-stitched them to the brim of her gardening hat.

Her mother shook her head and focused on quieting the baby.

Miri woke as the sky was changing from inky black to the blue-gray edge of dawn, the hour when animals of the night take to their dens, the birds have not yet begun to sing, and a hushed world waits for sunrise. Excitement surged through her. She hoped her decision to test her beekeeping mettle would not end in failure. Determined not to sink into a negative state of mind, she sent Philippe and Georgie off to their chores and got busy with her own tasks.

Portia arrived near noon. "I was too nervous to eat and afraid you'd be angry if I didn't show up," she said.

"You have to have something in your stomach," Miri said. "I'll fix you a sandwich. As soon as the casserole I made for supper is out of the oven we can go to the hives."

Portia fidgeted and fiddled with the flour canister cover.

"Stop that," Miri said. "My father's notes say the best time to remove frames from a hive is mid-afternoon."

"Why?"

Miri set the casserole on a trivet and said, "Let's go. I'll tell you on the way."

"Will I have to do anything?" Portia asked nervously. "You know I don't want to get too close to the hives."

"Stop worrying. You won't get stung. I have my father's journal and I'll explain every step to you." She picked up the book and read aloud. "Notes: In this tropical climate, flowering plants are plentiful throughout the year. Honey production of bees does not cease during the winter months and harvesting should be done in March and again in September."

It was May and the harvest was more than a month overdue. She wondered if a delay irritated bees the way late milking did with cows. She decided not to mention the delay to Portia. *Why give her a reason to avoid helping me?*

"Chores," she continued. "The brood chamber is three-quarters full and I have opened the honey chambers. Foraging activity is quite lively. With no heavy rains there has been no need for sugar water."

Since Portia wasn't listening, Miri read to herself, "Both queens are healthy and the brood chambers nearly full. Temperatures have been mild with an abundance of flowers though the area lacks Thyme."

Most of the honey sold in Spencer came from the flowers of wild thyme and had a distinctive reddish color. Clover honey was more common but she was fond of the deeper, stronger flavor of thyme honey.

She finished reviewing the notes, changed into coveralls and handed her father's hat to Portia.

"Why are you giving me this?"

"To protect you."

"I told you I'm not going near those hives." Her voice trembled.

"To protect you from the sun, Portia." It was a half-truth and Miri hoped Portia would accept it.

With her own hat and veil securely in place, Miri dampened a handful of wood shavings, mounded them on the smoker pan and laid it on top of an empty hive.

Portia watched, hat in hand.

"Will you stop acting like a child?" Miri said. "Put the hat on, grab a handle and help me take this hive to the field."

They were only a few steps into the field when Portia lost hold of her side of the hive and it thumped onto the ground. The sudden stop caused the hive to tilt and sent the smoker pan sliding. In a single move, Miri set her side down and reached for the pan, exasperated with Portia's timidity.

"For goodness sakes," she said. "Come on. You won't be any help to me if this is as far as you're going. I'll be doing the most dangerous thing. I have to find the queen's chamber and move it to the empty hive."

Portia's eyes, round as an owl's, were fixed on the bees flying about the field.

"Why do you have to move the queen?"

"Because worker bees will return to wherever the queen is, so she has to be transferred to an empty hive while the workers are off gathering nectar. Once the queen's moved, it'll be safe to take the full frames out of the old hive and replace them with empty ones."

"Then what?"

"Then the queen can be returned to her original location, and we can take the full frames to the shed to extract the honey. When that's finished, we'll do the second hive." Though Miri had never done more than partially uncap a frame, she told Portia, "I'll show you how. I know what to do."

"Sorry. But I'm not getting any closer to the hives than right here." Portia shook her head and crossed her arms, and Miri placed the smoker pan on the grass.

Trying to change Portia's mind was a waste of time. "We're going to need the wheelbarrow," Miri said. "So go back to the shed and get it."

Portia left, and Miri gripped one handle of the hive in both hands and tugged it across the field. She retrieved the smoker pan and placed a layer of crushed, dry leaves over the wet twigs. As she had seen her father do, Miri lighted a match with a flick of her thumbnail, and touched its flame to the leaves. Soon leaves and wood were smoldering. She stood there, midway between the two hives, each abuzz with activity. Her chest felt as though it contained a million bees struggling to escape. She was lightheaded and quaked with fear. She knew fear could cause her to make mistakes, and a mistake could agitate the bees. It was important to stay calm. She refused to admit she was incapable of harvesting the honey. She closed her eyes and concentrated on taking slow, even breaths and a minute or so later had her emotions under control again.

Portia was watching from the path. "Are you alright?" she asked.

Miri nodded and blew several puffs of smoke over the nearest hive. The bees circling around grew sluggish and settled inside. She removed the cover to search for the queen and found her immense body in the middle frame. Surrounding her in the brood chamber were hundreds of fat, squirming larvae.

Miri, no longer squeamish, took the frame by the corners. It didn't weigh much and she pulled it out and slotted it into the empty hive, isolating the queen. She paused to revel in her accomplishment.

"We can remove full frames from this hive now," she told Portia. "The workers won't bother us. Bring over the wheelbarrow."

Portia approached, chewing her lip. She nodded toward the hive. "How long will they sleep?" she asked.

"For a while," Miri said. She hoped the answer would ease Portia's anxiety. "I'll smoke the hive a little more to make sure." She was careful to limit the amount of smoke to prevent harming the bees. Keeping them sedated required a delicate balance of smoke and fresh air. Without an adequate amount of air, they'd suffocate in the smoke.

One by one she and Portia wiggled and jiggled sticky combs out of the hive and laid them in the wheelbarrow. When a full frame was removed, an empty one replaced it. Four partially full frames were left untouched to serve as food while the bees worked to fill the empty frames. Miri returned the queen to the hive and she and Portia trundled the loaded barrow to the shed.

"We need to hang the frames on those," Miri said, pointing to a number of large hooks, inverted metal question marks screwed into the rafters. "Then comes uncapping... pulling the wax covers off the combs."

"Everything is so sticky," Portia said. "And we aren't near tall enough to reach those hooks."

"Yes, we are," Miri said. She stepped onto a stool. "I'm determined to harvest this honey. Hand me a frame."

It turned into an awkward ordeal. She tried to be careful but the honey oozed, and when all of the frames were suspended, her coveralls and gloves were striped with honey.

She positioned collecting buckets beneath each frame and got the comb fork. She inserted the tip of the fork under the edge of wax that sealed the frame and pulled. With dismay she watched uneven pieces of parchment colored wax crack free and fall. Bits of it landed on the screen that covered the bucket and pieces were strewn on the floor. The wax should have lifted off in neat strips.

She recalled the time she tried to pare an entire apple in a single ribbon. That time Grandmother's advice saved her.

She reinserted the tool, adjusted the angle and drew it along beneath the wax cap with utmost care. Though not perfect, the improvement in technique allowed her to remove strips of wax without splintering it. Grandmother was right. Patience and practice brought success.

Chapter 27

May 1864

Amber liquid fell onto screens and seeped down into collecting buckets; carcasses of dead bees and fragments of wax accumulated atop the mesh. A second straining with cheesecloth would filter out smaller debris. The slow, painstaking cleaning process was necessary to produce clear honey.

"I have an idea," Miri said.

"What now?" Portia asked rolling her eyes heavenward.

"We should leave the rest of the honey in the combs, cut the combs and bottle the pieces. It'll be less work and eliminate the need for straining. Most people prefer comb honey anyway. They think it's purer. There's also the bonus of the beeswax for them to make a candle or two."

Portia applauded. "That's a wonderful idea," she said. "Straining is messy and takes forever."

One by one Miri pulled wax seals off six frames from the second hive and with Portia's help cut and bottled the entire batch of comb. Satisfied with what they had accomplished, Miri tightened the last bottle top in fading daylight. The jars gave off a golden glow, lit by the rays of the setting sun.

"We accomplished a lot today," she said. "But we're losing light and I'm tired and famished. Let's go home."

The second day of straining honeycomb through cheesecloth tested their strength and ability. Nevertheless, Miri decorated the first filled jar with a festive red ribbon and set it in a place of honor on the top shelf in the pantry. She sent Portia home with a dozen jars, and replenished her own supply. Her first honey harvest was a success.

Friday, the stitching group, reduced in number by illness, met for the first time in months at her house. Mrs. Barkley, hale and hearty, could not wait to gossip. "Miri, I hear you harvested the honey from your father's hives," she said.

With her face burning under the intense gaze from every eye in the room, Miri expected a lecture about proper activities for young ladies. Instead, Mrs. Barkley said, "I wonder if you could collect the honey from my hives?"

The request was a pleasant surprise and one she could accept. Mother was continuing to regain her strength and Philippe and Georgie were handling the bulk of non-household chores.

Thanks to Mrs. Barkley and the sewing group, knowledge of her skill spread in the community and requests multiplied. Before long she was respected for her expertise in the management of bees.

The next letter she penned to her father was full of details about the experience of collecting honey. She hoped he would be proud of her.

Gathering honey from hives in the community took her past abandoned homes and barns where entire families had perished from yellow fever. Houses with boarded windows looked blindly out on the knee-high grass that surrounded them and rippled in the breeze like waves on a green ocean.

Miri examined the hives in neglected fields. A few, not on raised platforms, had rotted bases caused by poor drainage. Some hives were full of honey but empty of occupants, the bees having swarmed. A fair number of hives were in decent condition with healthy bees. The hives were too spread out to care for where they stood. They would have to be moved into her field.

"When you finish today's chores," she told Philippe later, "I need you to help me move some hives. Hitch up the wagon and bring along some burlap bags and rope."

"Where are the hives?" he asked.

"Behind empty houses. I'm bringing untended hives to my field."

"This moving is safe?"

"Yes. By late afternoon the bees will have settled in and I'll smoke the hives to assure they'll be docile during the move."

Georgie, Philippe's ever-present shadow, heard the conversation and said, "I want to help, too."

Miri was afraid her brother would not be attentive enough to avoid causing problems with irate bees. "Georgie," she said. "There's going to be a lot of honey, and a lot of jars will be needed. I'm putting you in charge of collecting and cleaning jars and I will pay you if you do a good job."

"Real money, Miri?"

"Real money," she told him.

Twenty-eight hives dotted the field when she and Philippe levered the last one onto its base of bricks. Philippe wiped his brow. "So many will be much work," he said.

Miri contemplated what was now her apiary. "I think I'm up to the challenge," she said.

It was time to re-till and plant the fields. Portia, taxed with extra work because of the absence of her father, was no longer available to help harvest honey. Philippe, efficient in his tasks, took to coming to the shed after his work was finished. Georgie, was as always, at the elbow of his hero and mentor.

Philippe made small talk and observed Miri for three days as she bottled honeycomb. On day four, he said, "I have time. Please let me to assist you."

"Me too," Georgie added.

Miri accepted their offer without hesitation. Philippe was taught how to uncap and section honeycombs; Georgie got the job of bottling. He put each piece of comb into a jar, capped the jar and placed it in a crate marked with the customer's name. Customers could either pick up their honey or wait for it to be delivered.

Philippe understood Miri's goals and concerns. If Georgie was within earshot they spoke French and talked about her interest in college and a profession, things she could not discuss with her mother or Portia. Portia's thinking was more traditional. Her desires were for a husband and children. She had no sympathy with Miri's fixation on a career.

Philippe didn't try to dissuade Miri. He gave advice and offered suggestions. He often said, "There is no education or training available to you in Haiti. You must leave here to find them, perhaps in New York, or in Europe where I am going. I will be attending medical school in France."

"I won't be returning home until the war is over," she said. "Who knows when that will happen. Sometimes I'm afraid I'll never have any other life than this one. My mother thinks I'm foolish, not wanting to marry and settle down. Maybe she's right."

Philippe rested a hand on her shoulder. Warmth radiated from it across her back and down her arm. She didn't move and his hand remained where it was.

"You must be *fatigué*, Miri," he said. "This is not like you to give up on a thing you are feel passion for."

She did not look at him, afraid he might see what she was now aware of. She was falling in love. Ambitious, admirable and sensitive, Philippe had no foul or poor habits and his character and personality satisfied a need in her. In many respects, Philippe would make an ideal suitor and husband.

"I know," she said, moving from his side and his hand. She wondered if he harbored any romantic feelings toward her and quickly dismissed the question as foolish. Her practical nature knew he cared. Caring was a natural feeling between friends. She and Philippe were both in pursuit of career goals, but came from such different cultural and religious backgrounds a future together was impossible.

"A good night's sleep and I'll regain my *passion*." she told him. "In the meantime, let's get back to work."

The payment Miri received for the honey she was hired to collect was a portion of the harvest. Added to the amount from her hives, shelves in the pantry soon held a bounty of liquid gold.

Honey was stirred into coffee, tea, and lemonade...everything except drinking water, and was used liberally in cooking. Honey cake became a weekly dessert and honey butter replaced the plain variety on bread and biscuits.

Philippe was introduced to the novelty of chewing new wax until it was no longer sweet. And Miri donated surplus wax to anyone who wanted to use it for candle making, or for warm applications to ease the pain of arthritic knees, elbows and hands.

Throughout the spring and into the summer she was kept busy overseeing hives and collecting honey. One day in mid-August, she returned home to find on the table, an envelope with familiar handwriting. It was the first letter from Father in many months. Holding her breath, she opened it.

My dear daughter,

I am very happy to hear that everything continues to be well with all of you despite the harsh circumstances. It is likewise a great relief for me to know the unrest has ended and the colony is safe.

As for me, after my regiment was mustered in we went to Annapolis, Maryland by train. Our stay here may be brief as we await orders to proceed to some location where we will do battle with Johnny Reb.

Your mother's last note said you worry a great deal about me. Try not to fret Miri. Remember the reasons for this war. I am fighting to assure liberty and equality for freed slaves and freeborn people of color like us.

Now that Mr. Lincoln has deemed we are 'equal' enough to participate in the struggle; I must do my part to ensure victory. I fight for the certainty we will no longer be caught someplace between bondage and true equality.

Keep me in your prayers, Your loving father,
H. Whitfield, 26th United States Colored Troops, New York

She smiled at his use of the Johnny Reb label ascribed to pro-slavery southern secessionists. Northern sympathizers to slavery were sneered at and called "copperheads." As a free person of color, she stood proudly among the "Yankees," northerners opposed to slavery.

He didn't mention the harvest she had so eagerly written about and she was disappointed. He sounded too eager to engage in combat, and the idea reawakened her fear he would be injured or killed.

She wrote to him each week and waited. Return correspondence did not arrive and she began to worry again. Her mood descended into a brooding, gray gloom.

Philippe, unable to break through her despair gave up trying, and she was grateful. Except for brief exchanges related to the task at hand, they worked side by side in relative silence.

Months later she measured out cornmeal for the next day's muffins and looked at the calendar. It was almost Christmas. So much time had passed since the last word from her father, she wondered if her letters were getting to him or if he was in even in condition to read them. On December 20, 1864 she tried once again.

Dear Father, she wrote.

I hope you are well and are receiving the letters Mother and I send.

Not hearing from you for months makes it difficult not to be bedeviled with worry. The steamers bring newspapers from New York and though they aren't current, I read them to follow the progress of the war but don't know where you have been sent to fight.

As for family news, Mother has recovered her health and Georgie and I are both well. Livy scrambles about quick as a bug and will soon be walking. At this writing she is cranky because of sore gums but as soon as the new tooth breaks through, her sweet ways will return.

I am pleased to tell you the bees have produced a second crop of honey and another harvest is close. I have twenty-eight hives in our field and a good amount of honey left from the first harvest.

Philippe has been a boon as a hired hand. He and Georgie manage the garden and animals. Nonetheless my days are chock full of work which doesn't allow time to dwell long on troubling thoughts.

This wasn't the absolute truth but she wanted him to believe she had fortitude.

Well, Father, it is late and I must sleep and be ready to rise early and tend to the day's work. May the Lord watch over you and keep you safe,

Your loving daughter, Miriam

Sleep overcame her as soon as the envelope was sealed.

December, 1864
Dear Miri,

I hope you are well. This is the first opportunity in some time to write. After my last letter my regiment was sent by ship to South Carolina and landed at John's Island. We skirmished and battled with Johnny Reb.

The enemy had the advantage of knowing every swamp and gully here-abouts and though I believe to a man, this group of Billy Yanks fought bravely, we were defeated. A number of our men were injured and some lost to death. Thankfully I managed to come through unharmed.

Last week I was moved up in rank due to a shameful event in the squad.

Three men and a Sergeant went to a nearby farm and stole some chickens. They were found out by the Captain and made to wear signs that said THIEF for an entire day. The Sergeant was busted down in rank and I was promoted to Sergeant. One of my chief responsibilities is to set a good example for the men and I will certainly strive to do so.

We are bivouacked at Beaufort to defend the land we captured and protect ex-slaves. I must tend to my duties now, but will try to write again soon,

Your Father,
Sergeant H. Whitfield, 26th United States Colored Troops, New York

Chapter 28

January 1865

By now Miri had developed a pattern of household chores followed by tending the hives. She also helped a bit in the garden but, other than occasional oversight, left its care to Philippe and Georgie.

Though Georgie had grown more responsible with Philippe around, he required supervision and firm direction when it was time to pick ripe fruits or vegetables. They could not afford to lose any food.

"MaMa, MaMa, MiMi," Livy babbled as she ran to Miri on sturdy, dimpled legs.

Miri patted her sister's soft, black ringlets and smiled. "Proud of yourself, aren't you?" she said. She wiped a speck of oatmeal from Livy's chin and pinned her into a clean diaper.

Despite the harsh situation she was born into, Livy was a bonnie child and her innocent joy offset the extra responsibility she brought. As Miri watched her and heated water for tea, her mother came to the table and unfolded the newspaper, setting the pages aside after she finished reading them. Miri picked them up, ignoring most of the news from New York and Spencer. Instead, she scoured for information about the war.

Articles from reporters on the front lines were uplifting. The Union Army was achieving successive victories as it moved deeper into southern territory.

The information bolstered her belief the North would win the war, and the heaviness weighing on her heart lightened. In addition, her father's name was not on the lists of missing, wounded and dead soldiers and she took this as proof he was alive. There was a knock on the door. She stopped reading and drained her cup as Portia came in.

"Po Po," Livy said toddling toward her cousin with lifted arms. Portia scooped her up, tickled her chin. Livy squealed with delight.

"We're off to the river," Miri told her mother. "Stir the stew once in a while and slide the pot off the heat when it's done." She put her hat on and kissed Livy on the cheek before Portia sat the toddler on the floor.

The morning sun was warm and pleasant. As they walked she thought about her father and the war. A light slap on the arm startled her. Portia, a huge grin splitting her face, spun like a top and hopped over a wheel rut. "Race you to the shed," she said, and tore down the path.

Caught up in her cousin's silliness, Miri ran after her, twirled until she was giddy with glee, and sprawled on the grass. They laughed until their sides ached, for the moment children again, worry and problems forgotten. But Miri's brief period of pleasure soon ebbed away.

"Where do you suppose our fathers' regiment is?" Portia said.

"Probably still in South Carolina. If you had looked at the last headline, you'd know General Sherman captured Atlanta and is marching toward the sea. The rebels are going to retreat into places our Army has already captured, and they'll need to fight and hold on. I just wish for some word from Father that he's unharmed. These long periods without a letter are unsettling."

She stood and brushed a grasshopper off her skirt. "Come on, let's forget the war and go wading."

With shoes off and skirts tucked up out of the way, they splashed about in the shallows. Miri tried skimming stones, but her skills had gone rusty, and the first five sank as soon as they hit the water.

"I wonder why Philippe never comes down here," she said.

"If you're curious why don't you ask him?" Portia said. "Maybe he can't swim."

Miri launched another stone.

"Of course it's none of my business," Portia continued, "and I know you've told me you want a career, not a husband, but I think you're interested in him. Too bad. Your mother certainly won't approve of him as a beau," she said when Miri's cheeks flushed. "If your father were here, I don't believe he would either. Philippe is from another culture and practices a different religion."

"That shouldn't matter," Miri said. "He's a good person."

"But you know very well it does matter. A Catholic boy? A Haitian Catholic boy? The entire family would have a conniption. They would never accept him."

The painful truth stung, but not for long. Miri's practical and ambitious nature reasserted itself and she refocused on solving the problem of how to acquire skills necessary for a career. While lost in thought, the river soothed her cares, and things were pleasant for the rest of the afternoon.

Another letter arrived. This one written over a month ago.

My Dear Daughter,

I am sorry for such a delay in answering your letters and trust you are well.
Tonight there is a full moon and I'm using its light to scribble off a note before
bedding down.

    My regiment is still in South Carolina and now part of a brigade of colored
and white troops from Massachusetts and Ohio. We are busy skirmishing against
rebels. As soon as one battle is over, we break camp, march out and form up for
the next encounter. Moving thousands of men and a battery of artillery from
place to place takes time and coordination.

    Quiet moments to write are scarce but I was determined to set down this
note to commend you for harvesting the honey. You have always shown a lot of
pluck, and in this instance it served you well. I am proud you were able to accomplish a task not expected of a woman.

Miri reread the sentence twice. Her father's approval went beyond what
she had hoped for. Not only did he praise her, he also referred to her as a
woman. Tears blurred the closing lines of the letter and she wiped her eyes.

Dawn will arrive in a blink, daughter, and I must get some rest.
Say a prayer for me and for the success of the Union Army.

       Your loving father, Sgt. Henry Whitfield, 26th, N.Y.

· · · · ·

Her sleep that night was serene.

Chapter 29

January 1865

January 29, 1865

Dear Father,

I pray you are safe and well on receipt of this letter. The population of the colony is now less than one hundred but there have been no recent deaths and we pray the yellow fever does not return. I doubted we would survive in this inhospitable place without you, and yet, by the grace of God, we have. It pleases me to write that Mother, Georgie, Livy and I are all in good health.

Mother has resumed management of the house and most of Livy's care. Ever the blithe spirit, my sweet sister is now walking and has several words in her vocabulary.

The biggest change has been with Georgie. He has become a gangly young man and is no longer that cantankerous boy who had to be scolded before he'd do a lick of work. The army of tin soldiers he spent endless hours playing with have finished skirmishing and are off duty and stored away under his bed.

Thankfully, the shipping blockade ended and steamers are arriving regularly with food and supplies from the states. Our old cow still produces plenty of milk, we have eggs from the chickens and a second crop is growing in the garden. Our stomachs are once again full.

Mother and I follow progress of our valiant Army of the North in the newspaper. The last edition lauded General Grant's victories and hailed General Sherman's march through the south.

My fondest wish is for that rebel army to fall in complete defeat before long and end this terrible conflict.

But I will leave all thoughts of war here and move on to a more pleasant topic, the second honey harvest. The quantity of honey was larger than the amount in the first harvest because of the hives I have added. I am now at ease around the bees, my ability to uncap combs has greatly improved and collecting was accomplished without difficulty. I have Philippe hang some frames to drain the honey but the process is overly tedious. Bottling pieces of comb is much faster.

Last week Portia and I went to the Haitian open air market in Port-au-Prince with Dr. Lazarre and Philippe. Mother wasn't feeling up to the ride so Mrs. Barkley accompanied us. I suspect in addition to acting as chaperone, she was curious to see the market.

I took along two-dozen bottles of honey. The Haitians were eager customers and the entire lot sold for a decent sum. I was happy to sell some of the surplus that would otherwise sit in the pantry unused. Part of the money went to Georgie and Portia for helping with the harvest and I used a portion to buy fresh fish, meat and cheese.

We are managing fairly well, Father. You are sorely missed and I pray for you every day. Take care of yourself and please write to us whenever you find time.

Your loving daughter, Miriam

· · · · ·

A defeat of Union forces at Honey Hill, South Carolina was in the next edition of the paper. The article detailed numerous unsuccessful attempts to put down the rebels and her father's regiment was listed among troops engaged in a battle waged over two days. Though outnumbered, the enemy had the significant advantage of knowing the boggy terrain. A strategically placed earthwork fortress was used to shell Union soldiers with cannon balls and some soldiers were trapped between cannons and fields of grass deliberately set afire by the confederates. Hard hit, the Union Army ultimately withdrew from the battlefield. The number of Union dead and injured was described as "high" but no names were listed. Miri was sure her father participated in the battle, but his fate was unknown.

Seeing her mother read the article and break down, brought tears to Miri's eyes and she dabbed them away with her apron. "We must believe Father and Uncle Will made it through," she said. "To think otherwise is simply not acceptable."

Her mother nodded but her tears kept flowing.

Portia and her mother had also read the news and arrived at the door looking glum. Georgie joined the brooding women at the table while Livy, too young to understand the calamity, tried in vain to get someone to play patty cake with her.

Unable to tolerate the gloom, Miri said a silent prayer and went into the pantry. It was important to stay strong. Under the weight of this new worry, both her mother's health and her own could falter. Work was a tried and true method to prevent her mind from dwelling on any problem. She began to inventory their stock of foodstuffs, counting jars of honey, jams and canned goods.

Now that there was a source of money from selling honey, and fresh meat could be obtained, the tinned meat wasn't important although it would be kept since the ability to buy from the natives was never certain. The amount of flour, rice and dry beans could last for months and a steamer due in week was sure to have a supply.

Portia came to the pantry door and asked what she was doing.

"Taking a count of things and rearranging shelves."

"We're all fretting about the news. Hiding in here won't help."

"I'm not hiding. I need to stay busy."

"Well your mother thinks you're in here crying."

The thought she might be a cause of additional distress brought Miri back to the kitchen table. She said, "The pantry's in order, Mother. Here's a list of everything. I've got to check the hives and garden now and when I get back we can bake something for the sewing group meeting tomorrow. In the meantime, little Miss wants some attention," she said, handing Livy to her.

"Come on, Georgie. We've got work to do."

In the garden, Philippe was immediately aware of her dejection. She nearly fell to pieces telling him about the battle her father's regiment had been in.

"Your father will survive, Miri. I believe this. You must believe the same."

"I've tried to remain strong and appear hopeful," she said. "I do it so my mother and Georgie don't give up. But I'm drained by the constant struggle to hold in my worries about my father and the future of our family."

Philippe's arm circled her shoulder and she was immobilized. He was so close she could smell the Bay Rum in his hair.

"No, Miri," he said. "You have strength you don't realize, something I have admired since we met."

His words warmed her heart and flamed her cheeks. She looked up at his face and smiled. He was such a dear. He knew the right thing to say.

"Are you all right, Miri?"

Portia's interruption broke the fragile link.

"I'm fine," Miri said. She stepped away from Philippe and out of the garden.

"What was that about?" Portia asked.

"Nothing of concern," Miri said, setting a brisk pace to the hives.

"I saw Philippe's arm around you, Miri. That was nothing?"

"I said it was nothing, Portia. So leave it and stay out of my business."

"You needn't get snippy with me, Miri. I was only asking because I care."

"Sorry I was sharp, Portia. Can we just let it go?"

"Fine."

By the end of the day any thought Miri had entertained of Philippe as a beau had been erased. Though cultural and religious barriers could be surmounted, both she and Philippe had career goals. He would soon go to France to attend medical school and she hoped to attend college in New York or some place in the North. Her relationship with Philippe had to remain within the confines of a friendship. She put the cake she was making for the sewing circle in the oven and closed the door.

The sewing circle was smaller by three. Two women had left with their children on the most recent steamer for New York. Not knowing if their husbands were alive, they didn't want to risk the possibility of living as widows in Haiti. They felt the best chance for a decent future was in New York and had borrowed or used the last of their money to secure passage. The third was busy packing to leave on the next ship.

Mention of their names stirred a similar opinion from most of the women. Miri believed her mother wanted to go home too, but did not have enough money to pay the fares. For her mother, borrowing was out of the question.

The conversation gradually drifted on to everyday household topics. She stopped listening and turned her attention to her sewing project. She shook her head in displeasure at the crude, uneven stitches in her square, and began the slow process of ripping them out. Her needlework skills were still mediocre and she needed patience and attention to stitching detail to improve the look of her square. The idea to applique a honeybee next to her name came to her as she picked at a loose thread. A lovely pair of wings could be made with scraps of lace and a body cut from Georgie's old brown corduroy pants. The perfect, final touch would be the embroidered addition of "beekeeper" after her name. For the first time she felt enthused about needlework.

Chapter 30

February 1865

Dear Father,

We are all in fine health in this New Year and I pray you are the same.
Christmas without you wasn't quite as festive but celebrated nonetheless for
Livy's sake.

Philippe and Georgie went into the mountains and brought back a pine
tree that we decorated with homemade ornaments. You should have seen Livy's
eyes brighten at the sight. She is too young, of course, to understand the celebration and joy is because it is the birthday of our Savior. Her happiness is in
the treats and toys she received.

Haitians are quite clever at woodcarving, and craft all manner of toys,
trinkets and ornaments, and most of her new playthings were bought at their
market. I found a beautiful little mahogany box for Mother with the letter S, for
Sarah. The lid is inlaid with shells and it is lined with lapis-lazuli colored velvet.
She stores her necklaces and brooches in it.

I gifted Georgie with his very own shaving mug and razor because I
discovered him using your shaving equipment to attack a few springy hairs on
his upper lip and chin. My little brother is now a young man. He is as pleased
as punch with the gift and devotes an excessive amount of time honing the
razor. I'm sure the novelty will eventually wear off so I hold my tongue.

· · · · ·

She decided not to describe the gifts Philippe and she exchanged. Since
the incident in the garden, their conversation and interactions had
become a delicate, awkward dance. They were no longer at ease with one
another and had difficulty behaving as if nothing had happened.

She was keenly aware of the shift, and of Philippe's frequent
appearance wherever she was. She could sense his presence without having
to look, and was so afraid he would see what her heart felt, she often
avoided him.

She turned her attention back to the letter, and continued writing:

The newspaper is full of reports about the weak, poorly outfitted rebel army and mounting Union victories. General Sherman presented the city of Atlanta, Georgia to the President as a Christmas gift and presses onward to the sea, crushing all opposition in his path. Opinion is widespread in the north and here that the will the war will not last much longer. I eagerly await the end of the great conflict and the reuniting of our family.

Please write when you can and may Our Lord watch over you,
Your loving daughter, Miriam

She propped the envelope against her teacup as a reminder to mail it and turned Philippe's gift to admire its beauty again. At first the jar seemed merely a lovely token until she learned more of its story.

The orange sized globe was hand blown in France and purchased from a shop in Port-au-Prince. Philippe told her the original wooden lid was ordinary and not suitable for a gift, so he had it replaced. He commissioned a new mahogany lid locally, and its delicate, detailed work could only have been created by one of Haiti's most talented craftsmen. Decorative and symbolic, the carving represented a bee with outstretched wings landing on a flower.

The feelings she had about Philippe's thoughtfulness could not be defined. His gift to her was unique and the present she gave him, equally so. He had unwrapped the book, run his eyes and hand over the handmade cover and complimented her creativity and resourcefulness. She had found a broken book at the edge of the town dump, and repurposed its front and back covers. The worn, fabric-covered cardboard covers were removed, carefully cleaned with a damp rag and dried in the sun. Medical articles from newspapers concealed the original title of the book and three boxes of letter paper formed its pages.

Philippe blinked several times as he read the dedication on the flyleaf:

To Philippe, my dear, dear friend,

You have inspired and encouraged me not to lose sight of my goals and I will ever be grateful. In turn I hope this gift will assist you in your mission to provide medical care to your people. Best regards always,

Fondly, Miri

He turned to the first page. The Table of Contents listed Sections in the book along with their page numbers. In the section on Herbal Remedies was a sampling of recipes. Included under Compounds were ingredients and measurements for mixtures to treat colds, congestion and coughing. Formulas to use on bites and stings, aches and rheumatism, and salves to apply to eruptions and rashes were in Poultices, and pages on Potions contained concoctions to drink for headaches, fatigue, fainting and maladies of the stomach and intestines.

She had briefly debated about whether to include medications intended to treat maladies of the female system, and problems related to pregnancy and childbearing. In the final moment she decided to ignore societal rules forbidding an unmarried woman from addressing such topics with a man. She didn't feel inhibited about sharing her mother's knowledge and information with Philippe. It was necessary if he was to give women decent medical care.

In this, and in other ways she had matured from a fearful, trembling young girl into a skilled, independent minded adult. Philippe had offered advice along the way, and she hoped he would perceive her gift as a reward for his friendship and loyalty.

Chapter 31

April 9, 1865

"LEE SURRENDERS ~ WAR OVER"
There is great jollification and celebrating in the streets

When she read the headline, Miri's spirits soared. She laughed and danced in circles and Livy copied her, clapping in delight until she became dizzy and landed on her bottom.

"At last we can go home," Miri said. "As soon as Father sends money, we can take the first available steamer to New York."

"I am more than ready to leave," her mother said. "But we haven't received a letter or money in months."

"Have faith. They won't be long in coming," Miri told her.

Georgie and Portia, also joyous to learn the Northern was triumphant, began talking about going home to Spencer.

News of the southern surrender spread through the settlement like dandelion fluff on a spring breeze and raised the mood of the community. The Ladies Group of the church made plans for a celebratory lunch after Sabbath services.

Chapter 32

June 1865

Days struck off on the calendar became weeks. Nearly three months had passed since the war ended, and it was more than six months since they last heard from Father. Each day without a letter heightened Miri's concern for his wellbeing.

"I'm frantic with worry," she told Portia. "The war has been over for months and neither of our fathers has written."

"Their names haven't appeared among the dead and that makes me wonder if they were wounded or captured," Portia said.

"Wounded would be the better fate. The papers report colored soldiers captured by those despicable rebels were murdered."

"Don't say that. I can't bear the thought they might be dead."

"Neither can I. That's why I think of them as wounded and in a hospital. I don't know how else to explain why there hasn't been any word from them. I'm desperate to go home."

"So am I," Portia said.

"But until there's enough money to pay passage aboard a ship we'll have to stay here. Now rumors are flying again about political problems in Port-au-Prince. It will be bad for us if there's another eruption of violence among the Haitians. The colony's a poor, defenseless collection of females, boys and old men."

Philippe asked Georgie's age and said, "*Je suis desolé.*" He reminded Miri that at fifteen, Georgie was subject to conscription.

Days became filled with terrifying thoughts. Father might be injured, or worse, and there was a danger her brother could be drafted into the Haitian army. The idea of Georgie fighting at all, let alone in a foreign army on foreign soil, was repugnant. She had to find a way for the family to leave this odious island.

The next morning, dejected and drained from crying and lack of sleep, she didn't have much appetite.

"Do you think we'll get a letter from Pa today?" Georgie asked.

"I hope so," she said.

"Do you have an idea where he is, Miri?"

"No."

"What do you think he's doing? Why isn't he writing?"

Her patience broke. She snapped, "If I knew anything, Splinter, I'd tell you." Through the window she could see Philippe coming up the path and said, "Go meet Philippe and get on to the garden."

"Don't you think you were a bit harsh?" her mother said. "He's as concerned about your father as you and I."

"I know. I just wish he didn't ask questions that don't have answers."

She put a half-hearted effort into chores and after a light lunch went out to the hives. Flowers waved in the breeze, birds twittered and bees and insects flew about the path. Today the beauty and joy went unnoticed.

Once the hives were tended to, Miri changed out of her beekeeping clothes and sat on a stool. Her foot tapped the floor as she flipped the pages of her father's bee keeping journal. Frustration at not being able to leave Haiti ate at her. She desperately wanted to go home, and her foot tapped faster and faster as her feelings of annoyance and helplessness rose.

She slammed the journal shut, fighting back tears. Above her head sunlight flooded through the window and across jars on the shelf. The solution to her problem came from the golden light filling the room. She went over her plan several times and with each review grew more confident it would work.

It was late and she went to the garden, found Philippe and Georgie and joined them for the walk home. "Philippe," she said, "would there be enough room in the wagon to take all of the honey in the pantry to the next farmer's market?"

"I think so," he said. "Are you thinking of selling it all?"

"Yes, I am," she said, and offered no further explanation.

Before dawn on market day, they loaded the wagon by lantern light. Portia and her crates of eggs were onboard when Mrs. Barkley settled into her seat.

"I don't understand why we have to leave at such an ungodly hour," she fussed. Miri reminded her that early arrival was essential to secure a decent spot.

There was already activity when they got to the edge of the market area. Philippe stopped the wagon at the end of a row close to the entrance, an ideal location. He and Georgie set up a sturdy table by placing several planks across two stumps. Miri covered it with a red gingham tablecloth, and from the corner of her eye saw other vendors watching her. She arranged her wares, and the honey, glowing clear and pure in the morning light, lured customers to the table.

Today she was not going to barter or accept Haitian paper dollars. She set a fixed price per jar and only accepted gold or American money. She spoke sufficient French now to deal directly with Haitians. If they lapsed into *patois*, she stopped the transaction. Business was brisk and in no time she sold every single bottle.

Georgie fell asleep on the ride home while Mrs. Barkley and Portia gossiped about the sights, smells and sounds of the market. Miri ignored them and hardly paid attention to Philippe who carried on a largely one-sided conversation. Her mind was taken up with singular preoccupation: Spencer.

At home, she laid the money on the kitchen table.

"What is all this?" her mother asked.

"I sold honey at the market," Miri said. "I've paid Philippe, Portia and Georgie. This is what's left. It should be enough to pay our fares to New York."

Her mother smiled through tears. "I'm amazed," she said. "Although I'm not too surprised, Miri You have matured from a girl with a defiant streak of independence into a woman with determination and resolve."

Miri accepted the compliment as she squirmed out of her mother's embrace.

"First thing tomorrow we should look at the schedule for the steamers and pick a date to sail," she said.

"I'll write and let your grandparents know the name of the ship and when we'll be arriving," her mother said. She frowned. "What shall we do about this place and the animals?"

"I'm going to tell Philippe he can have the hives. He'll be here until he leaves for medical school next year. A year will be long enough for him to teach someone else how to care for the hives and harvest the honey while he's in France.

"No one in the colony is going to buy the house. They're all trying to get out of here just like we are. Maybe Philippe would like the house, and animals as well. He plans to return and set up a medical clinic when his studies are done."

She waited until the following Saturday to tell him she was returning to Spencer.

He wasn't surprised. "I thought it might be the reason you wanted to sell the honey," he said. I always knew your heart was in Spencer, so I understand your desire to go back."

The decency and generosity of Philippe's response increased her love for him and the regret she felt about their thwarted relationship. She held on to the belief if it was meant to be their paths would cross again. Then she moved on to discuss the house and property.

From a practical standpoint, Philippe saw the offers of house and hives as an opportunity, and was happy to accept. Honey from the hives would provide income and decrease his need of financial help from his uncle. A house of his own meant he could set up a clinic as soon he returned from France. He reached an agreement with her mother on an amount for rent and paid the first month in advance.

Some of the rent money was given to Portia's mother to supplement their funds. The entire family group made a day trip to the waterfront in Port-au-Prince to pay their fares.

Once that was accomplished, it took very little time to pack. Miri felt no remorse that furniture and household items would be left behind. Everything was replaceable except her books and her father's journal. Those she boxed along with her quilt square.

Four days later she stood on the deck of the brigantine Afton watching the anchor being raised. So much had changed during her time in Haiti. It seemed ages had passed since she landed on the beautiful, rugged, underdeveloped island as an untested, pampered girl. She was now a woman returning to her sorely missed home town, a woman capable of plucking a chicken, milking a cow, nursing the sick and dying, running a household and taking care of a baby. In her cabin, a jar with a red ribbon was evidence of another unique skill, one she was most proud of. The label read: produced by *Miriam H. Whitfield, Beekeeper.*

References

Abraham Lincoln, Complete Works: Comprising His Speeches, Letters, State Papers and Misc. Writings, Ed. John G. Nicolay & John Hay, New York: Century Co., 1894.

Africa America and Haiti: Emigration and Black Nationalism in the Nineteenth Century. Dixon, Chris; Greenwood Press, Westport, Conn., 1960.

African-Americans in New York State, N.Y. State Historical Assoc., 2001.

African Ancestry in Connecticut, www.afrigeneas.com.

A Gathering of Days: A New England Girls Journal 1830–1832, Blos, Joan, Scribners, 1980.

A Guide to Hayti, Redpath, James, 1861. Republished 1970, Negro University Press, Westport, Conn. [LAPL ref.].

All on Fire. William Lloyd Garrison and the Abolition of Slavery, Mayer, p. 47.

American Regionalisms, 18th, 19th and early 20th Ref., Century New England, Inglewood Pub. Library, Inglewood, Calif.

Antique Farm Equipment, *The Natural Farmer,* Fall, 1999.

"Association of Native Sons of Liberty," *The New York Times,* August 6, 2006.

A Year in the Beeyard, Morse, Roger, Scribners, 1983.

Before the Ghetto: Black Detroit in the Nineteeth Century. Katzman, David. University of Illinois Press, Urbana, Illinois, 1975.

Black Masters: A Free Family of Color in the Old South. Johnson, Michael P. and James L. Roark, Amo Press, 1970.

Black Separatism and the Carribean, 1860. Bell, Howard, Ed.

Camp William Penn. Scott, Donald Sr., Arcadia Publishing, S. Carolina.

Canning With Honey, The ABC and XYZ of Bee Culture. Root, Amos, Scribners, N.Y., 1877.

Classical Black Nationalism: From the American Revolution to Marcus Garvey. Wilson J. Moses, Ed., N.Y. University Press, N.Y., 1996.

The Complete Guide to Beekeeping. Morse, Roger, EP Dutton, N.Y., 1974.

Control of Communicable Diseases in Man. Benenson, Abraham, 11th ed., American Public Health Association, 1973.

Copy of Report and List of Passengers, Brig. Afton, of Halifax, November 1863. From Port au Prince, Haiti to Boston, Mass. Ancestry Library.

Cultures of The World: Haiti. NgCheon-Lum. M. Cavendish, N.Y., 1995.

Daily Life in Civil War America. Volo, Dorothy Deneen and James Volo, Greenwood Press, Westport, Conn., 1998.

"Emigration to Hayti: Sailing of The Janet Kedstone." *The New York Times,* Jan. 4, 1861.

"Free Inhabitants of the town of Fredericksburg, Virginia, 1850." U.S. Census 1850, *Godey's Lady's Book, Harpers Magazine,* 1860.

"The Great Centralizer: Abraham Lincoln and the War Between the States." DiLorenzo, T. *The Independent Review,* VIII, n. 2, Fall 1998.

Haiti: Enchantment of the World. Hintz, M. Grolier Press, N.Y., 1998.

History of the City of Troy. Weise, Geneology Ref. 974.72T83We, Los Angeles Public Library.

"Honey and Cinnamon Cures." *Weekly World News,* Canada; Jan. 17, 1995.

"Ice" poem from *The Common*. Mazur, Gail, Univ. of Chicago Press, 1995.

Invention of the Washing Machine. www.ideafinder.com.

James Redpath, 1833–1891. Dictionary of American Bibliography, American Council of Learned Societies, 1928–1936.

My Life in Camp. 1st South Carolina, vol. 33, USCT. Susie King Taylor.

The Negro Convention Movement 1830–1861. Bell, Howard, Amo Press, 1969.

The Pine and Palm Newspaper. Boston and New York, May 18, 1861. Boston Public Library Ref.

Profiles Out of the Past of Troy, N.Y. Since 1789 (Henry Highland Garnet, Troy's First Negro Minister and Abolitionist) Rezneck, Troy Chamber of Commerce, 1970.

Records re Suppression African Slave Trade and Negro Colonization 1854–72 Communications Relating to the Colonization Project at Ile a Vache, Haiti, Sept. 6, 1862–Jan. 18, 1869, National Archives, call no. 10-44-6, microfilm roll no. 9, pp. 21–24.

"Second Helping," *Country Home*, May 2005; pp. 154–6.

Search for a Black Nationality: Black Colonization and Emigration 1787–1863; Miller, Floyd, University of Illinois Press, 1975.

Slave Inhabitants of the Town of Fredericksburg, Virginia, 1850, U.S. Census 1850.

They Who Would Be Free: Blacks Search for Freedom, 1830–1861, Pease, Jane and William 1974, Atheneum, N.Y.

Uses for Beeswax. www.hampden-county-beekeepers.org

The Vanishing American Barber Shop: An Illustrated History of Tonsorial Art 1860–1960; Barlow, Ronald, 1966, Wm. Marvy Co., St. Paul, Minn.

2 1982 03150 2218

CPSIA information can be obtained
at www.ICGtesting.com
Printed in the USA
LVHW091034050719
623118LV00003BA/402/P